HILLARY'S BACK!

A gripping crime mystery full of twists

FAITH MARTIN

DI Hillary Greene Book 18

First published 2020
Joffe Books, London
www.joffebooks.com

ISBN: 978-1-78931-342-0

CHAPTER ONE

A rather grey Monday morning in October wasn't most people's idea of a good time, and former DI Hillary Greene was no exception. As she put on the kettle in the tiny galley kitchen of her narrowboat, the *Mollern*, she glanced listlessly through the round porthole window and watched as some fallen horse-chestnut leaves, a mixture of brown, red and gold, swirled about in a rising wind.

As if to add to the general ambience of chilly and miserable early-morning gloom, a few raindrops spattered against the glass, and she turned on the radio in a bid to bring some noise and life into her world. But the jaunty and uninspired DJ soon had her turning it off again with a muttered and rather uncomplimentary comment on what passed for entertainment these days.

She popped a slice of wholemeal bread into the toaster and sat down on the padded bench seat opposite the fold-down table. She was already showered and neatly dressed for work in a warm woollen trouser-and-jacket ensemble the colour of conkers, teamed with a complementary cream blouse, but she was debating whether to change her shoes for boots.

She wondered idly what the new boy at work would be like.

She sighed as she waited for her bread to brown and looked outside again as another gust of wind threw more raindrops against her home. She was hoping her boss, Superintendent Roland 'Rollo' Sale, would have another cold case ready for her, preferably an old unsolved murder inquiry. Since she'd presented her findings on her latest case last week, she was anxious to have something else to get her teeth into. These days, she dreaded boredom and unfilled hours more than anything else.

Her toast popped up and she got up and scraped some tasteless low-fat spread that was supposed to be good for cholesterol onto it, then bit into it, trying to pretend it was a bacon sandwich.

Outside, a moorhen, probably one of this year's fledglings and now more or less in full adult plumage, swam past and looked at her hopefully. She opened the window and tossed out a piece of toast, watching as the bird grabbed it and skedaddled with it as fast as it could into the nearest reed bed before a marauding mallard could steal it.

Wiping the crumbs from her fingers into the sink, Hillary gulped down the last dregs of her coffee, picked up her bag and edged through the narrow corridor towards the back of the boat.

She pulled on her raincoat and fastened it before opening the hatchway and climbing up the set of four steep metal stairs into the face of the wind. Luckily the rain had abated a little, but even so, her shoulder-length cap of chestnut hair was damp by the time she'd walked the short distance along the towpath to the nearby pub car park, where she kept her car.

Puff the Tragic Wagon, a rather rusting Volkswagen Golf of a greenish-grey hue, smelled damp when she sat behind the wheel, but so far, fingers crossed, he wasn't actually letting in water anywhere. She turned the ignition key and waited patiently while he coughed and grumbled and groaned. She trod the accelerator pedal a little in encouragement and tried again.

He continued to grumble and groan without success.

She swore at him and threatened him with the usual trip to the scrap heap. As ever, he seemed impervious to the threat.

'Oh come on, Puff!' she muttered wearily and tried again.

* * *

Gareth Proctor was having no such trouble with *his* car, a newer, specially adapted car that had come to him courtesy of the British Legion. He even had to turn down the heating a little as he made the short trip from his new digs above a fish and chip shop, down Kidlington's main road towards the Thames Valley Police HQ. A former sergeant in Her Majesty's Armed Forces, he still found many things sat oddly with him now that he was living in civvy street — such as attending his first day at his new job without the familiar comfort of wearing a uniform.

He drove carefully, grimly and still angrily aware of the weaknesses and frailties of his new body, but he had to admit that the automatic gears and power-assisted steering of his adapted car were a real lifeline. Though he never let himself think of his car as a 'disability' vehicle, he knew that subconsciously he still resented his reliance on it.

Only a few minutes after setting off, he turned into the car park at HQ, smiling at the tiny, almost laughable commute that he now had into work. In the army he could have travelled literally hundreds of miles to—

He shut the thought off ruthlessly. He was not in the army anymore.

Having finally left the hospital after months of rehab, he was still trying to get into the habit of not comparing his old life to the one he was currently living. Instead, he forced his mind to concentrate on the here and now, obediently following the one-day-at-a-time mantra his therapist had dinned into him.

He found and parked in a spot not too far from the main entrance. While he knew that he needed to walk and exercise as much as possible, he didn't want to arrive on his first day on the job looking washed-out already. He leaned forward to turn off the key, grateful, as a right-handed man, that all his injuries had been incurred on the left-hand side of his body. Which meant that at least he still had one good hand, one good arm and one good foot to rely on.

He sat for a moment, listening to the car click as it cooled, and eyed the big, uninspiring modern buildings around him.

Thames Valley, he knew, was a big police force, covering a lot of ground — much of it densely inhabited. He'd grown up in the north of Oxfordshire, and when he hadn't been overseas, he'd still called the market town of Banbury his home. It was where his wife . . . no, his *ex-wife* Trisha continued to live, along with their daughter Fiona.

So this area of the UK was the most obvious place for him to return to, in an attempt to build a new and different life for himself.

For a moment, Gareth Proctor sat in his car, a grim-faced, thirty-six-year-old man, contemplating his exciting *new* life, and his second career as a civilian working for the police force.

And a part of him *was* actually looking forward to it. There had been days in the hospital — when the skin grafts were itching and on fire, and each step he took had to be earned with sweat and pain — when he had looked forward to moments like this as the light at the end of a very long tunnel. Times when, instead of waking up in a hospital bed in a noisy, antiseptic-smelling ward, he would wake up in his own normal bed, in a normal room, where the day ahead would involve doing normal things — like getting up on a wet Monday morning and going in to work. And driving a car again. And—

A car horn honking angrily at someone reversing carelessly out of a space jolted him out of his reverie, and he grunted at himself. How much longer would he have sat there like a muppet contemplating his navel?

He opened the car door, carefully swinging his left leg out and around and onto the ground. He used the car doorframe to help him lever his six-foot-one-inch frame out of the car (seats helpfully elevated so he wouldn't have to bend his knees) and slowly stood up.

He winced only a little. He was reducing his painkillers more and more, determined to get off them entirely by Christmas, no matter what the doctors said. He tested his weight carefully, then reached into the car for a plain but hefty wooden walking stick. Again, he'd weaned himself off crutches early, and now only felt marginally conspicuous as he limped slightly across the car park.

His mates had all been quick to reassure him that he was walking so much better nowadays, and that he only looked like someone who'd suffered a bad tackle at a weekend football or rugby match, rather than someone who'd nearly died when an IED had exploded next to him.

But that didn't alter the fact that, unlike someone with only a pulled muscle or a sprained ankle, he'd never walk without the stick again.

He went through the main doors and paused in the hallway, looking around. The desk sergeant eyed him thoughtfully, but Gareth turned away from him. He knew, from his interview with Superintendent Sale last week, that he needed to head down the stairs into the bowels of the building, where the Crime Review Team (or CRT) were forced to make the best of the limited office space on offer.

As his commanding officer had said . . . No, Gareth corrected himself ruthlessly, as his *new boss* had said, cold cases were hardly a priority with the top brass.

Well, that at least was something that Gareth understood. When he'd first joined the army he'd initially started out as what a layman would think of as a common foot soldier, and he and his mates had hardly been a top priority with their superior officers either.

He held onto the stair rail and led off confidently with his right foot, his walking stick held less firmly than he'd have liked in his left. But then, he didn't have the strength in his left hand that he used to. Severed tendons and mangled digits, even when stitched together, were never quite as reliable as those that hadn't been lacerated by shrapnel.

He was still breathing normally when he reached the bottom of the stairs, and felt a flash of triumph. He didn't have far to go before he found the small communal office that he would be sharing with his new work mates. And as he stood silently in the doorway, contemplating the cramped space, he was glad that, for the moment at least, there was only one other full-time member in residence. Although there were three desks crammed in there, Superintendent Sale had mentioned that the unit . . . no, *team* was down to only the two of them, until some more youngsters could be found who were willing to take on the part-time, low-paid positions, which were all that was on offer.

Sensing his presence, the woman inside the room lifted her head and looked at him. She was, Gareth gauged, about fifty years old, built rather on the hefty side, with short black hair and sharp, near-black eyes. She smiled vaguely at him and rose from behind her desk, her hand thrust out.

'You must be the new man? Gareth Proctor? Or do you prefer Gary for short?'

Gareth moved forward a step or two, which brought him to the first of the desks. He held out his hand — his right, naturally, keeping his left hand half-concealed by his side and behind the black material of his civilian trousers. 'Gareth,' he said, with a smile. 'You must be Mrs Woolley?'

'Claire,' the woman said, shaking his hand with a grin. 'Welcome to the Black Hole of Calcutta.'

Gareth smiled, then glanced down. 'This my desk?' he asked. It was, unlike Claire's desk, totally clear of papers, stationery and the rather rampant spider plant that trailed across her space.

'Yeah, that's all yours,' Claire Woolley said graciously, slumping back down into her chair again and glancing at her watch.

The new recruit was ten minutes or so early. Which was a good sign. She glanced at him surreptitiously as he began settling himself in, seeing a lean man with short blond hair and a white line of scar tissue that cut across his left eyebrow. He moved carefully and with precision, as if every movement had to be calculated.

Rollo had already briefed Hillary and herself on Jimmy Jessop's replacement, of course, and so they already knew that he had been discharged from the army after suffering injuries. She only hoped that he wouldn't find life in the CRT too dull by comparison.

'Well, I know what it's like to start a new job from scratch, so let me fill you in on all the stuff that Rollo probably *didn't* tell you,' she began cheerfully.

'Rollo?' he echoed questioningly.

'Superintendent Sale. Our nominal boss,' Claire explained.

'Nominal?'

'Yes. The super's in overall charge of CRT, but that covers all the computer boffins and forensic folk in the labs,' she waved a vague hand at the open door. 'They're the ones who close the majority of open cases by checking them periodically to see where new steps in DNA testing can help catch perps who long thought they were home free. You know, a rapist of twenty years ago suddenly finds a copper knocking on his door because that decayed bit of whatever that was stored for years can now provide viable evidence.'

Gareth nodded. And smiled. 'That must ruin their whole day,' he said.

Claire grinned back at him happily. 'Better believe it. So, anyway, Rollo's main job is keeping on top of all that. But sometimes a cold case needs more than a simple review to see if new forensics can help clear it. It needs a proper investigation — and that's where we come in.'

Gareth looked at her, hoping his sudden unease didn't show. He had no experience whatsoever of what it took to conduct a 'proper investigation.' Although he'd done an induction course after he'd secured the position, and it had taught him the basics of what he'd need to know to do his job, it had obviously not included any actual police training. His job title was 'civilian consultant.'

For a moment, he couldn't help but wonder if a mistake had been made. But he couldn't see how. He'd gone through all the proper channels and sat through several interviews with the police and various other government bodies before being offered the job here.

'Which is where DI Hillary Greene comes in,' Claire swept on. 'Or rather *former* DI. Technically she's no longer a serving police officer, but to us, for all intents and purposes, she sort of is. Oh hell, you'll see what I mean,' Claire said with an encouraging grin.

And with that, Gareth felt himself relax a little. 'Yes, the superintendent mentioned that I'd be working under a former detective inspector. I take it we receive our day-to-day orders from her?'

Claire nodded. 'That's right. She should be in with the super now,' she said, glancing at her watch again. 'We just closed a case last week. Hillary reckons the killer was the victim's husband. The original SIO believed the same, but Hillary found the evidence.'

'So he's going to stand trial?'

Claire shook her head. 'Nah, he's carked it as well. Died three years ago. The cold case was fifteen years old when it came to us.'

Gareth blinked. 'Doesn't that seem a bit pointless then? If you can't prosecute the guilty party?'

Claire looked at him, her round face a little cocked to one side. 'Depends on your point of view. The victim's family, naturally enough, are glad to finally have some firm answers. Not to mention all those other poor sods who came under suspicion, and can now walk with their heads held high again.'

Gareth nodded, and could have kicked himself for being so obtuse. 'Oh right. Of course. Sorry, this is all very new to me.'

'Don't worry, we were all green as grass to begin with,' Claire grinned. 'You'll soon get the hang of things around here. Hillary will steer you right, you'll see.'

* * *

In Rollo's office, Hillary accepted the hefty folder he held out to her and glanced through its top pages, gratified to see that it was indeed another unsolved murder.

'The new boy's arrived,' Rollo informed her mildly. 'He's a smart man. Enlisted as a squaddie but worked his way up to Intelligence. Had his accident not long after though, so didn't get to do more than dip his toe in the water where that was concerned,' he added with a shade of sympathy.

The superintendent had just turned sixty, and was fighting to keep his slight paunch from spreading. An amiable-looking man, with mild hazel eyes and mousy brown hair turning grey, he didn't look like many people's idea of a seasoned police officer. And in truth, his career hadn't been particularly spectacular, but it had been solid.

And after his predecessor, the much more dynamic Superintendent Steven Crayle, had built the CRT into the active and successful unit it now was, the top brass had agreed that all it needed was a safe pair of hands at the helm to keep things going steadily.

And Rollo Sale had more than adequately justified their faith in him, mostly by keeping things running exactly as they always had been. Which included letting former detective inspector Hillary Greene take the lead with cold murder cases.

'How do you think he'll pan out?' Hillary asked absently, itching to get back to her office so she could read through the files and get to work.

'I hope he'll be OK. As you know, we're very short-staffed,' Rollo said flatly. 'And he was the best of the bunch. In spite of his disabilities and having no experience.'

Hillary sighed. She didn't need telling. What with government funding of the police at an all-time low, morale being driven into the dirt, and almost insultingly low wages on offer, it was not surprising that good candidates were hardly lining up to join the fight against crime. Especially when it came to niche, civilian-driven small enterprises like her own unit-within-a-unit.

In the past, she'd had four or even five members in her team. Now it was just down to the three of them. Still, at least Claire, who'd put twenty-five years into the job, was an old hand like herself. She could rely on Claire to help her teach the new boy all that he needed to know and keep him out of trouble.

She heaved a sigh. 'Well, we'll have to wait and see how it goes. He's obviously got guts, and the intelligence tests were a doddle for him, so there's no reason to think he won't be a good fit for us. I'm a little worried about his injuries though,' she added. It was not that she had a problem with a disabled person doing the job. What worried her was that, in the event of anything kicking off, she held herself responsible for her people's welfare — and there was no getting away from it: a man like Gareth was more vulnerable than most.

Rollo grunted. 'You and me both. But he's a civilian, and his work is going to be mainly paperwork and routine questioning of witnesses. It's not as if we'll be asking him to chase down villains, herd football hooligans or join the riot squad. And let's face it, poor old Jimmy was probably more of an invalid towards the end than the new boy is now.'

Hillary couldn't help but grin. Her former 'wingman' had been a retired old sergeant whose growing back problems had finally forced him to throw in the towel and leave the team a month ago. And Rollo was right — towards the end he could barely hobble in to work.

'Well, I'll read this through then get cracking, sir,' she said, waving the hefty folder in the air. 'I take it the rest of the boxes are in storage?'

'As ever,' Rollo said. Then he smiled. 'You can always ask one of the boffins in the labs to help you carry them up to your office.'

Hillary laughed out loud. 'Yeah right. And pigs might fly!'

She left, closing the door behind her, and Rollo Sale stared at it thoughtfully for moment, a slight frown playing across his face. She *seemed* to be back on top form. And she had begun to put on a little weight again after going so distressingly thin. And she'd finally begun to lose that lost, gaunt look to her face.

He sighed and turned on his desk lamp, telling himself that Hillary would be fine. It was over eighteen months now since her partner, and his predecessor, Steven Crayle had died.

And Hillary Greene was made of stern stuff. He had nothing to worry about.

Nothing at all, he told himself firmly.

* * *

'So you used to be a sergeant?' Gareth said, looking at his new work mate with respect.

'For my sins,' Claire grinned. 'I worked most of my twenty-five in the domestic violence and rape unit,' she added sombrely. 'And even with time off for having the sprogs, I decided to retire early. I'd just had enough, you know?'

Gareth nodded, although in truth he didn't think he did. He was too young to have suffered from 'burnout' and couldn't have imagined leaving the army early, given the choice. But he could understand how someone could only put up with so much human misery and depravity for so long.

He'd never liked men who thought women were punch bags, and he wondered how this seemingly normal, slightly motherly woman, could have coped with so much ugliness for so long.

'And then, after a year, I was bored out of my skull,' Claire continued with a laugh. 'So I looked around for something else to do, but somehow working in an office or stacking shelves at Tesco didn't really appeal. Know what I mean?'

Now *that* Gareth could relate to, and he smiled faintly. 'Yeah, I know just what you mean. When I finished rehab, I had my full army pension to live on, but I needed to find something to do — work that meant something, preferably. Like you, I thought I'd go out of my mind working down the local garden centre or sat behind a computer all day doing some mindless task or other. So my therapist suggested I apply for the job here.'

Claire nodded, but was looking at him closely. 'Well, a lot of this job *does* require sitting behind a computer,' she warned him. 'But the rewards make it worthwhile. Believe me, there's nothing like seeing a villain being taken off the streets to make your whole day.'

Gareth hoped she was right. In the army, the 'villain' tended to be more faceless and abstract — a problem to be overcome. But he could see how people like Claire would take things more personally.

'So, what do I need to know about DI Greene?' he asked seriously. In the army, he'd had to take orders off women on a regular basis, and unlike a few of his male colleagues, he'd never had a problem with it. Most of the female COs he'd dealt with had been clever, tough, driven women who knew what they were about, so when Superintendent Sale had told him he'd be working under Hillary Greene, he'd felt no qualms about it.

But it was rule number one to always learn all you could about the man or woman who gave the orders, so he was very interested in what his new work mate had to say on the subject.

Claire, aware of the new boy's pale blue eyes watching her closely, smiled knowingly.

'There's nothing scary, don't worry,' she said. 'In fact, as you'll soon learn, our Hillary is a bit of a legend around here. She's an OEC, but don't let that fool you. She worked her way up through the ranks and earned every promotion she ever got.'

'What's an OEC?'

'Oxford-educated cop,' Claire grinned. 'But like I said, that's practically irrelevant. When she was a full DI she had a solve rate next to none, and since she started working for CRT she's closed practically every case she was given. She also has a rep for standing by her people no matter what, and taking the flak for them when necessary. There was something a few years back now, about her having to go the extra mile for one of her colleagues called Janine Tyler, who worked on her team at the time. And, oh yeah, she also won a medal for bravery. Yeah, I thought that might interest you,' she grinned, as Gareth's pale blue eyes widened slightly. 'She took a bullet for her DCI — "Mellow" Mallow. But he's dead now,' Claire added flatly. 'In the line of duty.'

Gareth took a long, slow breath, and began to feel, perhaps for the first time, truly optimistic about his new job. It was beginning to sound as if he might have found if not a home from home exactly, at least a place where he could be of some use and not feel like a total waste of everybody's space. Whilst he was well aware that the police force was not the army, it clearly had its own heroes, lore and sense of honour and camaraderie — all of the things that he had missed so much that it was almost like another physical ache.

'Did you know him? DCI Mallow?' he asked quietly.

Claire shrugged. 'I knew him as well as you know people you tend to see around on a regular basis,' Claire said. 'He seemed a decent guy — always well dressed and smart as a whip, too. But he was Hillary's boss and best pal for, like, years and years. His loss hit her really hard. Mind you, not as hard as losing her partner last year. And by partner, I mean lover, not work partner. Although Steven was that as well for a while, since he used to do Rollo's job. That's how they met.'

Gareth nodded grimly. He knew all there was to know about losing colleagues. But not so much about losing people he actually loved. True, he'd lost Trish for all intents and purposes, but she hadn't actually *died*.

'It sounds as if she's had it tough,' he said quietly. 'What happened? Did he die in the line of duty as well?'

Claire sighed heavily. 'In a way, I suppose you could say that he did. When he got promoted from here, he was given the job of bringing down one of our really bad boys, Dale Medcalfe, a local villain we'd been after for years. He ran prostitution and protection rackets, car theft rings, drug running, all sorts. We knew multiple murders could be traced back to him, but he never got his hands dirty personally. Finally, though, Steven managed to turn one of his outfit against him. It took some doing, and it got really tense and nasty for a while, with threats, intimidation, you name it, but eventually the bastard was sent down for life. But it all took its toll, and Steven had a heart attack in his office, just weeks before the case came to court.'

'Shit,' Gareth said succinctly.

'Yeah. He was a fit and active bloke too, not overweight, didn't smoke or drink to excess. But I suppose the stress of it just did for him. Hillary was here at the office when she got the call. One of his work colleagues at St Aldates found him and called an ambulance. They managed to keep his heart going, but he had another attack in the ambulance on the way in. By the time Hillary got to the hospital, he was gone. She'd only just moved into his gaff a few months before. What a damned shame.'

For a moment, a grim, tight silence hung in the air. Then Gareth sighed. 'Is she over it now?'

Claire grunted. 'Hard to tell with Hillary. She's not the type to wear her heart on her sleeve, you know? But she doesn't talk about it, so if I were you, I wouldn't mention it.'

Gareth nodded. 'Got it. Thanks. Anything else—' He broke off abruptly as Claire's gaze went over his shoulder, and her sad expression turned into a brief smile.

'Guv, we got a new case?' she asked brightly.

Gareth half-turned in his chair and looked to the doorway. Standing framed within it, he saw an attractive woman, maybe a little older than Claire, dressed in a smart reddish-brown suit that matched her hair and sherry-coloured eyes.

Those eyes were on him and she nodded briefly. 'Mr Proctor, I presume?'

'Ma'am,' Gareth said smartly.

He'd heard Claire call her 'guv' but there was simply no way he could address this woman, watching him with such level, all-seeing eyes, as anything other than 'ma'am.' He felt his backbone stiffen as it tried to go to automatic attention.

'Welcome to the CRT and my team, Mr Proctor,' Hillary Greene said quietly. 'I take it you're ready to start work?'

'Yes, ma'am,' he said, trying not to actually bark out the words, as he would have done had he still been in the army.

He thought he saw her lips twitch slightly.

'Good, because Superintendent Sale has just given us our new murder inquiry. It's going to be a steep learning curve for you, so if you have any questions don't keep them to yourself — ask either Claire or myself. Clear?'

'Yes, ma'am.'

'All right, here's what we have.'

So saying, she walked into the office and dropped a hefty file onto the spare desk. It sent a stream of dust motes rising into the warm office air. 'Meet Andrew Feeley, a twenty-one-year-old man who was stabbed to death in the woods surrounding the village of Tackley in the summer of 2012.'

CHAPTER TWO

Hillary paused, drew out the spare chair and sat down. 'This one has all the hallmarks of being a bit of a bugger,' she warned them wryly. 'So we might be in for a long, hard slog. To begin with, our victim wasn't a very popular man, which means there are quite a few people who never shed any tears when a local dog walker by the name of Frank Tomelty found his body. Mr Tomelty was an old man at the time, well into his seventies, and is now deceased. He was never a serious suspect. Secondly, with the murder having taken place in country woodland, there is no helpful CCTV footage, and needless to say, no witnesses.'

She paused as Claire gave a long, slow sigh. The new man nodded, but he obviously had no idea yet just how bad these circumstances were.

'To make matters worse, forensics isn't going to be of much help to us either, and the pathology reports are very straightforward,' she added flatly. 'Andrew Feeley died as the result of a single stab wound to his chest. The knife, which was known to be his own, was left in situ.'

Again Claire groaned, and Hillary turned to Gareth to explain more fully this latest difficulty. 'Usually when a person has been stabbed more than once, especially if done in a frenzy or in quick succession, the perp more often than not also cuts himself. It's very hard to wield a sharp blade in close combat and not get nicked yourself. Which means that pathology can isolate blood samples that don't belong to the victim. In this case, however, a single stab wound, more or less straight into the chest, means one clean wound and no withdrawal of the knife.'

Gareth nodded. 'So no injury to the killer. Got it.' He could have added that he'd been taught all about knife fighting and hand-to-hand combat in basic training, but he didn't. Why bother? Both of these women were clearly intelligent enough to realise that without any reminders from him.

'The fact that the knife — a rather fancy but serious penknife — was known to belong to the victim also doesn't help,' Hillary swept on. 'Often, the choice of murder weapon is key. If it's a firearm it can often be traced. If it's something the perp brought to the scene, then it obviously shows the act was premeditated. And if, say, someone is hit with a specific or unusual-shaped hammer, and we later find a suspect who is also a woodcarver who uses specialist hammers . . .'

'Got it,' Gareth said again. 'The fact that it was his own knife closes off yet another avenue of investigation.'

'To make matters worse, the knife had a highly embossed and raised pattern on the handle, which means no fingerprints. On the plus side, there *was* a fair bit of blood at the scene, even though the stab wound would have proved almost instantly fatal. This means it's possible the perp got significant bloodstains on their clothing — not that there would necessarily have been anyone around to notice, the crime having occurred in the woods in the middle of farming land, during the afternoon. And as if all that isn't enough,' she continued heavily, 'when the murder was committed, which was . . .' again she checked the notes, '. . . mid-July, the summer weather had been fairly hot and dry for some weeks, meaning that there was nothing in the way of footprints or tracks to help us out. The area where the body was found was in a small grassy clearing in the woods, which had been trampled about a bit, but nothing else. Forensics found the usual plethora of guff you can always find at such places — months-old fag ends, a few crisp packets, used condoms, the odd beer bottle.'

She paused and Claire grinned. 'Don't tell me — the good locals of Tackley used it as a bit of a lover's leg-over place?'

Hillary grinned. 'Nice to know in this day and age there are still some nature lovers about, isn't it? Actually, the original SIO quickly ascertained that the victim regularly used the woods as a place to meet up with his punters and sell them drugs. The upshot is, what forensics evidence there was doesn't relate to our victim, and is sod all use to us. They did think, from the amount of trampled grass at the scene, that it was more than likely that several people had visited that glade in the woods around the time of the crime, as you'd expect, given what he was up to, but they couldn't prove it.'

Claire rolled her eyes. She had only worked with Hillary for just over a year, having taken over the job from the goth girl who had been here before and had left to become a social worker of all things. But although her own expertise had been almost exclusively confined to violent crimes against women, it hadn't taken her long, under Hillary's tutelage, to begin to think like a murder investigator. Which was why this long litany of setbacks was making her feel downright gloomy.

'So in other words, it's all going to come down to the suspects then,' she said flatly.

'Looks like it,' Hillary agreed. 'I obviously haven't had a chance to study the files properly yet, but that's my guess. And again, we're a bit up against it. Like I said before, Andrew Feeley was not well liked. According to the SIO on the original case . . .' she paused as she hunted through the paperwork for the document she was looking for, 'a DI Barker, he was suspected of all sorts. Car theft, a few local break-ins, and perhaps most significantly of all, being a low-level supplier of drugs to the local, mostly teenage community. He had nasty friends and was definitely considered to be the village lout. Girls lodged complaints about him, but then withdrew them a few days later, reluctant to actually go the whole hog and testify against him in a court case. Hints of threats and intimidation floated around, but nobody, in the end, was willing to do what it took to get him banged up and out of everybody's hair.'

'Lovely,' Claire moaned. 'Don't tell me — everyone they interviewed wanted to give the perp a medal?'

Hillary shrugged.

Gareth shifted just slightly on his chair, but Hillary was on to it instantly, her head lifting to look at him. 'Something on your mind, Mr Proctor?'

Gareth blinked and thought about denying it, but something in the level look she was giving him changed his mind. 'It just strikes me that people like that deserve what they get. Presumably there are other cold cases, with victims who deserve our attention far more?' He spoke somewhat tentatively. He was very much aware that he was still green as grass, but at the same time, he felt he was entitled to his opinion. 'I've seen my share of people like this Feeley character — they go about robbing and terrorising old folks and treating women like they're meat. For the most part, they're vicious and cowardly little ferrets, but they can turn the lives of people in whole neighbourhoods — or in this case a whole village — into a real misery.'

'And so we shouldn't investigate when one of these ferrets ends up killed?' Hillary asked mildly.

Gareth slowly shook his head. 'No, I'm not saying that as such,' he objected. 'I just think there must be other victims out there more worthy of our attention.'

Hillary smiled. 'Well, first of all, it's up to the super to dish out the assignments,' she said, smiling to herself as she saw the new boy nod to himself. Clearly, following the chain of command and obeying orders — no matter what you thought of them yourself — was something he understood very well. But she was not about to hide behind Rollo Sale's skirts!

'And secondly, it's not up to us to be judge and jury,' she swept on. 'That's what we have courts of law for. Our job is to take a second look at this murder investigation and see if we can't uncover something new. And if we can, follow where that leads us and, if possible, arrest the killer of Andrew Feeley. The fact that he wasn't exactly Mother Teresa has to remain strictly irrelevant. Is that clear?'

'Yes, ma'am,' Gareth said instantly.

Hillary hid a sigh. She rather thought being 'yes ma'amed' in such an emphatic fashion was going to grow old very quickly. But she could no more suggest that this man start to call her 'guv' than she could call him by his first name without first being given his permission. Unlike nearly everyone else she had worked with, she sensed that this man both needed and preferred formality. Besides, it was very early days yet — he might unbend a bit, given time.

'Right then, first things first,' she said briskly, 'and as always, it's mundane and boring. We need to have a spare copy of all the relevant details. So, get cracking with the photocopier.' She nodded in the direction of an ancient, clunky machine that sat in one corner. 'Let's hope we've got enough toner.'

Gareth, surprised, glanced at the old but serviceable-looking computers that rested on all three desks. Catching the look, Claire grinned at him. 'Yeah — we are digital, even down here. And we'll probably get the computer files emailed to us at some point from Records. But the one thing you're gonna have to learn and learn fast is that down here, we're right at the bottom of the pecking order. So we tend to do things the old-fashioned way, if that's what it takes to get things moving.'

Hillary got up. 'Right, and talking of Records, we need the evidence boxes and paper files. So I'm off down to Archives.' She paused dramatically and added, 'I might be gone quite some time . . .' Echoing the famous last words of one of the members of the doomed Scott polar expedition had Claire grinning in sympathy.

'If you're not back by lunchtime, I'll send a search party, guv,' she promised, calling out to Hillary's disappearing back.

Gareth watched her go, his face thoughtful. His first meeting with his new boss had, overall he thought, gone better than he'd had any right to expect. DI Greene was clearly a seasoned and successful investigator. And his first ever murder case sounded interesting.

Perhaps he was actually going to enjoy this job after all.

At least it would give him something positive to chat about to Jason Morley this weekend, when they met up to do some fishing.

As ever, thinking of his mate started Gareth worrying. A former member of his unit, Jason had been injured in the same incident that had caused his own injuries, but unlike himself, Jason's main problem had been mental rather than physical, and he still suffered from PTSD in particular. Since returning to civvy street, Jason couldn't seem to hold down a job for love nor money, and like Gareth's own marriage, Jason and Debs had split up when he'd left the army, leaving him more isolated than ever. He was currently sharing a flat in the nearby market town of Bicester with another former soldier, but he wasn't happy with that arrangement and was desperate to move out. The trouble was, Oxfordshire was such a notoriously expensive place to live in, and finding accommodation was almost impossible. Hence Gareth's own meagre digs above a fish and chip shop!

But at least they could escape the woes of life for a few hours every Sunday by taking their rods and tackle to the Cherwell, and seeing if they could lift a few roach, perch or bream.

It also meant that he could keep a regular eye on Jason and how he was doing. As someone who knew and understood what he'd been through, Gareth knew that he was the only one his friend would talk to about the dark things that sometimes went on in his head, knowing that he wouldn't be judged.

'So, you want to take the first stint?' Claire asked, pulling his mind back from his worries about his old mate and indicating the piles of paperwork that needed to be copied. 'You can have the first half hour, then I'll take over,' she offered cheerfully. 'I'll go and help Hillary lug the files up to her office.'

Gareth felt his face tighten at this, and tried to ignore the sense of shame and helplessness that threatened to swamp him. For it should, surely, have been his job to lug heavy boxes about. But it was outstandingly clear to his new work mates that he would be worthless when it came to that sort of task.

'Right,' he said tightly, and picking up the first of the files, he headed towards the old photocopier.

Claire, apparently unaware of any tension in the room, sauntered out.

* * *

By the end of the day, the bulk of the boring but necessary paperwork had been done, and they'd organised the wealth of material that was collected and collated in any murder inquiry into a more manageable order.

It was just gone four thirty when Hillary called a halt to it, and the three of them gathered together in the communal office, drinking much-needed mugs of coffee and itching slightly from the dust that seemed to have infiltrated most of the cardboard boxes surrounding them.

'OK, I think we all have a fair overview of the case now,' Hillary said, her voice sounding just slightly scratchy from the dust-clogged air. She coughed and took another sip of coffee, then consulted her notebook, which was already more than half full of notations and to-do lists.

'OK, so, Andrew Feeley then.' She got up and attached a photograph of a young man onto a cork notice board. 'Aged just twenty-one when he died.' She tapped the photograph, which depicted a reasonably good-looking and clean-shaven young man with dark blond hair and brown eyes. 'The only child of his mother Karen Feeley and her partner at the time, Malcolm Comer, known as Malkie. Malkie Comer, it seems, has been in and out of stir on a regular basis for most of his adult life, but not for anything too major. Nothing that involved excessive violence, for instance, or the use of firearms or knives. Drink and laziness seem to be the motivating factors behind his life of crime — but that doesn't mean that he's not a nasty piece of work. Got in trouble a few times for beating on his wife, too. Needless to say, Karen Feeley soon learned the error of her ways in taking up with him, and eventually got shot of him, later marrying one Sean Dalton.'

She broke off the recital to pin up a second photograph, this time of a handsome black man in his late thirties. 'Sean was thirty-eight years old at the time of the murder, a few years younger than Karen. He's worked on farms all his life, and has led a blameless life as far as we're concerned. Not even so much as a speeding ticket. Together, the couple had a little girl — Chloe — who was fourteen at the time of her half-brother's death.'

Hillary added the photograph of a pretty teenager to the board. She looked a little older than her years, and had a maturity about her eyes and expression that intimated that she had probably been one of those girls who had grown up fast.

'Now, this second marriage may have been the beginning of all Andrew's troubles and bad behaviour,' Hillary carried on, taking another swig of her coffee. 'According to the original SIO, Andrew, who couldn't have been any older than six or seven at the time his mother remarried, resented his stepfather right from the start. By all accounts, he worshipped his dad, Malkie, even though the man was more often banged up than at home caring for his family. Multiple witnesses told the investigators that as Andrew grew into a teenager, his resentment towards his stepfather grew, changing from childish tantrums into something far nastier. He was often heard to sling racial slurs at his stepfather, for example, and there were instances of vandalism of Sean Dalton's belongings that could almost certainly be laid at our murder victim's door. And probably a whole lot more that nobody outside the family ever knew about.'

Hillary paused and eyed the photograph of Sean Dalton thoughtfully. 'But Dalton, by all accounts, obviously put up with it, even though it must have been a strain on everyone in the family, because the marriage didn't actually fall apart until after Andrew's death.'

Claire sighed and nodded. 'You see it all the time. Not many marriages are strong enough to survive something as traumatic as a murder in the family, or the loss of a child. And in this case, it was both.'

Gareth nodded. 'I take it this makes the stepdad a viable suspect?'

'Only one of many, alas,' Hillary said. 'At the time of his death, Andrew Feeley was living in a large static caravan at the bottom of the family garden, along with his partner, a woman called Jade Hodson.'

So saying, yet another photograph was added to the cork board, this one depicting a nineteen-year-old girl. She looked petite and had a mass of red-gold hair, big blue eyes and a heart-shaped face. 'As you can see, Jade was — and probably still is — a pretty girl. She was raised in care for most of her life, which might go some way to explaining why she ended up with the likes of our Andrew.'

'Low self-esteem,' Claire snorted.

'Needless to say, their relationship wasn't known for running smoothly, and it was an open secret in the village that he was free with his fists. According to the witness statements, Jade was very often seen about the place sporting a black eye or split lip.'

'Like father like son,' Claire put in bitterly. 'It's learned behaviour.'

Gareth shifted a little on his seat. It had been a long day, his very first being out of his flat all day, and he wasn't used to doing so much sitting and standing without rest periods to lie down. Consequently, his leg was throbbing and his left hand was itching with pins and needles, but not for anything would he show his discomfort in front of the women.

Besides, the briefing fascinated him, so he merely shifted his body weight to a more comfortable position and waited.

Hillary, though, had noticed his difficulties, but made no sign of it. However, she began to speed things up a little. 'So she's another suspect for the list, especially since she was three months pregnant at the time.'

Claire saw Gareth frown, clearly not following the reasoning behind Hillary's words, so broke in helpfully: 'Women who put up with domestic violence when it's directed against themselves, sometimes for years and years, can finally stand up to their aggressor when they become pregnant. They worry about miscarrying, and turn their priorities to keeping the baby safe, rather than placating their abusive partner. But not always,' she added darkly.

Gareth nodded. 'Right. So Feeley might have started in on her, and instead of taking it, she fought back for once.'

Hillary nodded. 'But bear in mind, according to the files Jade is only five feet five, and slightly built. The chances that she could have got the better of Andrew in a knife fight are slim. Having said that, we can't rule it out. She could have taken him by surprise. As could any of our other suspects. And speaking of which . . .'

She pinned another photo to the board. 'This is Mrs Debbie Truman.' She stood back, revealing the image of a large, fleshy woman with brown curly hair and eyes. 'Aged forty-one at the time of the crime, she is the mother of . . .' Another photo was added, this time of a boy who looked to be a few years younger than their victim. 'Toby Truman. Now, the original SIO reckons that young Toby had probably got hooked on drugs around the age of fourteen or so, and was convinced — although he could never prove it — that not only was Andrew his supplier, but that Andrew was responsible for getting him hooked in the first place. It's not uncommon for small-time drug dealers to try and boost their client base by giving stuff away free to curious youngsters until they're well and truly hooked, and have to start paying for it. This was certainly his mother's belief, and she made no bones about the fact that she was sure Andrew Feeley deliberately targeted her son, and others. The fact that they had lived almost next door to the Feeleys for all their lives, and that the two boys had attended the same village primary school and then the same local comprehensive, apparently meant nothing to our murder victim.'

For a moment the room was silent as everyone contemplated Debbie Truman. 'Needless to say,' Hillary broke the silence, 'this woman in particular had reason to hate the dead man with a passion.'

She paused and then stretched, and determined to let the new boy get off in good time, faked smothering a yawn. 'All right, there's not much more to tell. Needless to say, none of the main suspects could prove alibis. Sean Dalton was working in the fields all day, but driving a tractor around on his own, he has nobody to vouch for his whereabouts at the time Andrew was killed. Mrs Truman, who had a part-time job where she worked only in the mornings, claimed to be alone at home at the relevant time. According to the post-mortem, it's believed that Andrew died sometime between two and four p.m. on the afternoon that his body was found.'

Hillary quickly scanned the pathology report. 'Normally time of death can't be narrowed down that easily, unless the victim is found shortly after death, as was the case here,' she added, strictly for the new boy's benefit. Whilst television shows very often blithely set times of death as if set in stone, everyone from the most experienced doctor down to the newly promoted constable knew that, in reality, it was a luxury to know with any real certainty when a victim had actually died.

She glanced at the cork board. 'Jade, who had been unemployed at the time, says she was at home in the caravan, watching telly. Karen Feeley backs her up in this, but DI Barker has been at pains to point out that Karen Feeley was clearly very fond of her son's partner, and probably wouldn't have hesitated to lie to protect her. As it is, with Karen also home alone in her own house whilst Jade was in the caravan, her word is not much use anyway, as Jade could easily have left her home without Andrew's mother being any the wiser.'

Hillary, somewhat wearily, pushed a wave of hair off her cheek and sighed. 'We have to bear in mind that Karen has lived in the same council house for all her life, since her parents were the original inhabitants, and the council agreed to her staying on after they died. And as with lots of buildings put up in the late 1940s in small villages, the property has an abnormally large garden, which can accommodate a large static caravan with room to spare. And according to the map of the garden made by DI Barker at the time, the caravan was located right at the bottom of a rather overgrown garden, and the direct line of sight of it from the house was mostly concealed by large shrubs.'

She finished her mug of coffee and stood up. 'Right, I think that's it for the day. Nobody's going to mind if we knock off a bit early. Tomorrow we start work in earnest,' she warned.

Claire got up gratefully. 'Well, I dare say my better half will appreciate having something hot and ready waiting for him when he gets home from work,' she laughed. 'And it wasn't myself I had in mind, so much as a microwaved Sainsbury's hotpot.' She winked good-naturedly at Gareth, who grinned back at her.

Hillary watched the interaction with a smile of her own. If anyone could make the new boy feel at ease it would be Claire. The mother of three grown children — two of them boys — she had a way of smoothing over any awkwardness that might arise in the male breast.

As Claire began to tell him all about her husband, Bobby, who was a telephone engineer for BT, Hillary turned and walked back to her own stationery cupboard, which was supposed to pass for her office. Although the other two members of her team were set to leave, she would stay on for hours yet, doing unpaid overtime, getting to know the case inside out.

She'd got into the habit now of avoiding being alone for too long on the narrowboat, with nothing to do.

CHAPTER THREE

Gareth was so sure that he would be the first one in that when he walked into the small communal office at just gone eight o'clock the next morning, he stopped short in the doorway at the sight of Hillary Greene sitting at the spare desk, industriously reading a file. Every now and then she paused to scribble notes into her notebook. But that didn't mean that she had failed to notice Gareth's arrival, for in the next instant, she glanced up at him and smiled briefly.

'You're quick off the mark,' she greeted him. 'You don't have to arrive early to impress the boss you know. If the super didn't tell you, there's no such thing as paid overtime around these parts.'

Gareth smiled and took his own seat. 'I know that, ma'am. I just wanted to get a head start — and working odd hours isn't unusual for me. Well, I mean, in the past it wasn't,' he added, a shade clumsily. In the army, the concept of a 'normal working day' had been more or less non-existent.

Hillary, though, didn't seem to notice his momentary unease. 'I dare say it'll take you some time to find your feet. Being in the army must be a hard way of life to leave behind.'

Gareth's lips tightened, but he said nothing.

Hillary looked at him thoughtfully, not really surprised that he hadn't taken her up on her unspoken offer to open up a bit and talk about himself. No doubt it would take him some time to begin to feel comfortable in his new environment. And she knew from experience that a lot of people, but men in particular, never liked to admit any weaknesses — even when they were glaringly obvious.

But then, she couldn't really take the moral high ground on that score either.

She carried on working, watching him surreptitiously as he went about settling in at his desk. The thin white scar that cut a line from his forehead and neatly bisected his left eyebrow made it obvious at first glance that this was a man who'd had a few knocks in life, but the scar wasn't disfiguring in any real sense. It didn't, for instance, pull down his eyelid, or pucker his skin. In fact, she mused, with a wry inner smile, it would probably be the sort of scar that the romantic novelist Barbara Cartland would have ascribed to her plethora of heroes. It seemed to accent his rather austere good looks rather than detract from them.

She knew from his personnel file that Gareth's marriage had recently broken up, but she didn't think that either his noticeable limp or the weakness in his left arm would be any real deterrent in him finding a new partner. Always supposing he was looking to find one.

Catching her scrutiny at last, Gareth took a slow deep breath and said quietly, 'I just wanted to say that I appreciate being given my job here, ma'am. I know I couldn't have been an obvious choice, but I can promise you that my . . . physical condition won't affect the quality of my work. I'm determined to learn on the job and to do it well. And I also just wanted to say, ma'am, that I have no problems taking orders from a female commanding officer.'

During his somewhat restless night, he'd debated the pros and cons of making such a speech, wondering if talking about the elephant in the room was even necessary. He'd finally dozed off having come to no particular conclusion, but finding himself alone in the quiet building with his new boss, it felt as if the decision had been made for him.

Hillary met his steady gaze with one of her own. His eyes were that shade of very pale blue that some people could find disconcerting. She occasionally saw that pale shade in the eyes of some dogs, and for some reason, they had always struck her as being slightly sinister.

She smiled at herself for the whimsical thought, and nodded at him. 'First of all, you got the job strictly on your merits, and I had nothing to do with the hiring process. Secondly, I'm not, strictly speaking, your commanding officer, since we're both civilians. Which means I'm not, technically, a DI anymore, although the title is still mostly respected around here, in an honorary sort of way. Most people know me from the twenty-odd years I worked here on the force, and still think of me that way. Thirdly, I have no issue with your physical abilities one way or another, so long as you can do the job that needs to be done. And if you can walk, talk, listen, use your brain and do as you're told, I don't see why either one of us should have any problems. Fair enough?'

Gareth smiled. 'Fair enough, ma'am.'

* * *

When Claire came in dead on time at the dot of nine, she found her boss and the new boy deep in the files, making notes.

'Morning, Claire,' Hillary said amiably. 'Right, first order of the day is compiling up-to-date information and contact details for our main suspects and witnesses. Since the murder didn't happen that long ago, I'm hoping that most people involved are still around, and haven't moved to the Outer Hebrides or remarried and changed their names more than once.'

Claire rolled her eyes. 'From your mouth to God's ear, guv,' she said with feeling.

'However, I daresay some will have changed address and phone number, so that's a nice day on the computer for someone,' she said, glancing from Claire to Gareth.

Normally, she would always give the new recruit the scut work on their first real day of work. It was partly because seniority had its privileges, and Claire might object if she didn't, but also because it taught them, right from the start, that police work wasn't all *Sweeney*-style 'banging up the villains.' Let alone did it resemble some of the more slick CSI shows, which had their leading characters swanning around in Armani suits, making use of state-of-the-art tech.

But in this instance, she knew that she was going to cast tradition aside, and give the boring, painstaking job to Claire. And since it was the new boy himself who had brought up the issue of his physical limitations, she needed the chance to assess for herself just what they were, plus his possible strengths. And there was no better place to find out what someone was made of than in the field.

'Claire, perhaps you could do that?' she looked at the former sergeant, who grinned back at her good-naturedly.

'An easy day in the office, guv? No worries.'

'You can also set up the Murder Book while you're at it,' Hillary added. She felt, rather than saw, the new boy stiffen into alertness at the admittedly attention-grabbing phrase, and turned to look at him.

'The Murder Book is a running record of everything we do while working the cold case. Every task you complete, you need to make a note of it for the book, keep track of it, and add to it as you go along. You also need to keep apprised of what others have added to it, so that you always have an overview of the complete state of the investigation. That's because we'll be splitting our tasks throughout the course of the next few weeks, and everyone needs to have *all* the facts at their fingertips, not just those details that they themselves have unearthed. Clear?'

'Yes, ma'am.'

'Right then. Now that we're more or less organised, it's time to get out and about and give you your first taste of fieldwork. Which sounds far grander than it actually is,' Hillary added with a wry smile. 'Basically, we go out and talk to people and listen to what they say. What we're looking for is something missed by the original team. Often, with the passage of time — especially when it's been years, as in this case — witnesses are less reluctant to speculate than they are at the actual time of the crime. They're less worried, less nervous, less inclined to be cautious. They feel more removed, and therefore less involved. Which means that things they felt reluctant to say at the time, in the heat of the moment, don't seem so important to them anymore, which makes them far more willing to open up to us now. Do you understand what I'm getting at?'

'I think so,' Gareth said.

'What's more, most people, when a crime is committed in a small community,' Claire took up the lesson, 'rightly or wrongly think they probably "know" who did it. And often they can be right. But obviously, they can also be wrong. But what most people *won't* do is stick their neck out and give an opinion when they don't have any proof. It's just human nature. You don't lift your head above the parapet. You keep schtum. You don't get involved. The coppers are around, sniffing about, asking questions. You scuttle home and keep the curtains closed. There must be a killer about somewhere. You want nothing to do with any of it. But then, time slowly passes. Nothing else bad happens. People forget the dead person — and in this particular case, when nobody's actually mourning the victim much, they forget them very quickly — and they fade easily into the background and become just ancient history. Life goes on. And now, years later, somebody comes around, bringing up the old history, and it's interesting more than worrying. People remember things they never mentioned at the time, and are now willing to say who they always thought must have had a hand in it. People open up . . . And that's where we step in and reap the rewards of what they now think of as little more than gossip.'

Claire paused for breath and shrugged. 'It's not just gossip, of course, but actual testimony that might be used in court, if it's relevant, but we're at pains to keep that aspect of it to ourselves.'

Gareth nodded but said nothing. Clearly, Claire mused with an inner smile, nobody was going to be able to accuse the new boy of being a chatterbox.

'So,' Hillary said, 'as you can see, we have something of an advantage over the original team. But always keep in mind, this is not a competition. DI Barker, as far as I can see, conducted a thorough and efficient investigation. We're not out to prove him incompetent, or to score points. What we're looking for are *new* leads — the odd stray bit of apparently random or irrelevant information that he didn't have the time or the resources to follow up on, but which might, just *might*, lead to something more substantial for us. We're also looking at it with totally new eyes too, the value of which shouldn't be underestimated. It's very easy to develop tunnel vision when working a case, or to get fixated on one or two set ideas. And when that happens, an investigation can easily go off the rails. But we come to this fresh, with no preconceived ideas and no agenda of our own. And the combination of all of these things can sometimes give us something new to work with. But not always,' she warned him seriously. 'During the next few days and weeks, you'll get really caught up in the case, and you'll want to solve it so badly you'll be able to taste it. But there's no guarantee that we'll be able to close the case any more than DI Barker was able to. Failure is always an option.'

'Yeah right, like *you* know all about failure, guv,' Claire grinned, mock-rolling her eyes.

Hillary grunted but said nothing, turning instead to the new boy.

'OK, get your coat, Mr Proctor,' Hillary said crisply. 'Where do you think we're going?'

The question clearly threw him. He blinked at her, realising he'd been caught out, and not liking it at all. His very first and instinctive response was to say Tackley, since that was where the crime had been committed. But something told him that might well be the wrong answer.

But where else would they be going?

The pause lengthened, and Gareth began to feel alternately stupid and annoyed. But it was clear that he couldn't stand there like a dummy all day. Best simply to admit what was now obvious.

'I don't know, ma'am.'

Hillary nodded. 'Good answer,' she surprised him by saying flatly. 'Don't ever think you know it all. It can get you into all sorts of trouble.'

Gareth blinked again and began to feel slightly angry. Was he being patronised? Or had he just been given one of the best pieces of advice in his life?

He met Hillary Greene's clear, faintly amused sherry-coloured eyes and instinctively made up his mind which it was. 'I'll remember that, ma'am,' he promised.

Hillary nodded. She had the pleasant feeling that the new boy was going to work out just fine.

* * *

Tackley lay only a couple of miles from Kidlington as the crow flies, and it took them barely ten minutes to get there. They took Puff, who was happier with the new, drier day, and started first time, thus saving his owner from embarrassment. Although the skies were still predominantly grey with only the odd interlude of sunshine, and the wind was definitely blustery, it was a warm wind, as if summer was saying goodbye, rather than the approaching winter saying hello. Consequently she had donned only a lightweight tweed jacket that morning, and had left it unbuttoned.

As they passed the impressive village green, Hillary looked at a large Georgian-style house with a massive front window and felt a small tug of nostalgia. If that hadn't been a village shop in days of yore, she'd eat her hat.

The village was fairly large, and had probably once boasted two or more pubs, before the smoking ban, cheap supermarket beer and the proliferation of large-screen televisions had all but put them out of business. As it was, she could now only see one that remained open.

She knew the Feeley house belonged in a small development of council houses built on the far side of the village. And as they turned a sharp bend and began to climb up the hill that would take them out of the village at the far end, she saw the unmistakable grey concrete buildings rising up on a bank to her right. The main village 'street' was little more than a country lane, clogged as such arteries always were by intricately patterned deposits of mud left from the passage of huge tractor wheels. Clearly the surrounding farmers used the road often.

If she had wanted to test Gareth Proctor's stamina, then the winding, steep little pathway that led up the hill to the cul-de-sac of council houses at the top couldn't have been a better set-up.

But although he walked with a simple wooden walking stick, and favoured his left leg, he kept up with her easily, and without any breathlessness. She did notice, however, that his left hand, which he occasionally used to hold on to a smooth, rounded handrail, was criss-crossed with severe scarring, and looked misshapen. But he hadn't actually lost any of his fingers.

At the top of the path, she paused to look behind her. As expected, the elevation gave them a pleasant view of the lie of the land. Mostly brown fields, which had recently been harvested and now lay in attractively ploughed furrows, stretched to the left and right, whilst the odd patch of green denoted pasture — mainly for a herd of mixed cattle that munched and meandered contentedly in the distance. A copse of trees that ran away from the village to the horizon caught and held her interest. Not because of the lovely display of autumnal colours, but because it was the site where Andrew Feeley's body had been found.

'You can see why it would be a popular place to walk your dog. Especially in the summer,' Gareth said quietly, clearly following her line of vision and thought. 'In the middle of July, it would provide welcome shade.'

Hillary nodded. 'Yes. It's also a good meeting place — out of the way of prying eyes.'

'You think the victim arranged to meet someone in there, ma'am?'

'I don't think lazy young lads like Andrew would voluntarily walk anywhere for the fun of it, do you? And I can't exactly see him being a nature lover, at one with the birds and the butterflies. He'd be more likely to take his motorbike to the pub a hundred yards down the lane. No, if he was in those woods, I think it's fairly safe to assume he had a reason to be there.'

Gareth nodded. It made sense. 'Which would make his death more likely to have been premeditated then?'

'Unless someone else spotted him heading into the trees, followed him, and then did for him before he met up with whoever it was that he'd arranged to meet there. Or else hid in the trees and waited until the meeting was over and the other participant had left, and then challenged Feeley,' she pointed out. She thought that scenario was a bit unlikely, but you never knew.

'That would have been a bit risky though, wouldn't it?' Gareth mused.

'That would depend on the circumstances,' Hillary said succinctly. 'Anyway, speculation only gets us so far. Let's start where you nearly always start on cases like this — with the victim's immediate family. We know that at least Karen Feeley, the boy's mother, hasn't moved residence.' It was one of the first things she'd checked the first night of the case.

'Is that usual, ma'am? I'd have thought most people would want to leave the place where their kid was killed.'

Hillary shrugged. 'There is no "normal" when it comes to grief and mourning and human nature, I think you'll find,' she said flatly.

And Gareth, suddenly remembering that Hillary Greene knew a lot about grief and loss, could have kicked himself.

'Ma'am,' he said smartly.

Hillary gave a little sigh, and led the way around the cul-de-sac, checking house numbers. It didn't take them long to find the Feeley residence.

The front garden wasn't particularly big, but the plain concrete path that led off from the gate seemed intent on leading them away from the front door and to a side entrance. Passing obligingly down a narrow passageway, they soon found themselves walking out into a huge, overgrown but beautiful back garden.

It was long and wide and more generous than even its immediate neighbours, due to the semi-detached house's placement on the rounded end of the two rows of buildings. The end of the garden terminated in a line of tall mixed deciduous trees, behind which was a farmer's field, currently full of sweetcorn but in the process of being harvested, if the noise of the large combines was anything to go by.

Close by the hedge, a large static caravan was just visible. But forsythia bushes, some large blackcurrant bushes and a patch of mallow all but hid it from sight, and Hillary saw at once that DI Barker had been right to be sceptical of Karen Feeley's testimony that Jade Hodson wouldn't have been able to leave the caravan without being seen.

A straggling but productive vegetable patch, badly in need of weeding, was flanked by a ramshackle collection of sheds, which were probably used for storage. A large, rather worse-for-wear black plastic water butt took advantage of the rain water dripping from the inadequate guttering. A stand of fruit trees, small and bent and old, made for a haphazard orchard in one corner. Patches of Michaelmas daisies, chrysanthemums and dahlias provided the odd splash of bright colour. The grass needed mowing. A blackbird helped himself to blackberries that grew wild down one side of the boundary. It was, all in all, a charmingly messy sort of garden that the wildlife probably loved.

'What a mess,' Gareth said disdainfully.

Hillary nodded. No doubt in the army neatness and precision was king, even when it came to the grounds of the barracks. Had she read somewhere that soldiers actually had to paint stones white, so that they'd look neat? Or had she imagined that?

'Well, it obviously suits the lady of the house,' she said amiably. 'Which is surely all that matters.'

'Yes, ma'am,' Gareth said, clearly acknowledging the slight reprimand implicit in her voice, whilst not moving from his stance by one inch. He was happy to follow her to the door and turn his back on the garden, because he could feel himself itching to get hold of a pair of garden shears and a lawnmower.

CHAPTER FOUR

Karen Feeley opened the door to their knock and stood looking at them without any apparent curiosity.

Hillary sometimes phoned ahead when she was going to visit the family of the bereaved. It was a courtesy, and it was also practical, in that she could be sure that someone would be in to receive her. But in this instance she'd decided to take the chance of a wasted journey, because her desire to see how Karen reacted to the reopening of her son's case without having prior warning was much more important.

She knew from the research done by her team so far that Karen had, for nearly twenty years, worked from home, running her own small business offering her sewing services, so it wasn't that surprising that her luck was in.

'Yes?' Karen prompted, her eyes going from Hillary to Gareth, clearly trying to place them and no doubt wondering if they were potential customers, but looking unconvinced.

Perhaps, Hillary mused, neither one of them looked as if they were in need of having their hems lowered, or their waistbands let out. She just hoped that they didn't look like double-glazing salesmen. Or worse — estate agents.

She dug into her bag to produce her ID, and Gareth, following suit, quickly opened up his own wallet, for the first time ever displaying the laminated card he'd been given, proving his identity and the fact that he worked as a civilian consultant for the Thames Valley Police. It was quite a moment for him, and he wasn't unaware of its significance.

His new life had, for better or worse, now well and truly begun.

Hillary introduced them and told Karen why they were standing on her doorstep. She knew that at the time of her son's murder this woman had been forty-one years of age, but she now looked more like a sixty-something than someone who could only be in her late forties.

At five feet eight, her formerly blond hair had now gone almost completely grey, and she had the scrawny look of someone who smoked too much and ate too little. Her big brown eyes, which had probably been her best feature in her youth, looked dull and, as Hillary's words penetrated, decidedly fearful.

'Our Andy's case? You're working on that again? Why? I thought that the case was closed.' She shot out the words in a series of sudden bursts, as if she had no control over them. She looked puzzled and dismayed, and clearly felt shocked.

'We don't ever really close an unsolved murder case, Ms Feeley,' Hillary explained gently. 'I'm a former DI, and now I work cold cases. Every now and then, after a period of time has elapsed, we review unsolved crimes, such as your son's, and take a second look at them. We sometimes find the passage of time can be more of a help than a hindrance. May we come in?'

Karen Feeley blinked, then finally seemed to get a hold of herself. Hillary wondered how much, if anything, of what she'd just said had been fully taken on board.

'Oh. Yes, of course, come on in. Sorry to keep you standing about on the doorstep, it's just . . . I never . . . Er, would you like a cup of tea?' Once again, the words seemed to shoot out of her as if she had no control over them.

They stepped into a small but neat hallway and without waiting for an answer to her question, Karen moved off down the corridor towards the far end, shepherding them into a small but equally neat and clean kitchen. The tiling on the walls had been recently done in a multi-coloured geometric design, and plain mock-marble white worktops gleamed. A small pine kitchen table was tucked away in one corner, one side of it pressed up firmly against the wall, and Karen indicated with a vague wave of her hand the three chairs that were grouped around it. 'Please, sit down. Do you want tea or coffee?'

Hillary opted instantly for coffee. Gareth asked for tea, decaf if she had it. Karen had to admit to only having bog-standard teabags, and set about filling the kettle with quick, nervous movements.

Her shoulders were tense, and Hillary could almost hear the wheels in her brain whirring maniacally as she set about spooning instant coffee into a mug and dropping two teabags into proper cups. She paused, as if for a moment unable to think where she kept the sugar and milk. She was clearly still very rattled.

Eventually, she made her way to the fridge and withdrew a plastic bottle of milk, and then, in another cupboard by the sink, a slightly chipped porcelain sugar bowl. By the time the kettle had boiled, and she was forced to finally sit and stop dashing about here and there, she looked a little calmer.

'So,' she said, with forced brightness, as she drew back her chair and sat down. 'What can I do to help?' She had her hands wrapped around her cup of tea, and Hillary wondered how she could stand the heat of it. It must be burning her fingers, but the woman didn't seem to notice.

Hillary smiled gently at her. 'What can you tell us about what you remember from that day, the day Andrew died?' she began calmly.

'Well, it was hot,' Karen said at once. 'I mean, really hot. Even though it wasn't what you'd call high summer yet, we were having one of those mini-heatwaves that we've started to get nowadays. You know what they're like! I had all the doors and windows open, and made sure that the dog had an old tin tub full of water in the garden, so that he could keep himself cool. He's not with me now, the poor old chap.'

'I'm sorry,' Hillary said. 'Was Andrew fond of the dog?'

'Hmm? Oh, no, not really. He never walked him or anything. I did that. But not that day — I took him out in the evenings when the weather was that hot.'

'Good idea,' Hillary said. 'Dogs can really suffer in the heat, can't they? What was his name?'

'Barney.'

She could tell from the way Gareth looked from her to the witness with a studiedly blank gaze that the new boy was finding the tone and content of the interview surprising. No doubt he was wondering why they were talking about dead dogs and the weather.

But he'd learn.

Hillary was happy to listen to anything at all the boy's mother wanted to tell her. Always, of course, with one inner ear alert for all the things that she *wasn't* saying or was taking pains to avoid mentioning.

'So, what else stays in your memory about that day?' Hillary prompted, taking a sip of her coffee. It wasn't the good-quality stuff Steven used to . . .

She stopped the thought right there, took another sip, and forced herself to concentrate on her witness.

'I had a big order in — some bridesmaids' dresses, in a lovely shade of champagne. Two of them, when delivered to the bride-to-be, were in a right state. It was a rush job, as the wedding was that weekend and I was busy shortening both sets of sleeves and re-sewing a load of little crystal beads that didn't lie flat properly. A right fiddly job that was, I can tell you.'

Hillary nodded. 'Sounds as if you were busy.' So much, she thought wryly, for this woman's insistence that she'd have noticed if Jade Hodson had left her caravan. If she'd had that much work on, she doubted that Karen would have left her sewing room until the dreadful news about her son had been brought to her door by the responding officers.

'I take it Andy was living in the caravan with Jade at the time?' she put in.

'Yes. That's right. He moved out of here when he was eighteen. He'd have preferred to go and live somewhere like Oxford or Banbury, a place with a bit of life, you know, but house prices around here . . .' Karen shrugged one bony shoulder helplessly. 'As it was, he was lucky that a mate of his had this static caravan he wanted rid of. Andy was able to buy it, and I said he could have the bottom end of the garden for his own space, like. We got it all plumbed in and hooked up to the electric. Jade moved in when she got together with Andy.'

'How long had they been living together?' Hillary asked. She was casually jotting down notes as she did so, glad that her home-made variety of shorthand was still pretty good. She only hoped she would be able to read it back later, when it came to updating the Murder Book! Usually she relied on the junior members of her team to do this work, but with such an important witness, and with Gareth so new to the job, she didn't want to take any chances.

'Oh, it must have been since just before Christmas the previous year,' Karen said, having had to think about it for a few seconds.

'And Andrew wasn't at work that day?' Hillary slipped in nonchalantly. She knew, of course, that the victim had never in his life had what could be called a 'proper' job, with regular hours and a boss and a pay cheque. Instead, he belonged to that group of rather diverse people that magistrates tended to refer to as 'having no visible means of support.'

Such people could range from professional gamblers, to odd-jobbers who always did cash-in-hand jobs, to buskers, beggars, and, of course, people like Andrew Feeley. You couldn't, after all, list petty larceny, drug dealing and a bit of pimping on the side as your main source of revenue when filling in your tax return.

'No, like me, Andy was self-employed,' Karen said, her eyes very carefully not meeting Hillary's own.

Hillary didn't push it. Her son had been murdered, and whilst nobody in the room had any doubt that Karen must have been well aware of how her son acquired his money, she didn't see any need to belabour the fact. Well, not at this stage, anyway.

'Did you see Andy that day at all?' Hillary asked next. She knew that the original SIO had gone over all this, but she wanted to see if Karen's story now varied in any significant way. She also wanted to see and hear for herself just how the woman reacted to her questions. It was one thing to read dry facts from a report, but it was a vastly different thing to be able to witness body language, tonal changes and little nuances first-hand.

'I saw him around breakfast time. He came in about half past nine for a bacon sandwich,' Karen said. 'It was his favourite, and Jade was finding the smell of frying bacon was making her feel sick. So he came over here for me to do the cooking instead.'

Gareth, who was perfectly capable of making himself a bacon sandwich one-handed, wondered why the lazy sod hadn't cooked his own breakfast.

'Yes, I understand she was three months pregnant at the time?' Hillary interposed.

'That's right, poor thing. Suffered terrible from morning sickness, she did. And I just don't know how she's going to cope with all this,' Karen put in, looking at Hillary with the first signs of imminent anger. 'She and little Briana don't need this upheaval in their lives right now. Briana's getting on well at school, but everybody knows about her daddy. They haven't had it easy, either one of 'em, bless 'em, and this will just rake it all up again. And you know how cruel kids can be . . .'

'I'm sorry, Ms Feeley . . .'

'Well, it's just . . . you and all this have come as a bit of a bolt from the blue. I feel all upside down, and no doubt they will too.'

Hillary nodded. 'I understand, and like I said, I'm very sorry we're causing you distress. I can understand that it's a bit of a shock, but surely it's also a good thing?'

For a long, long moment, Karen Feeley stared at her blankly. Then a look of slow panic filled Karen's face as she realised that she simply didn't understand what this strange woman could possibly mean.

Hillary found that interesting. Very interesting indeed. 'I mean, your son's killer was never found. So you must be pleased that another investigation is getting under way? It means that now there's at least a chance you can get justice for Andrew at last,' she elaborated.

Karen still looked blank.

Beside her, she again sensed that Gareth, who had yet to speak, was finding it all a bit baffling. He was no doubt wondering if it was usual for a family member of a murder victim to be so unenthusiastic about the news that their loved one's case was to become a priority once more.

Hillary could have told him that it wasn't.

And it made her wonder why the dead boy's mother was so distinctly underwhelmed by it all.

'Oh, yes, I see what you mean now,' Karen finally said feebly. 'It's just . . . I suppose I've become so used to the fact that we'd never know . . .' She stopped, took a long shuddering breath, and then another. Her brown eyes shimmered with unshed tears, and for a moment her lower lip trembled in warning.

But then she seemed to pull herself back from the brink of tears. 'And it's just that having it all brought up again . . . I'm not sure it'll be . . . I don't know what Chloe will say about it all,' she finally wailed helplessly.

'Chloe is your daughter with Sean Dalton, yes?' Hillary said briskly. Her witness was all over the place, barely able to complete a sentence, and the interview was in danger of descending into chaos if she didn't get a firm grip on it.

'Yes. She's all grown up now, and is studying to be a solicitor,' Karen said, Hillary's no-nonsense attitude helping her to pull herself together and organise her thoughts. Unfortunately, the new topic only set her off down a familiar theme.

'She doesn't need all this . . . horror . . . starting up again. She was only fourteen when it all kicked off the first time, and it affected her so badly. Her schoolwork suffered, and she hardly went out, not even to the sports club, and she used to love trampolining and gymnastics. It took her years to get back to normal — *for all of us* to get back to normal,' Karen emphasised, her eyes big and wide with appeal. 'Can't you see, I'm dreading it starting up all over again?'

Hillary nodded. She could understand this woman wanting to protect her family, but was it just emotional defence? Or was she hiding something?

'It sounds as if she's a very smart young woman,' Hillary said, deliberately trying to keep the topic on safer ground. The last thing she needed was for Karen to become hysterical or break down altogether.

She also needed to get as much information from Andrew's mother as possible, before she had time to gather her wits and stonewall her. Instinct told her that that was what was going to happen sooner or later, and she gave herself a mental pat on the back for getting to this woman before she'd had a chance to put up any defences.

'Oh she is,' Karen said, with evident pride. 'Chloe's smart as a whip, and pretty as a picture. She lives in Woodstock with her partner, and like I said, she's training to become a solicitor. She already works in a solicitor's office, and the partners say they'll take her on when she passes her final exams, or articles or whatever it is she's working on now. But I don't know if they know about Andy . . . being murdered, I mean. I just hope they won't hold it against her when they find out! They have to be so careful about scandal, don't they, those kinds of people. Oh, you don't think there'll be any publicity again, do you?' Again, the big brown eyes looked at her in horror. 'The last time the papers were horrible. Hinting at all sorts, and making our lives a misery! We even had reporters going through our rubbish bins and—'

Abruptly, Karen stopped speaking. A wave of what could have been shame, or maybe guilt, crossed her face. 'You must think I'm awful,' she finally whispered. 'My poor boy, nearly ten years dead, and me going on about . . . But Chloe's all I have left, you see. And little Briana. And you have to look after the *living*, don't you?' she said forcefully.

Hillary smiled gently. 'Of course, Ms Feeley,' she agreed mildly. But although it might be this mother's job to look after her family, it certainly wasn't *her* job. Her job was to find out who had killed Andrew Feeley and why.

'Do you have any idea who killed your son, Karen?' Hillary asked softly.

Karen went pale. For another long moment she seemed incapable of speech. Then she said, in a small, tight voice, 'I don't know.' She paused, swallowed hard, then said in a rush, 'My boy . . . I loved him . . . but he wasn't . . . he wasn't . . . he wasn't a *nice* boy. Do you understand? I loved him, I *did*,' she insisted fiercely, 'from the moment he was born. But his father, his natural father I mean, Malkie, he was never no good. Not to me, and not to Andy. He never took him out anywhere, fishing or to play football or nothing like that. He never showed him any affection. Not that it ever mattered to Andy — he just adored his dad. And when Malkie went down that last time, to prison I mean, and we split up . . . it seemed to really affect the little tyke. He went all quiet and locked up inside himself and became, well . . . mean.'

She stopped talking, and Hillary noted that Karen was panting a little, probably with both the effort of talking so much and so fast, coupled with the no doubt overpowering rush of emotion that she must be experiencing.

'I always tried my best for him, I swear,' Karen began again, her voice as forlorn as the look on her thin, tired face. 'But he wouldn't *let* me love him. You know? I'd try to hug him, or josh him along when he got moody, or try and play card games with him or what have you, but he wouldn't have it. He'd just push me away and become right snide. He seemed to blame me for his father leaving us — but of course, I couldn't stop Malkie from going to prison, could I?' she appealed, her voice rising a notch. 'And when I married Sean it just all got so much *worse*. Andy hated Sean, you see, right from the off. At first, when he was only little, we convinced ourselves that he'd grow out of it. All the tantrums and tears, and the threats. But he never did. And when he became a teenager . . .'

Karen threw her hands in the air in despair. 'I mean, being a teenager's bad enough, ain't it, having to cope with all your hormones and puberty and what the teachers call peer pressure and whatnot. But with Andy . . . it was a nightmare. A right nightmare.'

'I imagine it must have put a severe strain on your marriage,' Hillary put in gently.

'Oh yeah, it did,' Karen admitted candidly. Then she smiled. 'But Sean was wonderful. You won't find me saying a bad word about him,' Karen said a shade aggressively, as if Hillary had somehow impugned her ex-husband. 'He put up with no end of shit . . . sorry, pardon . . . no end of nonsense from Andy. But he never raised a finger to him. Well, sometimes maybe he'd tan his hide, but Andy could be such a little bugger. But I mean Sean wasn't ever free with his fists, not like Malkie . . .' Suddenly, realising that she was wandering onto potentially dangerous ground, Karen shifted tack. 'Anyway, like I said, Andy moved out the moment he could, into the caravan like. Things got a bit easier then, what with them not having to live in the same house. They could avoid one another. It gave us some peace at last.'

'Yes, I see. That must have been a relief,' Hillary said. 'So, let's get back to the day Andrew died, shall we? You said he came in for a bacon sandwich. Then what happened?'

Karen shrugged. 'Nothing much. He said he had someone to see, and left.'

Hillary felt herself tense. Now *that* was new. DI Barker hadn't mentioned that, and Hillary knew he wouldn't have missed such an important indicator. 'Did Andrew say who that was?' she asked, careful to keep her voice calm.

'Nah. He was a closed-mouth sort, Andy was.'

'Did you get the feeling he was looking forward to the meeting? Or did he seem anxious?'

Karen sighed. 'Don't think so — he just mentioned it, in passing like.'

'What time do you think that was?'

'I dunno for sure. Around eleven o'clock?'

'And then?' Hillary pressed.

'Nothing. I got on with my sewing. I had a peanut butter sandwich for my lunch, and something cold to drink. Like I said, it was hot that day. I had the radio on — they was playing one of those songs from the sixties, I remember that — when I got the knock on the door about four o'clock. That one about the bus stop. A boy meets a girl at the bus stop and they share an umbrella . . . Funny, I can remember the tune, even now. It was still playing when I opened the door, and this copp— this policeman in a uniform was standing there. I could see by the look on his face . . . I thought at first it was Sean, see? I thought he might have had an accident, working on the farm. His tractor turned over onto him and crushed him flat or something like that. But no. They told me it was Andy.'

She paused, and turned and looked out of the window. 'My boy was dead. And that's all I can tell you,' she concluded with an air of finality.

Hillary nodded. She knew there would have to be a second interview at some point — but right now, the woman was clearly exhausted. And there was a hint of stubbornness to that last sentence that told Hillary's experienced ear that the witness had had enough and was likely to become truculent and uncooperative if she was pressed any further right now.

'All right, Ms Feeley, I think that's all for now. Could you tell me where Jade and her daughter are living at the moment? Do they live here with you?'

'Nah, they're still in the caravan out there. I asked her right from the beginning to move in here, thought it'd be good for her and the baby, but she wouldn't have it. Said she wanted her independence and didn't want to get under me feet. Shame, though. It does seem a bit quiet in here sometimes, now Chloe's moved out and Sean isn't here anymore.'

'Right then, I'll go down and find her now.'

'Oh she won't be in. She's at work. Won't be back until she's picked Bree up from school,' Karen said quickly.

Hillary nodded. 'All right. I'll come back this afternoon then.' And no doubt by then Jade Hodson would have been warned and would have had ample time to rehearse what she was going to say, Hillary mused cynically.

She slowly got up, and Gareth did the same. As he rose, he put his injured hand on the tabletop to help support his weight, and Hillary saw Karen eyeing his disfigurement.

She winced slightly, and quickly averted her gaze. Gareth pretended not to notice.

'I'll keep you informed of our progress, of course,' Hillary lied smoothly as the other woman showed them to the door.

'Yeah, thanks,' Karen said listlessly.

Once outside, Gareth carefully planted his walking stick on the path, and waited for Hillary to speak.

'So. Your first ever interview,' Hillary smiled at him. 'What did you make of it?'

Gareth frowned. 'I'm not sure. I felt sorry for her though.'

Hillary nodded. 'Good. If you didn't feel sorry for her, it would mean you've got no compassion. What else?'

'I'm not sure I believe everything she said.'

'Good. If you did, it would mean that you've got no brains. As a general rule, scepticism never hurts,' Hillary said dryly. 'Now there's a motto for a T-shirt for you. Anything else?'

'It was clear that she knew her boy was a waste of space,' he said brutally.

Hillary nodded. 'And?'

Gareth thought some more, then shrugged. 'I don't know, ma'am,' he said, mindful of the lesson he'd been given earlier.

Hillary grinned approvingly at him. 'Well, since we're in the area, let's see if Debbie Truman is at home. According to Claire's research she's still living in the village.'

Gareth nodded. 'Must take some courage, that,' he remarked. 'Staying in Tackley, I mean. Local opinion must have had either her or her lad down as one of the main suspects in the murder. It takes some guts to look your peers in the eye and face down something like that.'

Hillary nodded. He was a fast learner, this new boy.

CHAPTER FIVE

Debbie Truman lived more or less in the middle of the village, just down a small lane lined with picturesque cottages, which had probably once been the exclusive domain of farm workers. Nowadays, of course, most of the cottages were privately owned, their original farmer landlords having cheerfully sold them off during the property booms, and had been renovated and extended to within an inch of their lives — and their boundaries. Since a railway line flirted past the outskirts of the village, Hillary surmised that it must be commuter heaven around here, which would mean that even the most modest of two-bedroom terraced dwellings would change hands for eye-watering sums.

From the background checks completed so far, she knew that Debbie Truman's now deceased husband had been a lifelong inhabitant of the village, and had inherited his home from his parents. No doubt they had had the good fortune to buy the place back in the mists of time when such rural backwaters were not so desirable, and houses could be purchased for mere hundreds of pounds. Otherwise, she doubted that someone who had worked as a railway porter for nearly thirty years, as had the late William Truman, could ever have hoped to buy a place in a village such as this.

'What can you remember about Debbie Truman, Mr Proctor?' Hillary shot the question at him as they walked down the narrow lane towards a small detached cottage set back in a neat garden. It was attractively tiled in grey slate, and built of the local ironstone. Unlike Karen's garden, however, here the tiny handkerchief-sized lawn was neatly mown, and the shrubs had all been trimmed back to wait out the winter months. Not a weed dared to grow between the old-fashioned crazy paving that led to the no-nonsense front porch, situated directly in the centre of the house, and even the fallen leaves had been raked and cleared.

'She's an old-fashioned cleaning lady, ma'am,' Gareth said confidently. 'Widowed, with one child. No previous record.'

Hillary nodded. So he'd checked the Murder Book, but that didn't mean that she wouldn't be checking up on his memory and testing his attention to detail throughout the case.

'At the time, she had three regular clients in this village, and two others in Rousham,' Hillary mentioned the neighbouring village casually, wondering if Gareth had had time yet to familiarise himself with the immediate area. 'So she works irregular hours — she might be out in the morning or afternoon, or both, depending on the preference of the people she "does" for. And she was doing so on the day Andrew Feeley was killed. According to DI Barker's reports, that day she'd only done a morning stint in Rousham — which means she has no alibi for the time of death, which, as you know, the pathologist put somewhere in the mid-afternoon. According to her original statement, she was at home during the relevant time, doing some washing, since it was such a hot day that she wanted to take advantage of the heat and get everything well aired. One of her neighbours confirmed that washing was up and out on her clothesline just after lunchtime. For what that's worth,' she added dryly.

Hillary rapped smartly on the door, hoping that today, unlike on that other fatal day eight years ago, Mrs Truman would not be doing a morning round. By her watch, it was barely eleven o'clock.

She was in luck, however, for the door was yanked energetically open almost immediately. The woman who stood looking at them from the threshold had been forty-one at the time of the murder, and didn't look that much older now. That was probably partly due to the fact that she was a large and fleshy woman, standing at nearly five feet eleven, with a chubby face that looked mostly unlined.

She had a lot of brown curly hair and deep-set brown eyes, but a small button nose and a cleft chin which lent her an oddly chipmunk-like and cute face that didn't sit well with the rest of her appearance. She was dressed in baggy denims and a chunky grey jumper that was sagging at the neck and just starting to fray at the cuffs. Probably old clothes that she wore when about to set out for work.

'Mrs Truman?' Hillary asked with a bland smile. She was already reaching for her identity card, as was Gareth beside her.

'Yes?' Debbie Truman looked questioningly from Hillary to Gareth. Her eyes, Hillary noticed, quickly took in her companion's walking stick, the way he half-hid his left hand by his side, and the white scar on his face. Unlike Karen, however, she had no trouble meeting his eyes without giving any impression of feeling pity, curiosity or embarrassment.

It must, Hillary thought, be a refreshing change for the ex-serviceman, who had probably become used to people not knowing quite how to act around him.

'We're civilian consultants with the Thames Valley Police, Mrs Truman. We're currently conducting a further investigation into the murder of Andrew Feeley,' Hillary explained concisely. 'Would it be possible to have a quick word with you?'

For a moment, the large woman stood silent and thoughtful. Then she said, 'Civilian consultants? You're not regular police then?'

'No. I retired from the force as a detective inspector several years ago,' Hillary admitted. 'I now help my former colleagues by working cold cases.'

Debbie slowly nodded. 'So I'm not obliged to talk to you then?' she clarified carefully. Her tone wasn't so much belligerent or challenging as careful and considered.

'No, Mrs Truman, you're not,' Hillary reluctantly confirmed, aware of how quickly and without much effort this woman had succeeded in putting her on the back foot. 'But we are, of course, hoping that you will.'

Debbie grunted and the merest hint of a smile tugged at her lips. 'I dare say,' she acknowledged. And then said nothing.

Again, Hillary found herself forced onto the offensive, for not many people could remain silent for any length of time. People, as a general rule, felt compelled to talk, especially to strangers representing authority, and Hillary began to sense, more and more, that she was dealing with someone here who could seriously test her mettle.

'I can assure you, it's nothing too terrible,' Hillary tried again, with her best unthreatening smile. 'We only want to go over your original statement and see if you've remembered anything new about that day over the course of the years.'

'I doubt it,' Debbie said, again after a moment's thought. She had a careful and stolid way of talking that most people might think was indicative of a slow mind.

But Hillary wasn't most people. She also didn't like the way the woman was beginning to look comfortable, wedged firmly in the doorway, and making no sign of inviting them in.

'As I'm sure you can appreciate, Ms Feeley is anxious that we get to the bottom of what happened to Andrew,' she tried again. Sometimes an appeal to someone's empathy worked wonders, but Hillary, in this case, wasn't about to hold her breath.

'Is she? Really?' the other woman asked sceptically.

This time it was Hillary's turn to pause and think. Was Debbie Truman being deliberately provocative, or did she genuinely know — or could make a good guess — that Karen Feeley hadn't exactly been overjoyed by the thought of her son's case being looked at again? And if the latter, then just what had made her think so?

Hillary wasn't forgetting that here, too, was a mother whose son's life had been blighted by misfortune.

'I think most mothers would want justice for their sons, don't you, Mrs Truman?' she finally asked, careful to keep her voice casual.

Debbie Truman's lips twitched again as she conceded the deftness of Hillary's wording. 'Depends just whose son you're talking about, don't it, Mrs . . . what was your name again?'

'Greene. Hillary Greene.'

Hillary, by now, wasn't at all surprised that this woman had picked up on her ambiguously phrased question. Or that Debbie hadn't been afraid to call her on it.

'Well, Mrs Greene,' Debbie said laconically, 'for myself, I've long given up on expectin' life to be fair or just about anything. As for Karen, I can't rightly believe that she's thrilled to have her son's case opened again. And nor will anybody else be around here, I reckon.' She paused, glanced around at the deserted country lane, and shrugged.

'Mind you, come to think on it, most folks now weren't even living here when Andrew Feeley died,' she mused, her Oxonian country accent thickening slightly as she became more and more pensive. 'Most folks round here nowadays are from London or Birmingham or where-have-you. Most of the true village families are dying out. These newcomers come in and buy a house, then set off for work early on the train every morning and come back late every evening. The only time you sees 'em, if'n you see 'em at all, might be on the weekends at the pub, or when they're out walking the dog. And then, after just a year or two, they get fed up of walking in the cow shit, or having to put up with the stench of the muck-spreading, or watching the corn grow, and then they sell up and move back to London again. And then another yuppie couple move in and it starts all over again. And I can tell you for nothin' that none of them could give a fig whether or not Andrew Feeley's killer gets nabbed or not.'

It was a long speech, and for most of it Debbie had been staring absently over Hillary's shoulder, watching a dove having a bath in one of the rain-filled pot holes that littered the lane.

'And what about the old-time village residents that are still clinging on?' Hillary challenged her quietly. 'Those who remember what a real village community is all about?'

Debbie's slow smile came and went again. 'Oh, they don't want to know either. Them 'specially, I reckon.'

'You really think so?' Hillary, resigned by now to conducting the interview on the doorstep, sans notes, mentally settled herself down to doing things the hard way. 'Funny, I would have said the opposite was true. I can't imagine it would be very pleasant for people living here, never knowing the truth but suspecting that one of their neighbours, one of their *friends*, might be a killer.'

'Who's to say they are?' Debbie asked, after a moment's thought. 'You know that little toad was a drug dealer, right? And a pimp? A thief?' The litany of the dead boy's sins came out flat but bitter. 'We reckon around here that types like that make a lot of enemies. We reckon the little bastard just trod on somebody's toes that he oughtn't to have. Somebody from the city, maybe. Somebody handy with a knife, like, as that type all seem to be. We in the village reckon that some bigger drug dealer was prob'ly just getting rid of the competition. And that's nothing to do with us, is it?'

Hillary did see — very clearly. So that was going to be the official line was it? *Nothing to do with us, officer. We're all white as the driven snow round here. Just law-abiding, country-yokel types who wouldn't hurt a fly. Let all the big-time boys from the cities get on with their horrible, illegal, dirty little ways, and leave us be.*

And who was to say that she wasn't right? Hillary was well aware that, as a theory, it was no better or worse than any other. Perhaps Andrew Feeley *had* got on the wrong side of someone higher up the food chain.

And just how impossible would it be to prove any different, so long as everyone in the village followed the ethos of the three wise monkeys?

'I see.' Hillary's own smile was now slow and laconic — and very nearly respectful. She wondered how often Debbie Truman, with her large fleshy body and slow, careful way of talking, had been mistaken for someone who had just fallen off the apple cart, when it was becoming very clear with every moment that passed that the exact opposite was true.

One thing was for sure: if Debbie Truman *had* killed Andrew, then she would have made a very good job of it, and Hillary was going to have the devil of a time proving it — especially after all these years.

Well, it was time for them to stop the verbal fencing, Hillary decided. Fun though it had been.

Hillary went straight for the woman's weak spot. 'So, can you tell me what your son Toby was doing on that day, please? According to DI Barker's reports, he would have been . . . what, eighteen years old or so when Andrew was killed? He should have been at school studying for his A levels, but had been off sick, I understand.'

The only sign that she had scored a direct hit was a brief shift in Debbie's weight distribution, as she leaned slightly onto her right side and settled her right shoulder more firmly against the doorjamb.

'That's right. He had a cold,' she admitted flatly.

'In the middle of a heatwave?'

'Summer colds are worse than winter ones, I says,' Debbie opined.

Hillary nodded. 'At least he'd have no trouble keeping warm,' she said. 'I dare say he was out and about enjoying the sun?'

'He was in bed,' Debbie said. But her eyes had briefly flickered.

Hillary nodded. 'Of course he was. And you . . . ?'

'Well, I did my morning round in Rousham — I clean some houses there. But then I came right back and stayed in to look after him, of course.'

'Didn't go out at all after that?' Hillary met the other woman's bland gaze with a bland smile of her own.

Again the weight shifted slightly. 'Can't remember exactly, not after all this time, can I?' Debbie gave vent to a long-suffering sigh. 'I might have done some gardening. Might have walked the dog. Might have gone out and picked some strawberries. Can't say for sure. But I weren't out long enough not to know that Toby stayed at home all that day,' she insisted.

'Of course. Did you see Andrew Feeley that day at all? Passing by in the lane perhaps, on his way to the woods?'

Debbie shrugged. 'You can get to the woods in all sorts of ways, without passing by here,' she pointed out laconically. 'Just cross the meadow, for one. Or take the footpath up to the ridge and follow the old bridleway. Or even cross the stile at the hollow and go over the old bridge then hike up.'

'That would be a no then? You didn't see him?' Hillary pressed.

'That would be a no. Yes.' Again the big woman's lips twitched. But Hillary was sure that any real sense of humour she might once have felt was now long gone.

'So how *is* Toby doing nowadays?' Hillary persevered, going back to the weak spot. 'I understand he had a problem with drugs when he was younger. According to our records, his first brush with us was when he was sixteen.'

Debbie's eyes flickered again. 'He's doing all right now,' she insisted, her voice going hard.

'Only, from what we've learned, he lost his place at university. Wasn't he set to do a course at Reading? And then lost the opportunity when he got his first three-month suspended sentence that summer? The same summer that Andrew was killed?'

'Yes, but he's got a job anyway. And now he's got another girl — a nice girl, works in a building society. He's living in Bicester now, in his own flat. He's doing all right.' She listed these accomplishments stubbornly, unwilling to admit the severity of the blow that Toby's loss of a university place must have been.

'I'm glad to hear it. Wasn't he going out with a local girl at the time? The daughter of one of the farmers around here?' Hillary persevered. She knew that he had been, because DI Barker had mentioned it in his initial report. Along with the follow-up fact that the wealthy daddy in question had insisted that his darling girl broke it off after it became clear that Toby was an addict, and about to do time for possession of drugs.

'That didn't work out,' Debbie dismissed with a brief shrug. 'They was only eighteen, the pair of 'em. Too young to be serious,' she added nonchalantly.

Hillary nodded. But she would have bet her next year's worth of pay cheques that, for all her blasé dismissal of this budding romance, this woman had been hoping against hope that her boy would make a match of it. After all, marrying the daughter of a local landowner must have been a glittering prospect for both of them — not to mention a mammoth step up the social ladder and local standing.

'Do you know how Toby came to get addicted to drugs in the first place, Mrs Truman?' Hillary asked mildly. She glanced around the deserted lane, the barren, brown fields, the cawing of rooks in the woods beyond. 'I mean, it's not the sort of place where you'd expect there to be a drugs problem, is it?'

'And nor was it, until Andrew Feeley started pushing them onto the youngsters,' Debbie said quickly. Her voice was bitter, but matter-of-fact. Clearly, she wasn't about to lose her iron-tight control of her anger. Which was impressive. And worrying.

More and more, Hillary was beginning to sense that a very formidable personality indeed lay behind this woman's misleadingly cute and chubby face.

'So you blame Andrew Feeley then?' she finally asked outright.

'Of course,' Debbie admitted at once, and without any apparent apprehension. 'Everyone knew that if there was ever trouble in the village, that little toad was behind it. His mother knew it. His stepdad knew it. That poor lass he got pregnant knew it. Hell, even some of the yuppies knew it. Not that they cared one way or the other, obviously. If *they* wanted to snort coke or what have you, I expect they had people in London who could get it for 'em.'

Debbie's grim smile flashed across her wide mouth and then was gone.

'Did you kill Andrew Feeley, Mrs Truman? In order to put a stop to him supplying Toby with drugs?' Hillary asked the question without any particular emphasis.

Debbie Truman watched her quietly for a few moments. Then sighed. 'I told that other copper who came asking. No, I didn't. But I ain't sorry he's dead. And you won't find anybody around here who *is* sorry he's dead — not even now, after all these years. You won't find no sympathy for the likes of that toad. Now, if that's all, I've got to get a move on. I'm due at Mrs Blandish's place in ten minutes.'

And so saying, and before Hillary could react, she took a swift step backwards and softly shut the door.

Hillary stared for a moment at the red-painted wooden barrier, then turned around and began to walk back down the path. Once they were out in the lane, she took a much-needed deep breath.

'Well, that was interesting,' she said to Gareth wryly.

Gareth looked at her and grinned. 'Wasn't it just? So do you think she did it?'

Hillary smiled. If she had a ten-pound note for every time some raw new recruit had asked her that . . . 'I'm not psychic, Mr Proctor, nor do I have a crystal ball,' she gave the standard reply. Then added, 'But I think that if she *did* do it, then she won't have made a hash of it. She's clever, she's in control of herself, and she's not the type to panic. Which might explain why the original team couldn't close the case.'

Gareth nodded, but one look at her closed, thoughtful face had him quelling any more questions. Well, save for one. 'So where to now, ma'am?'

'Back to HQ for some lunch, I think,' Hillary said, rather prosaically, leaving the former soldier with a distinct sense of anticlimax. But then she added, 'This afternoon I want you to find out all you can about her son, Toby. Let's just see how well he's *really* been doing. I have a feeling that he won't be such a hard nut to crack. Maybe I'll even let you take the notes when I interview him.'

'Yes, ma'am!'

* * *

As they walked back to where Puff patiently awaited their return, Debbie Truman stood in the window of her cottage and watched them disappear.

She wasn't happy. That woman copper had the look of a terrier about her. Unlike that other copper, Barker, she seemed the sort who wouldn't give up so easily. And the other one — the one who looked like he'd been through a mangle — he didn't exactly seem like a cissy either.

Debbie bit her lip. How many people in the village would they talk to? And how many of them, after all these years, might just come out with something, in all innocence, that sent the coppers sniffing in the right direction?

It was impossible to say. But surely, after all this time, there couldn't be *that* much that the coppers could get a hold of?

Well, one thing was for sure, they'd get nothing out of *her*!

She thought back on the interview, and thought she'd covered herself well. If somebody *did* happen to mention that they'd seen her walking the dog that afternoon . . . well, she had said she might have gone out, hadn't she? And she was fairly confident that's what she'd said in her original statement too. So they couldn't catch her out in a lie. Not her.

She was far too wily for that. From girlhood, Debbie had learned how to look out for number one, all right. No other bugger was going to, were they?

But what about that young girl? The one Debbie had seen that afternoon, crying and sobbing helplessly, her face all white with shock and walking across the meadow like a zombie, her dress all covered in blood?

Debbie sighed. She hoped they wouldn't learn about her. And they certainly wouldn't learn about her from Debbie. She'd keep mum about that to her dying day.

* * *

Back at HQ, Claire cheerfully informed them that she'd finally managed to track down the whereabouts of Malkie Comer, Karen Feeley's ex-partner and father of the murdered lad. Of all the main players in the case, he had been the hardest to pin down.

'He's been in and out of clink a few times since his son died, guv,' Claire said, surprising no one. 'Now he's holed up in Swindon, no doubt living off some poor woman who's yet to learn better.'

'Great. We'll go and talk to him tomorrow. Mr Proctor, you can get on with that research into Toby *after* you've typed up a report on our interview with Debbie Truman for the Murder Book. Later this afternoon Claire and I will go and talk to Jade Hodson.'

'Bloody hell, guv, you gonna keep on calling Gareth Mr Proctor forever and a day?' Claire asked, grinning as she looked from one of them to the other. Her grin only widened when both Gareth and Hillary glanced at each other with mutually disconcerted glances.

Hillary said, 'Mr Proctor hasn't indicated that he wants me to call him by his first name,' at the same moment as Gareth said, 'I thought superior officers used surnames . . .'

Both broke off in confusion, whilst Claire howled with mirth.

Hillary smiled wryly. 'Do you prefer to be called Gareth?' she asked the new boy thoughtfully.

'Yes, ma'am,' Gareth said, but was not at all sure that he did, really. But in the face of Claire's derisive laughter, he knew that he'd feel a right prat if he said so. In the army, the distinction of rank was always maintained — and the use of first names between differing ranks was unusual.

'All right, Gareth it is then,' Hillary said. But, very wisely, she didn't ask him to call her 'guv.' She had the feeling the poor lad would probably choke on the word if she did.

CHAPTER SIX

Claire drove an old dark green Renault that was still Puff's junior by a good six or seven years, and whenever they went out together she preferred to take her own transport. Probably because, on their very first case together, Puff had disgraced himself with a rare breakdown, which had taken an AA man several hours of impressive patience to fix.

She drove well, but with a sometimes worrying appearance of not seeming to be paying attention to the roads at all. This impression was, as Hillary had slowly come to realise, a completely false one. So now, as Claire drove them back to Tackley, chatting all the time and once overtaking a tractor on what — from the passenger side — looked like a blind bend, she barely noticed. She certainly didn't grip the dashboard with white knuckles every five minutes or so, or entertain perpetual terror that they were about to find themselves parked in a ditch or wrapped around a telephone pole, as she had done in their earlier car journeys together.

As they turned off onto a single-track lane that would take them to the village, Claire, getting her first glimpse of the place, kept looking around at the deserted farming landscape, noting everything from the newly harvested fields to the colourful displays of autumn leaves. She looked a bit like a demented owl, but was hampered somewhat by not quite having a neck that rotated 180 degrees.

'Nice area, this,' she noted cheerfully. 'A bit isolated though, not being on the way to anywhere particular. Not sure I'd like to live here in the dip like this. I suppose, living in Weston-on-the-Green, I'm used to having a ruddy great main road bisecting everything, and having a bit of life and bustle about me.'

She lived in a village that was indeed on the main thoroughfare between Oxford and the soon-to-be 'garden city' of Bicester, largely because her husband had inherited a house there from his parents. And who was going to look a gift horse like that in the mouth?

'How are the kids?' Hillary felt obliged to ask, and listened, vaguely nodding in the appropriate pauses, as Claire lamented the lot of a modern-day parent. Her mind, though, was definitely on other things.

It would probably be a good idea to call on the now-retired DI Barker and get his take on the Andrew Feeley case, but talking to the original investigator was always a double-edged sword, Hillary had found. True, they almost certainly, as first responders, had more insight into the immediate events surrounding a case. But against that was the fact that it was very easy to let yourself become persuaded into looking at things from their point of view, instead of developing one of your own.

On the whole, Hillary preferred not to have her mind clouded by preconceived ideas, but knew that, if they got stuck, she might well be forced to go to Barker as a last resort.

'Up there, are they, guv?' Claire interrupted her musings as she tucked the car as close to the hedge as she could get, and peered up the hill at the faces of the council houses looking down on them. 'Must be a nice view from up there. Bit windy though, in a storm.'

Hillary nodded, and retraced her steps up the steep path. Beside her, Claire panted a little. Being in her early fifties and roughly the same height as Hillary, she easily packed another four stone or so onto her frame, and her motherly-looking round face quickly became pink with effort as the gradient began to pull on her calf muscles. 'Bloody hell, guv, you wouldn't need to go to the gym if you lived here,' she puffed.

Hillary grinned. The picture of the stalwart, down-to-earth and happily plump Claire sitting on a rowing machine, or jogging on a treadmill, was literally unthinkable. Not that Hillary used a gym either. What a pair of bad adverts they were for a health-conscious society, she mused, her grin widening unrepentantly.

At the garden gate belonging to the Feeleys, Hillary paused to let her colleague get her breath back, then led her through the odd dogleg arrangement that led them to the back of the garden.

Here Claire paused and glanced around. The sun was out and still packing quite a warm punch for early October, and its rays picked up and reflected the glories of every red, yellow, orange or copper-coloured leaf. The messy, colourful patches of Michaelmas daisies and earwig-strewn dahlias also glowed like neon.

Claire, whose own former council house consisted of more concrete parking space than lawn, nodded in approval. 'Very nice,' she opined judiciously. Her eyes moved automatically to the back of the garden, where the large static caravan was barely visible. 'Hard to see what sort of place it is from here,' Claire observed. 'It might be a right shack — but even that's better than nothing.' As someone who'd often dealt with women who came from either broken homes or had come through the so-called 'care' system, she'd dealt with her fair share of people who lived rough. From bus shelters to public toilets, and even all-night supermarkets, if they could manage to hide from store managers or security.

By comparison, a woman living in a caravan could think herself lucky. In Claire's experience, very few of those who started off underprivileged to begin with ever managed to pull themselves very far from the bottom of the ladder.

'Let's go and see if Jade's in then, shall we?' Hillary said.

The two women picked their way, with some care, down a very uneven path made of square concrete slabs, which were overgrown at the edges with couch grass. 'Bloody hell, guv, this must be fun to walk down when it's got a frost on it,' Claire complained.

The worn concrete was already slippery enough, given the damp weather of autumn and the slick, greasy patches of fallen and decomposing leaves. Twice Claire nearly took a header, once into a withering patch of rhubarb, and once into the old black plastic water butt, next to one of the sheds. Luckily, Hillary had quick reflexes, and both times managed to grab her arm.

But once they'd got past the last of the mallows, and could see Jade Hodson's home for the first time, they were both taken slightly aback by both the size of it and the state of good repair it clearly enjoyed.

Wide and long, it probably had the same square footage as a modest bungalow. Its exterior had recently been painted a pleasant shade of mint green, and had white-painted windows and door. The flat roof looked soft grey with recently applied felting, which didn't have any visible patches of mildew, moss or water damage. An obviously home-made but wide and well-constructed wooden veranda stretched from halfway in the middle and went all the way around one side. No doubt in the summer this added much-needed outdoor living space.

They climbed up to the front door on low, sturdy steps made out of old railway sleepers, with a handrail on each side for safety. They didn't even have to knock on the door, for as they stepped onto the wooden veranda, it began to open.

As Hillary had suspected, Karen Feeley must have warned her about their earlier visit, and told her to prepare herself for a visit of her own.

Jade Hodson had been only nineteen when her partner was murdered, and she didn't look that much older now. Her mop of slightly damp, reddish-gold hair indicated that she had not long had a shower, and she looked at them out of a pair of troubled big blue eyes.

'Hello?' She was wearing a pair of leggings in bright fuchsia pink and a fluffy pale pink jumper with sparkly bits strewn about it, which had probably been the choice of her young daughter.

Hillary and Claire reached for their ID cards almost simultaneously. Hillary noticed no surprise on the pretty, slightly freckled face as she gave their names and the purpose of their visit. Instead, Jade merely nodded and stepped aside to let them in.

The front door opened directly into the kitchen. Not huge, it nevertheless had everything in it that you would need. The walls had been painted a pretty shade of primrose yellow, whilst apple-green cupboard doors complemented black and white spotted Formica work surfaces.

The door leading to the room beyond was firmly shut. Jade, noticing Hillary glance at it, sighed slightly. 'My daughter, Briana, is doing her homework. I'd prefer it if we didn't get in her way. Please, sit down,' Jade said, indicating a small square table in the middle of the room. It was serviced by stools rather than chairs, which fitted neatly away under the actual table, offering more space and cleverly allowing the table to serve a second function as an 'island' when needed.

Claire and Hillary pulled out a stool each and perched on them somewhat awkwardly, watching as Jade set about putting on the kettle. 'Karen told me you'd come,' she said, her voice neutral and casual as she worked at the sink, pulling down three mugs and then holding aloft a coffee jar in one hand and a box of tea bags in another, shaking them in a silent question.

Both of them opted for coffee, Claire asking for two sugars and plenty of milk in hers. As she listened to the kettle warming up, Jade stared through a large solitary window. Hillary, sitting almost directly behind her, could see the eccentric but picturesque garden scene beyond, where a nearby apple tree, old but heavy with attractive red-and-green fruit, shone in the sun, as if in a spotlight. Hillary wondered if they were Bramleys or Pippins, and if they were cookers, did Jade use the fruit for pies or crumbles? Or did she just buy them ready-made at the supermarket like nearly everyone else did nowadays?

Coffees made, Jade deposited them on the table and pulled out a stool for herself and sat down wearily. 'So, is it true that you're looking into Andy's case again then?' she asked. Waiting for their reply, she listlessly pulled at some damp strands of hair that were clinging stubbornly to her cheek. It was obvious with her every gesture that here was yet another of Andrew Feeley's 'women' who didn't seem to be all that happy at the thought that his case was being looked at anew.

'Yes, it is,' Hillary confirmed. Although she knew that Claire, having worked with abused women for most of her career, might be a more obvious choice to lead this interview, when it came to murder cases, Hillary always took the lead. However, that didn't mean that she didn't trust Claire to watch and listen and step in if she picked up on something that Hillary might have missed.

'What can you tell me about him, Jade?' Hillary said, starting off with a deliberately broad and non-threatening question. 'What was he like?'

Jade looked slightly startled by the question, but then smiled down sadly into her coffee mug. 'Like most blokes, I suppose. He had his good points, and he had his bad.'

'How did you meet?'

'At a nightclub in Oxford. I was couch-surfing, and the mate I was staying with was making noises about me needing to move on, because she wanted to move her fella in. I'd gone to that particular nightclub because I was looking for another friend of mine who worked there, hoping she might be able to put me up for a while. But she wasn't in that night, and later on, I got talking to Andy. He seemed all right, you know?'

Both of the women did. No doubt to begin with he was all puppy-dog charm and eager to please. But how long, Claire wondered cynically, before his true colours started to show?

'When I told him about needing a place to crash, he offered me the spare bedroom here, right off. Of course, at first I was proper leery,' Jade added hastily, lest they suspect her of that most unforgivable of all social blunders: naiveté. 'I thought . . . well, you know. Why would a bloke offer to let you live with him if he didn't expect . . . well, like I said, you know. But the truth was, I was desperate. I'd already been told by the hostel that I'd been staying in sometimes that I couldn't expect a room to be available whenever I needed it. So I took him up on it. I planned on only staying one or two nights, three at the most, before I found somewhere else.'

Jade laughed bleakly. 'I can tell you, I spent the first night in this place wide awake, just waiting for the bedroom door handle to start sliding downwards. You know?'

'But it didn't?' Hillary guessed.

'Nah, it didn't. Next morning, I felt kind of bad for thinking the worst of him, I can tell you. Especially when he told me to use as much bread for toast as I wanted, and then just left for work.'

'Work?' Hillary echoed, and Jade flushed.

'Well, that's what he called it. He was gone all day anyway. At the time I thought he had, like, you know, a regular job. Later I learned he was self-employed, like.' Her eyes slewed back to the window and she stared once more at the illuminated apple tree. Her look was oddly concentrated, as if she expected the tree would know the answers to life, love, the universe and everything.

If it did, it wasn't sharing.

Hillary forced her attention back to the matter in hand. 'But you didn't move out after three days?' she prompted, and smiled to show that there was no judgement intended in her remark.

Jade turned back to face her and gave a shrug. 'No. Like I said, he was nice. Good-looking too. And he treated me right. We just . . . sort of drifted into becoming a couple, I suppose. There was no big eureka moment or nothing. It helped that I got on really well with Karen and Sean. And then I got pregnant — still not sure how that happened. I was on the pill and everything, but . . .' Jade shrugged. 'They say, don't they, that sometimes the pill doesn't always work, but you never think you're going to be the one caught out, do you?' she asked philosophically.

For a moment, all three women were silent as they contemplated this. Claire, the happy and contented mother of three, all children planned for; Hillary, childless and more than content with that state of affairs; and Jade, made a mother by a faulty pill.

'I was upset and angry at the time, I suppose, but I wouldn't be without my Briana now,' Jade admitted with unmistakable conviction.

'How did Andy take the news?' Hillary asked casually.

Jade shrugged, her eyes skittering away from hers and sending her gaze out through the window once again. 'Oh, you know. Men!' She tried for a valiant smile, but it was hopelessly strained. 'But he would have come around to it . . .' she trailed off, as if the weakness of her argument was unsupportable, even to her own ears.

'Did he ever hit you, Jade?' Hillary asked quietly, and saw the other woman stiffen. It seemed to take her a while to be able to process the question.

'No,' she said eventually.

Claire's and Hillary's eyes met in shared silent disbelief.

'So, what can you remember about the day he died? Talk me through it, from the moment you woke up,' Hillary said, deliberately turning her tone a shade more brisk and bright. 'You were three months pregnant by then. I expect you were beginning to be plagued by morning sickness?' she prompted.

'Yes, I was,' Jade made an obvious effort to rouse herself. She sat up a little straighter on the stool, and brought her shoulders back. 'I remember he left to have breakfast at his mum's.' She nodded toward the roof of the council house, just visible beyond the jungle outside. 'The smell of frying bacon made me heave, see. He was thoughtful like that,' she said defensively, but it was clear she didn't really believe it.

No doubt in reality he had cursed her and stormed off, slamming the door behind him, Hillary mused. 'Yes, Karen mentioned he wanted a bacon sandwich. So what did you do then?'

Jade sighed. 'I got up about ten. I was trying to find work — I only wanted something for a couple of months, just to tide me over until Briana arrived — but I was having no luck.'

'So you had all day to yourself? That must have been nice,' Hillary smiled. 'What did you do?'

'Oh, the usual. It was a hot day, so I did the washing and put it out on one of those old rotary dryers we had back then. Did a bit of housework, but not much, to be honest. Had the telly on — some awful programme about making over houses or what have you. Had some salad for my lunch. Then I took a nap in the afternoon. It was so damned hot that day, and in a heatwave, this place,' she waved a vague hand around, 'can feel like an oven. It's great most of the time, don't get me wrong, and it's surprising how warm it is in winter. It's not damp or nothing. But in the heat . . . well. It made me so sleepy. So I took a nap. I woke up . . . I dunno, around four or so. I was just peeling some spuds for Andy's tea when the police came . . .'

She paused and looked down at her cooling coffee. 'Karen was in a right state. Well, she would be, wouldn't she? He was her only son. And poor Chloe was as white as a ghost, bless her, shaking so hard she couldn't drink the glass of milk Karen gave her. She was only . . . what . . . fourteen at the time? I couldn't believe it. None of us could. We just sat in Karen's house, not taking it in.'

Jade shook her head at the memory and then got up and poured her unwanted drink down the sink. Once more, she stared outside, her gaze fixed on the old gnarled apple tree. 'I just couldn't believe it. They told me Andy was dead, but I couldn't register it.'

She shook her head again, then dragged her eyes away from the window, but clearly reluctant to face them. 'And that's all I know.'

Hillary nodded. 'So you didn't go outside that day at all?'

'Nah. Only to hang out the washing, like I said. It was just too hot, see?'

'So you didn't sit out in the shade, under a tree, to make the most of any breeze?' Hillary asked.

Jade smiled. 'I would have done, if I'd had the sun lounger then. But I didn't get one until a couple of years ago. And I didn't fancy lying on a towel in the grass. The red ants around here would eat you alive!'

'And you didn't see Andrew again after he left that morning?'

'Nah. Andy could be gone all hours. You'd never know how long he might be or just when he'd be back. Sometimes he'd be in and out all day, other times he'd be out the whole day, and even the night too.'

'You didn't think to ask him where he was?' Hillary asked. 'When he stayed out all night?'

Jade shivered slightly. 'Nah. He didn't like it . . . I suppose it felt as if I was keeping tabs on him. Men don't like that, do they? So I was careful not to ask him.'

Claire nodded. No doubt she'd quickly learned, after he'd thumped her for asking, that it paid to be incurious.

'Do you know who might have wanted him dead, Jade?' Hillary asked next.

Jade stared down at her feet. She was wearing dirty white trainers with a pink trim. She sighed and then looked at them. 'You know how he made his money, right?' she asked reluctantly.

'We suspect he dabbled in drug dealing,' Hillary said, again careful to keep her tone neutral. 'Burglary, the odd bit of car theft. Anything to turn a profit, and if it was illegal, he didn't care. Do you think that's a fair assessment?'

Jade sighed. 'I suppose. Then you know . . . he must have stepped on quite a lot of people's toes, mustn't he? But people wouldn't tell me about stuff like that, would they? Around here, they were always nice to me.'

'So did you ever meet any of his shady friends?' Hillary asked.

'Nah, not really. And Andy didn't have *friends*, as such. Well, except for that bloke Frankie, I met him once or twice, but I never really knew anything about him or what they did together. I suppose Andy thought the less I knew the better.'

Hillary recalled a Frankie from DI Barker's initial report, although he was never a person of interest. Barker hadn't been able establish a motive for him, and the lad had had an alibi backed up by more than one of his mates. Still, she made a mental note to look into him further and see if she could unearth anything useful.

'And is there anything you can tell us now that you didn't mention at the time?' Hillary asked. 'Sometimes, over the years, things come back, and we remember stuff that didn't seem relevant at the time.'

'Sorry, no, I can't think of nothing,' Jade said.

Hillary, who had a degree in English literature, bit back a sudden irritable urge to explain to the younger woman about double negatives. Then she had to smile. Since when, she wondered wryly, had she become such a stickler for good grammar? She knew why she was feeling disgruntled and out of sorts, of course. It was because, so far, they were coming up empty, and she was beginning to feel frustrated.

It was becoming obvious that nobody was going to be in any hurry to help them out in their new investigation, which, given the nature of the dead man, wasn't exactly surprising. But that didn't mean that she had to like it.

'Well, if you *do* think of anything . . .' She rose, handing over one of her cards. As they stepped back out onto the veranda, Hillary glanced around. 'This is really very nice, isn't it? It's almost as spacious as a bricks-and-mortar place.'

'Oh yes,' Jade said, with her first genuine smile. 'That's Sean's doing mostly. He makes sure the insulation is up to date, and the roof is really watertight. And he built this,' she patted the wooden railing that kept the raised veranda safe for children — a must when you had an eight-year-old in the house. 'He's really a great handyman. He even fixes the plumbing and the radiators when we need it.'

'You still see a lot of him then?' Hillary asked, making a mental note of the stepfather's handyman credentials. 'I thought Sean and Karen's marriage broke up a while ago?'

'Yeah,' Jade said sadly. 'Yeah, it did. About a year or so after Andy died. It was really sad. But Sean still lives in the village, and they've remained good friends, him and Karen. He's still Briana's granddad. I mean, not really — not blood, like. But Bree calls him granddad, so . . .' She shrugged and broke off. Once again, her eyes went to the apple tree in the corner of the patch.

'Well, we'll keep in touch, Ms Hodson,' Hillary said. 'And please don't hesitate to call me, any time.'

'Thanks,' Jade said uncertainly.

She stood on the veranda, watching them until they were out of sight, then slowly went back inside.

Hillary waited until they were walking back down the steep path towards Claire's car before saying briskly, 'Well?'

'Definitely a battered wife, guv,' Claire said flatly, confirming her own reading of the situation. 'We know Malkie Comer used to hit Karen, and I'm afraid it's the same old story. Learned behaviour. Like father like son. Bad blood. Call it what you like.'

Hillary sighed. 'She had motive and no alibi.'

Claire shrugged. 'From what we've learned so far, the same goes for a lot of people around here,' she pointed out pessimistically.

* * *

Back at HQ, Claire got busy typing up the Jade Hodson interview for the Murder Book, and Hillary walked down the corridor to report to Rollo.

As she walked into his office, he looked up from signing off on a pile of DNA reports from the boffins due to be used in an upcoming court case. He smiled a greeting, then leaned back in his chair to stretch, giving a slight groan of stiffness as he did so.

'So how's it going?'

Hillary went through what they had so far. It wasn't much, but Rollo wasn't disappointed. He knew if there was anything new to be ferreted out, Hillary would find it.

'And how's the new boy working out?' he asked next, as he signed off on yet another report and tossed it into his 'out' tray.

'No problems so far.'

'Fine, fine. Well take off early if you like,' Rollo said, after a quick glance at the wall clock showed him it was just gone four thirty.

Hillary grunted. As if! She got up, and then paused by the door. Then, as if debating with herself, she hesitated for a moment, and turned back to look at him.

'Sir?'

Rollo glanced up, one eyebrow raised in query.

'Can you get me the go-ahead to dig about a bit in the Feeleys' back garden?'

Rollo's eyebrow rose a shade higher, and his lips twitched slightly. 'What? The *whole* garden? I understand it's quite a size. I doubt if the budget-pushers will stand for it. How many flatfoots would it take?'

'Oh, only a couple, sir. And it won't take long. I only want to have a rootle about in one particular spot.'

'Where?'

'Around an apple tree in the back of the garden.'

'Any particular reason?' Rollo asked, sounding amused.

Hillary grinned vaguely back. 'Just my spider-sense tingling, sir. It's probably nothing.'

But Rollo was far too wise a bird by now to ignore Hillary Greene's spider-sense — or any other sense she might want to indulge. 'Well, it won't be top priority for anyone. It'll probably take me a few days, but I dare say I can find some judge who owes me a favour.'

'Thanks, sir,' Hillary said. But even as she said it, she wondered if she wasn't being a bit paranoid.

It was just that there had been *something* about the way that Jade Hodson had kept being drawn back to staring at that apple tree that niggled at her.

* * *

The last of the sun's rays were setting as Hillary parked Puff in the pub car park and made her way down the towpath towards her narrowboat. The next weekend but one the clocks would go back, and then she'd find herself coming home in the dark.

It almost seemed to become instant winter then, but right now, with the last of the warm sun dipping below the horizon, it still felt like an Indian summer.

As if sharing her view, a large emerald-green dragonfly darted past her, its whirring wings sounding like dry paper as it chinked its erratic way across the khaki-coloured water, hawking for the last of the season's flies amongst the reeds.

It was very late in the year for them to still be out and about, Hillary mused, as she watched it fly out of sight. She wasn't an expert, but she didn't think these ancient insects hibernated throughout the winter. If so, its days must be numbered.

She shivered slightly as she stepped onto the back of the *Mollern* and searched in her bags for the key to the padlock.

As soon as she made her way through the narrow corridor to the galley, she automatically switched on the radio. Then she reached into the cupboards in search of a tin of something or other to heat up for her supper.

CHAPTER SEVEN

The next day Hillary awoke the moment it started to get light and discovered that the sunny weather of yesterday was still holding. She got up, showered, forced down a bowl of cornflakes and got into the office at just gone eight o'clock.

There, she took an hour to go over everything DI Barker had had to say about Malkie Comer. Not surprisingly, none of it was particularly flattering. A petty criminal for most of his life, he'd always been rather free with his fists, especially around women and the elderly people he preferred to mug. And you didn't need to be a genius to figure out where his young son had gained his racist leanings.

At the time of his son's murder though, he'd already long since left the village. He'd recently come out of his latest spell in prison, and had been shacked up in a hostel in Northampton. Of course, Northampton wasn't that far away, and although he had no official car of his own, it wouldn't have been that difficult for him to borrow or even steal a vehicle.

What's more, the owner of the hostel couldn't swear to it that he'd been in on the afternoon of the murder, since he was officially supposed to be out and about actively seeking work. Although, almost certainly, any supposed 'job interviews' that he'd gone out for had been spent in the local pub.

Which meant he had no alibi for the sunny afternoon his son was stabbed to death. But as DI Barker had pointed out, why would the man want to murder his only son?

Hillary, sitting in the stationery cupboard that passed for her office, heard the others start to drift in, but made no immediate move to rise and join them in the communal office. Instead, she turned her thoughts to people who killed their own children. And why they did it.

The majority of these terrible cases consisted of suicidal or depressed women, perhaps suffering from postnatal depression, who simply lost it, and in a moment of blind madness suffocated or shook their infant babies to death.

Then you had the real cold-blooded types who insured their offspring and then helped them to have an 'accident.' Or, on finding that a new partner really wasn't happy with having little ones around, found a fatal way of ridding themselves of their nuisances.

None of those fit in this case, obviously.

But whenever you considered that a man like Malkie Comer was in the frame, with his casual attitude to violence and his world-owes-me-a-living mentality, the most obvious scenario had to include a sudden bout of anger and an impulsive use of his fists. With the incident ending, perhaps, more fatally than had been intended.

So was it possible that Malkie had come down from Northampton on the day in question, maybe to 'touch' his son for a loan? Newly out of prison, he might have run out of beer money. And he'd have known that drug dealers were rarely short of money. So yes, she could see good old Dad deciding to come down and ask for a 'loan.'

But Andrew Feeley wouldn't have been a little kid anymore. Karen had said that, as a young boy, he'd hero-worshipped his dad. Which had almost certainly been the main reason why he had played such merry hell with his stepfather.

But kids grew up — and kids like Andrew probably grew up quicker, and meaner, than most. Plus, with all the time that Malkie had spent at Her Majesty's pleasure in various nicks over the years, it was doubtful that Malkie would have seen much of his son as he grew into a man. So the bond couldn't still have been so strong.

What's more, a little kid's hero-worship of his father could very easily turn into contempt or indifference during their teenage years.

At the time of his death Andrew had been twenty-one, and probably considered himself to be not only all grown up, but a 'big man' in his own right, and in more ways than one. A pregnant girlfriend as proof of his virility would almost certainly have swollen his head, even if he hadn't been particularly looking forward to the responsibilities that came with fatherhood. And most of the village probably went in fear of him, if only because they didn't want to get their houses burgled or their cars pinched and crashed. And such begrudging deference must have massaged his ego enormously.

And, of course, as a drug dealer — even a minor one — he must have been earning more money than most people his age could even dream of. And all of that certainly put him a rung above his low-life father on the scumbag's ladder of success.

So would he have been that happy to see his good old dad — his small-time, loser, ex-con dad — coming around, cadging some cash?

Hillary thought that Andrew had never been caught, let alone prosecuted, for any of his crimes, but she checked the notes just to be sure. No, her memory wasn't at fault — he did have a clean rap sheet. So he'd always managed to keep the law from catching up with him. It would only have been a matter of time before it did, of course, Hillary knew, but still, at the time, it would have given him yet one more reason to look down on his good old dad, who seemed to get nabbed with monotonous regularity.

Had the boy made that attitude plain? Because, if he had, she couldn't see any displays of contempt sitting well with the likes of Malkie Comer. Brutish, not particularly bright, and with the ego and sense of entitlement that invariably came with a swaggering male who liked to knock women around, she could well see how Comer and his son might have struck aggressive sparks off each other.

Hillary leaned back thoughtfully in her chair and closed her eyes, picturing the scene.

Malkie begs, steals or threatens someone for the use of a car. Drives back to his old haunts. What does he do when he arrives in his old stomping grounds? Well, go to the house of course. And Karen, by her own admission, was in that afternoon, sewing. Malkie knocks on the door and demands to see Andrew. But Andrew isn't in, and his mother says she doesn't know where he's gone.

OK, so first problem: how does Malkie find out where Andrew went?

Unless, of course, Karen had lied to Barker during the original investigation and Andrew *had* mentioned that he would be meeting someone in the woods later on. So Karen, intimidated by Malkie and not wanting a beating, tells him where her son is. And later, when she learns of the severity of what has happened and fearing reprisals from her now 'killer' ex, she keeps quiet about Malkie's visit. And is still keeping quiet about it, even now.

Second problem. Would the mother of a murdered son really not tell the police who she suspected had murdered him? Especially when, if convicted, it would mean Malkie going away for life, leaving her safe from him for twenty years at least?

Hillary sighed. She didn't like to think so. But she wasn't sure. She knew that battered wives could become all but brainwashed by their attackers, robbing them of all will and leaving them hopeless and convinced that they could do nothing to help either themselves or others. Even if they were lucky enough to get out of the abusive relationship, the conditioning in some cases could still stay with them for the rest of their lives. But wouldn't someone who'd been *that* traumatised show signs of it, even years later? She certainly hadn't got that vibe off Karen Feeley, but then she was no expert in that field.

Hillary made a mental note to ask Claire about her thoughts on that later, and got back to her imagined reconstruction of the scene.

OK — for argument's sake, say Malkie comes back but *doesn't* go to the house at all, because he's lucky enough to spot his son making off over the fields towards the woods. Or he's somehow found out his son's routine of selling drugs in the woods.

Hillary gave a mental wince. Yes, that was stretching coincidence too far. Besides, Jade Hodson had made it very clear that Andrew didn't keep to any kind of routine.

OK. Scratch that. Perhaps Malkie phoned his son before setting off from the hostel and Andy arranged to meet him in the woods? Now that might make more sense. That way, Malkie could be sure that he wouldn't have a wasted trip, and, even better from his point of view, he wouldn't have to see his ex at all. For Karen would have been almost certain to guess that he'd come on the cadge, and men like Malkie didn't like to be shown up.

It would also explain why Andrew had gone to the woods — in order to meet his old man. The original team had always assumed he'd gone to either meet his buyer to receive a stash of drugs, or to make a sale to one of his customers. But there were always other options as well, Hillary reminded herself.

OK, so say on that particular day, he went specifically to meet his father. Andrew, maybe expecting just a father-and-son reunion, soon learns that Dad wants more than that — he wants some cash. Naturally, Andrew says no. Why should he support his loser of an old man? Maybe he says 'no' not too politely. Maybe with enough scorn that Malkie takes umbrage. Hillary can just see the old lag saying something really stupid, like, 'You ain't too old to get a slapping, son' or some such other threat.

But he hasn't fully taken into account that Andrew isn't a little kid anymore — he's all grown up now. And maybe Malkie's gone a little to seed. Too much stodgy prison food has turned him a bit soft? Whilst Andrew is fit, lean, and decades younger.

So maybe Malkie wades in but quickly finds himself coming off the worst. That would surprise and anger him even more — maybe even frighten him a little?

Hmmm. But where did the knife come into all this?

Hillary frowned. The knife, Barker had established, definitely belonged to Andrew. So presumably at some point Andrew must have produced it — regardless of whether or not it was Malkie he'd met in the woods that day.

But sticking with the boy's father for the moment, Hillary shifted thoughtfully on her seat. OK, so far, it was all sounding plausible enough. His father touches him for cash, he says no. His father gets a bit physically insistent. Andrew, now thoroughly pissed off, produces a knife, telling him to back off.

What then?

From Hillary's experience of bully boys and the not-too-bright, most of them, when presented with a knife, would indeed back off. It was just common sense, and every con she knew had a very strong sense of self-preservation, developed from their years inside.

But maybe Malkie had just been *too* enraged? Or simply didn't believe his own son would actually stab him? So he makes a grab for it, or a lunge, or whatever. They fight, and Malkie's bulk and desperation helps him to win the fight. During the struggle, Andrew is fatally stabbed.

So what can he do about it now, except leg it back to Northampton, cleaning up somewhere on the way and keeping schtum about it?

That would work. In theory.

Hillary sighed, got up, slung her bag over her shoulder and walked down the corridor. Speculation was all well and good, but until she'd had a chance to talk to Malkie Comer and assess him for herself, it was all so much pie in the sky.

When she popped her head around the door, Claire and Gareth instantly stopped talking and looked at her. A little uneasily, she wondered if they'd been talking about her.

'Gareth, how are you coming along with the background search on Toby Truman?'

'Nearly finished, ma'am.'

'Right. Well, you and me will go and talk to him after lunch. Claire, you up to coming to Swindon with me to talk to Comer?'

Claire rolled her eyes. 'Can't wait, guv. He sounds like a right prince.'

Hillary grinned. 'Bring a truncheon. You never know your luck — you might get to use it.'

Claire rolled her eyes. 'I doubt we could get that lucky, guv. His sort, when dealing with the law, are more likely to try and turn on the charm.'

'Ugh! Don't,' Hillary said, with a genuine shudder.

Gareth began to look concerned. He glanced from one to the other, his fair hair almost white under the artificial lighting that they had to keep on all day, being down in the bowels of the building as they were. 'Do you think I should come, ma'am?' he asked quietly.

Claire automatically shot him a look. She opened her mouth, clearly about to say something sardonic about the likelihood of him needing to save the poor helpless females from the big bad man, when she suddenly changed her mind. A look of slight confusion and embarrassment crossed her face instead.

Hillary saw it, and realised her dilemma at once. No doubt, had the new recruit been an able-bodied man, Claire would have done just that — given him a ticking off for thinking they couldn't handle a suspect themselves. But, just in time, the former sergeant saw how the new boy could easily take such a comment the wrong way. That Gareth might think she was having a dig at him and his disability, and be intimating that he'd be more of a hindrance than a help if it came to a fight.

Hillary interjected smoothly, 'If I thought we'd need you, I'd ask,' she told him, her voice carefully toneless. 'See you later.'

'Yes, ma'am.'

Claire, a little red-faced, went past Hillary at a trot. Outside, both women pretended that the awkward moment hadn't happened, and instead walked in companionable silence to her Renault.

* * *

Malkie Comer lived just outside the centre of the town, on the top floor of a small, uninspiring block of flats. Probably built in the 1960s, they had once all been owned by the council, but in recent years a lot of the residents had taken advantage of laws making it easier for them to buy their places from the housing association.

As Claire and Hillary checked the doors for the right number, it was sometimes easy to see which of the clone-like dwellings were privately owned and which were still rented, since as a general rule, people who owned property tended to take more pride in their upkeep.

Number 52, which according to their records had been rented out to one Doreen Salton for the past six years, was situated at the end of the outdoor concrete corridor, and overlooked a large supermarket car park.

Hillary knocked on the door sharply, not surprised to find that it was eventually opened not by the lady of the house, but by Malkie himself. No doubt, Hillary mused cynically, Doreen had been at work for a good hour or so by now — maybe stacking the shelves of the supermarket on her doorstep. Whereas Malkie looked as if he'd just roused himself out of bed.

It was just gone ten thirty.

Malcolm Comer had been forty-eight at the time of his son's death, and the intervening years hadn't been particularly kind to him. At not quite six feet tall, he was bulky, but more in a soft way, like someone who had been padded all over with wadding. He was fast losing his greying hair, and he looked at them with wary, pale brown eyes.

He was dressed in slightly baggy black trousers, and a grey knitted sweater, the sleeves of which had been pushed up to reveal hairy forearms littered with bad tattoos.

'Yeah?'

'Mr Comer? Malcolm Comer?'

For a moment, both women could see him wondering whether or not to deny it. Then he shrugged. 'Yeah?'

Hillary and Claire showed their IDs. Instantly he stiffened, but after another pause, he gave them a resigned look and stood back a pace. 'Better come in then. But I didn't have nuffing to do with them toasters, no matter what that sonofabitch Taylor's been sayin'. I got mates who could swear I was with 'em at the betting shop . . .'

'We're here to talk about your son, Mr Comer,' Hillary cut across the waffle. Not that her copper's nose wasn't interested in stolen electrical goods, mind, but that wasn't her job here.

Still, that wouldn't stop her, when they left, from detouring to the local station and passing on the gen. She had no doubt they would know instantly who this 'Taylor' chap was.

'Who? What?' Malkie said, staring at them with an unlovely gaping jaw.

'Your son, Mr Comer. Andrew Feeley,' Hillary reminded him heavily. They were standing in a tiny hallway, and she turned to glance through the half-open door behind her. 'Living room in here is it?' she prompted.

Malkie grunted and pushed it open further, revealing a compact room. A two-seater sofa was placed in front of a gas fire. A small glass coffee table was set to one side. An old-fashioned record cabinet, used nowadays to store bits and bobs instead of LPs, was the only other piece of furniture, which was just as well, as the tiny room wouldn't have held much more.

'Suppose you'd better sit down,' Malkie grunted gracelessly.

The two women eyed the settee for a moment, and then Claire, without needing to be told, moved instead to the far wall and leaned one shoulder comfortably against it. It wouldn't be a good idea, as they well knew, for both of them to be confined together in one space. In the event of anything kicking off, you needed to be able to come at a threat from a position of strength.

Hillary took one of the seats, and was glad when Malkie, instead of sitting beside her, pushed aside the few cheap ornaments that were sitting on the top of the cabinet, and perched on that instead. Luckily, the brown wooden frame was sturdy enough to take his weight.

'Our Andy's been dead for years,' Malkie said suspiciously. 'So what're you here for then?' Obviously he was still worried they might be here about the toasters.

'Yes, sir, we know. We work for the Thames Valley Crime Review team. We take a look at cold cases to see if the passage of time and fresh eyes can discover something new.'

For the first time, Malkie looked interested. 'Yeah? Well, that's good then. I always said that copper what investigated our Andy's case was about as much use as a fart in a colander. He should just have arrested that bastard Dalton right at the start, and it'd all be sorted by now. But would he? Nah, buggered if he would, no matter how much I told him who'd done it.'

Hillary nodded. 'You're talking about Mr Sean Dalton, Karen's husband at the time?'

'I was her husband,' Malkie snapped back.

'Really? We have no copy of a marriage certificate in our files, Mr Comer,' Hillary said mildly. 'If you can provide us with your wedding date, and the church or registry office, I'll amend our files.'

Malkie's jaw thrust out for a moment, then he grunted. 'Well, we never made it official like. But I was her partner,' he insisted. 'Common-law, weren't we? Or don't you say that nowadays? Unpolitically correct is it?' he sneered.

Hillary nodded. 'You *had* been her partner at one time, I understand. But at the time of your son's murder, she'd been married to Mr Dalton for some time, hadn't she? They had a child of their own — Chloe.'

'Huh, and no doubt *she* was a right spoilt bitch an' all.'

Claire, busy taking notes, heaved a heavy and audible sigh. Malkie shot her the evil eye, but Claire made a great show of failing to notice it, let alone be impressed.

'Do you have any reason for suspecting Mr Dalton of murdering your son?' Hillary asked doggedly.

'Stands to reason, don't it?' Malkie said sulkily. 'Our Andy hated the black—'

'Mr Comer, I'm not prepared to put up with any racist remarks,' Hillary interrupted sharply. 'So let's just stick to facts shall we? Now, stop messing me about, please. Do you have any proof that Sean Dalton killed Andrew?'

'Nah, course I don't have any bloody *proof*!' Malkie spat at her. 'If I had, I'd have given it to that wanker detective at the time, wouldn't I? But like I said, he was useless. Kept saying they couldn't arrest Dalton because they had no witnesses, and no forensic evidence and all that other crap,' Malkie said disgustedly. 'But everyone knew that Dalton and Andy hated each other's guts. Who else would kill our Andy 'cept him? Eh? Tell me that!'

'Your son dealt drugs, Mr Comer,' Hillary pointed out. 'He was also a pimp, in a minor way. He made enemies left and right in the village where he lived. There are any num—'

'Oh don't give me that,' Malkie interrupted with a sneer. 'No silly prossie is going to stick Andy because he helped her out by finding her Johns to feed her habit, is she? And as for that lot in Tackley — a lily-livered, law-abiding, pussy-footin' load of tossers to a man.'

'And rival drug dealers, Mr Comer?' Hillary put in quietly. 'Not many lily-livered pussy-footers amongst them, I think.'

For a moment Malkie looked discomfited. Then he shrugged. 'Nah, I can't see it myself. Andy was too smart to get on anyone's bad side. 'Sides, if one of them did it, they'd have made more of an example of him, wouldn't they? Stands to reason. They'd have bashed him about more, left his body somewhere in the town where it would make more of a splash. Sent the message loud and clear to the others, like, reminding them what would happen if they crossed the big boys. If Andy had done something stupid and upset a bigwig, they wouldn't have just stabbed him once and left him in a bloody wood in the back of beyond, would they?'

Hillary, in spite of herself, had to reluctantly concede that he probably had a point. In fact, it had been something that she'd already reasoned out for herself.

Besides, the killing of Andrew Feeley felt too private, too personal, to be the work of a disinterested party. Even so, there was no way she could dismiss the possibility altogether.

'Did you see much of Andrew before he died, Mr Comer?' she asked casually.

'Nah. He was all grown up, wasn't he? Was even shacked up with some bird. Didn't need me anymore,' Malkie said, with apparent sincerity. ''Sides, I was too busy living me own life.' Malkie shrugged.

'Yes, I understand you'd not long come out of prison,' Hillary said dryly.

Malkie flushed. 'All right, all right. So, anyway, I was living it up a bit, weren't I? Out on the town, having a bevvy down the local with the boys. Going to watch the footie. Putting some money down on 'osses.' He smiled in happy remembrance.

'So you didn't come to Oxfordshire to see Andrew?'

'Nah. Like I said, I was busy having a good time. You dream of doing stuff like that when you're banged up. Can't wait to let your hair down a bit. Course, if I'd have known the poor sod was going to cark it, I'd have been down like a shot to see him,' Malkie said self-righteously, bristling a little as he shot her a dirty look. 'I was his father, wasn't I? If I'd known what was up . . . I'd have protected him, like. I'd have given that bastard Dalton a taste of this all right,' he said aggressively, showing his clenched fist.

Over by the wall, Claire shifted slightly and broke off from jotting down notes. She did, indeed, have a short truncheon in her large bag, and she surreptitiously slipped her hand inside, just in case.

But Hillary, who would back her instinct any day, felt no sense of impending danger.

'You seem sure that Sean Dalton was responsible. Any reason for that, apart from the fact that he's black and had the temerity to marry Karen?' she pushed.

'The tem . . . what?' Malkie asked suspiciously. But went on without a pause. 'Like I said, Andrew and him were at daggers drawn. He was making Dalton's life a misery, Andy was,' Malkie said with pride. 'He never liked his mum shacking up with the likes of him. And Dalton, he didn't like Andy standing up to him. Nah, it was Dalton who killed my boy, I'd bet you any money you like,' the other man said, nodding vigorously.

Hillary sighed slightly. 'Did you travel down to Tackley the day Andrew died, Mr Comer?'

Malkie sighed elaborately. 'I told you — I was living it up with my mates.'

'And that takes money,' Hillary put in silkily. 'And as a newly released con, I don't suppose you had much of that to spare? Did you go and ask your son for some spending cash? Did he say no? Did that make you mad? Before you knew it, had things got out of hand, and was Andy waving a knife about?'

Malkie's eyes had got slowly wider and wider as she'd talked, and now he looked fit to burst. 'Eh? What you talking about? Here, d'ya think I did for my own boy? You mad or what? And I never asked him for no money, see, because I had th—'

Abruptly he stopped speaking, looking almost comically surprised to find himself on the verge of saying something incriminating.

But Hillary was already smiling. 'Yes, Mr Comer? You were saying?'

'Nothin'. I was saying nothin',' Malkie grumbled.

'Oh? Because I have the feeling you were going to say something about you having no need to cadge off your son because you had some money stashed away of your own. Proceeds of whatever crime it was that you'd just been sent down for was it? Or did some poor sod owe you money? Or had you just done a job flogging toasters, say, and had just had a big pay day?'

Malkie flushed. 'Now you're putting words in my mouth. And I ain't gotta put up with this. So go on, sod off. If you can't even arrest my son's murderer when he's staring you in the face, then what use are you? Go on, sod off,' he added, getting to his feet.

Again Claire's hand went into her bag, but Hillary merely shrugged and stood up. 'If you have any real evidence, or know of anything even remotely useful to us, here's my card. Don't hesitate to get in touch.'

She handed it over, and Malkie snatched it from her hand with ill grace. He muttered something inaudible.

At the door to the flat, however, Hillary suddenly remembered something and turned to look at him. 'Oh, by the way, you wouldn't happen to remember your son's friend Frankie, would you?'

She wasn't expecting anything to come of it, so she was very pleasantly surprised when Malkie said, 'Frankie Lamb, you mean? Yeah, he was Andy's so-called best mate, I think. Bit of a wanker if you ask me. I dare say he only hung around Andy because Andy used to give him stuff.'

'What kind of stuff?' Hillary asked sharply.

But Malkie only shrugged. 'I dunno. Just a feeling I got. I only saw him a couple of times, the few times Andy and me met up. He looked the sort who used to hang around, you know, like a puppy dog, hoping for the odd pat or two. I think Andy found him useful sometimes.'

Yes, Hillary thought, reading between the lines. I bet he did. A not-too-bright wannabe friend could often be relied on to take messages or do a bit of dealing, or act as a backup in the event things turned a bit iffy. 'Know where I can find this Lamb character?' she asked hopefully.

But it was there that her luck ended. Malkie shook his head. 'Nah. He might even have carked it himself by now. He didn't look the sort who was living too healthy a lifestyle. Know what I mean?'

Unfortunately, Hillary did.

CHAPTER EIGHT

Gareth looked around the small empty office that already, after only a couple of days, was beginning to feel both comfortable and familiar. Although it was still very early days, he had far more confidence now that his return to a full-time working lifestyle was something that he could achieve and maintain.

What's more, he was beginning to see himself working in this environment, and with his two fellow co-workers, for some time to come. Claire was like everybody's idea of a favourite aunt — good-humoured, motherly, comfortable, experienced and wise. Of course, not many people's favourite aunts were ex-police sergeants who'd had to deal with the darkest extremes of human nature on a regular basis. And Hillary Greene was showing all the signs of being an exceptional CO. She was clearly very bright, experienced and competent. All right, he had a feeling that he wasn't seeing her at her best right now, given she was in mourning for a man she'd loved and lost. Sometimes she looked too thin, too pale and hollow-eyed. Even so, he could sense real steel in the woman's backbone, and a grim determination not to let the excrement that life could throw at you get the better of her. And Gareth could appreciate and respect that.

If his long-term physical fitness held up, he was definitely beginning to get the feeling that he had found an acceptable billet here. And he was finding his first ever murder case fascinating. He'd had no real idea what to expect of the job when he'd applied, and certainly hadn't expected that he would be pitched in at the deep end quite so soon. Mind you, all he was doing at the moment was watching, listening and keeping quiet. He knew he had a steep learning curve ahead of him, but watching Hillary Greene at work — especially when interviewing witnesses and suspects — was an education all of its own. She had a way of fitting her approach and manner to whoever it was she was talking to. Gentle but firm when dealing with the victim's family, but showing a weird kind of ironic patience when it came to less likeable characters. And all the time, you could almost hear her mind ticking away, thinking, cataloguing, querying, but above all, missing nothing.

And thinking of the two new women in his life made Gareth realise that Hillary and Claire would be back soon, so he'd better take advantage of the empty office while he could. Quickly, he reached for his mobile phone and dialled one of the few numbers saved in his contacts.

It rang for some time before it was answered, and when it eventually was, the male voice sounded sleepy and slightly slurred. Gareth glanced with concern at the office clock, which confirmed that it was nearly noon.

'Hello, Jase, you lazy sod,' he said cheerfully. 'It's all right for some, lying in bed at all hours of the day! Some poor sods like me have been at work for hours.'

'Gar?' the voice said a shade uncertainly and after a brief pause. Gareth could easily picture his friend, blinking at his phone and struggling to get his brain in gear.

'Who else, mate?' Gareth said. 'Just ringing up to make sure we're still on for Sunday. You, me, the fish, a pint at the local? You still up for it, yeah?'

'Yeah, sure.' He didn't sound highly enthused, but then Jason Morley never did nowadays.

Over the line, Gareth heard a deep sigh and a rustling sound, and he could imagine his old comrade now sitting up in bed and yawning. Unlike himself, Jason had yet to find full-time work. But that wasn't all that surprising. He just couldn't seem to stomach having to answer to a boss who, in Jason's opinion, didn't know his arse from his elbow. Gareth had heard all the excuses — all the jobs that hadn't quite 'been right' for him, and all the reasons for finding himself suddenly fired. The boss was too young, too snotty, too stupid, too up his own arse, too fixated on working his employees to death for a lousy minimum wage.

Sitting in his own new office — which, let's face it, was small, cramped, ill-equipped and was hardly a penthouse office overlooking Canary Wharf — Gareth nevertheless was suddenly very aware of how lucky he was in comparison.

At least he wasn't still lying in bed at lunchtime with nothing to get up for.

'So I'll pick you up at sparrow fart on Sunday and we'll get some angling time in. Then we'll have lunch at the pub — my treat, now I'm earning again. Yeah?' Gareth pressed on, careful not to sound too upbeat. He knew from his own experience of depression that listening to well-meaning, bright-eyed and bushy-tailed friends trying to force you out of your rut could be about as welcome as a dose of malaria.

'Yeah, OK.'

Gareth hesitated for a moment, aware that he was clutching his phone too tightly now, but he couldn't stop himself from saying casually, 'And you haven't been thinking about . . . you know . . . what happened in Reading, have you, mate?'

There was a long pause, and then a harsh bark of laughter. 'What? You my mother now, Gar? Clucking anxiously over her poor, wayward chick? Piss off! I've got better things to do with my time.'

Gareth winced at the obvious lie, but forced a laugh of his own. 'Fair enough. See you in a few days' time then, mate.'

'Yeah, sparrow fart, Sunday,' Jason agreed. But beneath the sardonic undertone, Gareth could tell that Jason was glad to have something to look forward to, and to know that he hadn't been totally forgotten by those closest to him.

Gareth ended the call and leaned back wearily in his chair. He wished Jason's family could help him, but he knew that they couldn't. They simply didn't understand, since none of them had been army brats themselves. Jason wasn't one of the lucky ones who were second, third or even the umpteenth-generation of soldiers. He'd joined up because he couldn't find a job, was sick of living in Britain and had thought joining the army would at least broaden his horizons and let him see a bit of the world.

Well, it had done that all right, Gareth thought sourly, and then instantly felt guilty. After all, nobody had *made* them sign up, had they? And doing relief work for poor sods who'd had their homes flattened by hurricanes and earthquakes had been very rewarding. And if you got sent to a war zone, you made the best mates ever — you had to fight side by side, your life in your mate's hands, and his life in yours. Of course, you knew it was possible you could get killed. Or injured. But you never thought it would really happen to *you*. And when it did . . . well, there was no rulebook for coping with catastrophe, was there? You just had to try and get through it in your own way, the way that best suited you.

And some coped better than others. Gareth had lost his marriage, his old way of life and his old way of looking at things. But he still had Fiona to take to the zoo or the cinema, and know that he would always be the 'best dad in the world' to his eight-year-old. Well, at least until she became a teenager! Plus he'd found a new place to live, and he had this new, challenging job.

But not everyone was so lucky. Some let the darkness overwhelm them. And Jason was one such lost soul. Gareth sat for a moment, thinking about what had happened in Reading, and worrying. Of course, he might have it all wrong and be worrying for nothing. Jason might have had nothing to do with—

'Hello, daydreaming away in a nice warm office while the rest of us have been working our backsides off, chasing down leads out in the cold?' Claire's mocking voice brought him abruptly out of his gloomy reverie, and he grinned across at her as she slumped down wearily into her own chair.

'More like slaving over a hot keyboard while the rest of you have been out and about gallivanting around Swindon and having a good time,' he shot back.

Then his eyes went to Hillary Greene, who was standing watching this banter from the doorway.

Noticing, she smiled, and said briskly, 'Right, Claire, type up the interview notes with Comer for the Murder Book. And, Gareth, before you go home every night, get into the habit of checking the book, to make sure you keep current with the state of the case. You said you'd made progress with that background check on Toby Truman?'

'Yes, ma'am,' Gareth said smartly.

Hillary hid a smile. He still had the habit of shooting out her title as if he were on the parade ground, but at least he wasn't shouting it out too loud now. Which, Hillary supposed, had to be an improvement. It didn't make her feel quite so much like one of those beleaguered sergeant majors in a *Carry On* film!

'Toby's life since Andrew Feeley's demise has been no great shakes, no matter how well his mother thinks — or says — he's been doing,' Gareth informed her.

'Probably wishful thinking on her part,' Claire muttered darkly from behind her monitor.

As if she hadn't spoken, Gareth swept on concisely, 'He never got back with that wealthy farmer's daughter that dumped him, and as far as I can tell, he's had no real long-standing relationships with anybody else either, although having said that, he's still young.'

Hillary nodded. 'Hmm, his mother said he had a steady girlfriend who worked in a building society. She never said she'd met her, though, so it's possible it's a fabrication on his part,' she mused. 'He's, what, in his mid- to late twenties now?'

'Yes, ma'am. He did go through a major detox and rehab shortly after Andrew Feeley was murdered, and for the most part it seemed to have taken, if you don't count two minor slips when he had to go on Methadone for while. By all accounts though, he's been clean for the past couple of years. No arrests for being under the influence of narcotics.'

'More likely he's just never been nabbed with anything on him,' Claire offered cynically, her fingers not even pausing in their flight across her keyboard as she typed furiously.

Again, neither Gareth nor Hillary gave any sign of having heard the interruption.

'He lives in a flat in the Glory Farm area of Bicester, which he shares with two other men — one works in Bicester Village flogging designer gear to all the Japanese and Chinese tourists, the other is a mechanic in a garage. Toby works part-time in the big Tesco supermarket on the edge of Bicester Village, but he supplements that income doing bar work at that big pub on the main road that does cheap meals, and is open all day long. Know it?'

Hillary didn't, but wasn't particularly interested. 'So he's got no real record worth mentioning?'

'No, ma'am. A few drunk and disorderlies, and a few traffic violations.'

'Nothing for violence?'

'No, ma'am.'

Hillary sighed. 'All right. Do you know where he'll be this time of day?'

Gareth checked the time and did a quick mental calculation. 'At the pub I reckon, helping out in the lunchtime rush.'

'Right. Well, we'll break for lunch ourselves then drive out and see him this afternoon. No point dropping him in it with his boss by hauling him out for questioning when they're busy.' She glanced at the clock. 'Anybody fancy a pie from the shop on the corner?'

* * *

It was nearly two thirty by the time they pulled into the car park of a large chain pub overlooking a busy roundabout. As a backdrop for fine dining it didn't have a lot to recommend it, Hillary mused, but then the clientele here had no need of such pampering. A selection of grilled meats, chips and plenty of it were probably all they required.

The smell of cooking food when she'd not long eaten a steak-and-kidney pie herself made her feel slightly nauseous, but she ignored the unwelcome sensation as she pushed open the door and made her way to the bar.

They found Toby there, serving a customer a glass of Australian lager. He had his mother's brown curly hair and eyes, but had been spared her chipmunk-like features. Tall, lean and reasonably good-looking, she suspected that Toby wouldn't have much trouble attracting female company. The fact that he couldn't seem to keep it, though, made her wonder if his early brush with drugs and addiction had scarred him in ways that weren't physically apparent.

'Mr Truman?' She spoke quietly, and discreetly showed him her card. 'We'd like a word. Can you take a break?'

Toby Truman stared at her for a moment in dismay, looked at the tall silent man beside her with his scarred face and stiff way of standing, then gulped, nodded and turned to a young blond girl who was serving another customer at the far end of the bar. The lunchtime rush was indeed over, but the large room, filled with multiple tables, still housed a fair few customers. 'Laura, I have to take a break,' they heard him say, and her complaining voice followed them as Toby led them to the far end of the room, to a conservatory area where large windows overlooked the unlovely roundabout.

'Er, would you like something to drink?' Toby asked diffidently, indicating an empty table and then automatically reaching for the white cloth that was tucked into his trousers and wiping the table clear of drink smears and food residue.

'No thanks. Please, take a seat with us. We want to talk to you about Andrew Feeley,' Hillary said.

'Andy?' Toby squeaked, bending his body into a chair. He sounded almost comically surprised, and then a moment later looked very relieved. Hillary hid a world-weary sigh as she contemplated just what it was that Toby had been expecting them to say. Obviously, his conscience was hardly as pure as the driven snow, and she wondered, vaguely, what it was that he'd done recently which he thought might have brought the law to his door.

'Yes. We're looking at his case again.'

Toby leaned back into his chair, looking more curious than cautious now. 'Andy, huh?' he mused. 'Funny, I haven't thought about him for years.'

'No? That surprises me,' Hillary said mildly. 'According to your mother, he was the reason you got hooked on drugs in the first place. I wouldn't have thought many people could so easily forget the man who ruined their life.'

Toby paled a little, and shot a look around, but nobody was in earshot. 'That's all in the past now,' he said quickly.

Hillary's lips twitched. 'Sure it is, Toby. If you say so. But your mother isn't the forgive-and-forget type, is she? She had a lot of harsh things to say about your old mate when we talked to her yesterday.'

Toby briefly met her level sherry-coloured eyes and then quickly looked away again. 'You shouldn't listen to Mum,' he muttered. 'She always hated Andy.'

'From what we've been learning about him, she wasn't the only one,' Hillary said dryly. 'He was a bit of a blight on the village, wasn't he? Stealing their cars every now and then, indulging in a bit of burglary here and there. And selling drugs to anyone who wanted them.'

'Don't forget pimping out their daughters,' Toby said with a snort.

Something in the sudden silence had his eyes swivelling back to hers, and then he paled again, and looked quickly away.

'Tell me more about that,' Hillary said quietly. She didn't think DI Barker's original investigation had made any mention of significant prostitution activity involved in the case. Maybe that had been a mistake, and instead of just pimping out the odd girl or two, the dead man had had a far larger sex racket going on.

'Oh, it was nothing much really,' Toby said with a shrug and an appalling attempt at nonchalance. 'I mean, it wasn't anything serious.'

'Not serious?' Hillary echoed. 'Just how "not serious" was it, Toby? Did he have a string of girls? If so, how many? Were they all local? Did he put them out in Oxford or nearby cities?'

'What? Hell no, nothing organised, not like that!' Toby hastened to assure her.

'No? Because if he'd been doing something like that it would give a lot of people a motive to murder him, wouldn't it?' Hillary grated relentlessly. 'Fellow pimps who didn't like him muscling in on their turf. Not to mention the fathers, brothers or boyfriends of the girls he pimped. And let's not forget the girls themselves,' Hillary pointed out, her voice going hard and flat. 'Some of them must have borne a grudge against him?'

'No, no, you got it all wrong. I didn't mean nothing like that!' Toby insisted. 'I mean, it was more of a lark, sort of thing.'

Toby was sweating now, and looking around nervously. 'And please keep your voice down. I've got a good job here, I don't want to lose it. If my manager knows the cops have been talking to me . . .'

Hillary smiled and nodded. 'Sure, Toby. So why don't you just quietly and clearly tell me what you *did* mean by it, and we can get out of your hair.'

Toby swallowed hard. 'Well, I dunno for sure, do I? I mean, I wasn't in his confidence like. I was just . . . a customer. He didn't confide stuff in me, but . . . well, you can't help seeing or hearing things, can you?'

Hillary nodded patiently at this rambling waffle. Beside her, she could feel Gareth's tension was rising. No doubt he found the direction the interview was taking distasteful. Perhaps the thought of men using women for their own sleazy ends — and profit — made him want to punch someone. He probably also wanted to make his displeasure known, in no uncertain terms, to the man in front of them.

But he would learn, Hillary thought. You had to develop patience and control. More than anything, you had to keep your eye on the prize. And the prize didn't have anything to do with appeasing your anger. It was all about gaining information. No matter what you had to wade through or tolerate in order to get it.

'No, you can't help but learn stuff,' Hillary agreed patiently. 'So what did you learn about Andrew and his, shall we call them, ladies?'

Toby unexpectedly blushed. It took Hillary a little by surprise, since, given this man's history, she hadn't supposed there could be much that would trigger such a phenomenon within him.

'Well, they needed his gear, didn't they?' he muttered. 'And sometimes, quite often, they didn't have money to pay him. So he sort of . . . offered to sell them to his mates for an hour or two. Like that nasty sidekick of his, Frankie Lamb. Or even to other male customers who were flush. He had some customers who drove sports cars, you know, and were well able to spread the dosh around.' Toby sounded suddenly pleased by this memory.

Then he frowned. 'Sometimes they paid the girl, right, and then she just handed the money straight over to Andy, which made him laugh. He got a kick out of it, see? Having the power to make them . . . you know . . . demean themselves.'

Toby paused and swallowed hard. 'Andy was . . . I dunno, sometimes a bit weird about things. I often thought he had something twisted, you know, up here,' he tapped his own temple, 'when it came to girls. He liked to see them really desperate for the gear, like. He never made the men beg for a fix, but he often made the girls do it.'

Hillary heard Gareth let out his breath in a hiss beside her, and caught his eye. She shook her head slightly in warning. Yes, her eyes told him, it was disgusting and sickening. But Hillary knew that they couldn't afford to spook the witness by letting him see how much they despised him.

In her experience, people didn't like it when they were suddenly forced to see their own shortcomings in the eyes of a stranger.

'It sounds to me as if Andy had a bit of a sick streak in him,' she said mildly, turning her attention back to the complacent man sitting opposite her.

Toby snorted. 'You ain't kidding! Some of the things he said made me feel sick to my stomach. I was glad that I always had the cash to pay him I can tell you! Not that he seemed to care about tormenting the men so much . . . Even so . . .' He shuddered.

Beside her, she could sense Gareth's lips twisting in a sneer.

'Do you know the names of any of these girls?' she asked abruptly, forcing Toby to keep on his toes. It wasn't a good idea to let them forget who was in charge of the interview.

'Nah,' Toby said at once — far too quickly. And again, he wouldn't meet her eye.

'You're not a very good liar, Toby,' Hillary said, her voice light and chiding.

Again Toby surprised her by flushing. 'Look, I ain't no nark, all right? Those girls, well, they had their own problems. I ain't gonna add to 'em by dropping them in it now with the likes of you. 'Sides, most of them are probably dead now. Or married or moved away, or who knows what? Leave 'em alone, can't you?' he finally hurled at her.

Hillary looked at him with a measure of surprise, and a brief, warm flicker of hope. Who'd have thought that even a spark of gallantry could still exist in the world according to Toby Truman?

'All right. I won't press you for names,' Hillary agreed. Not that she was making much of a concession. As Toby had just pointed out, she doubted that they would now be able to locate any female one-time drug addicts willing to talk about what they'd suffered at the hands of Andrew Feeley.

'So, what can you tell me about the afternoon he died? From what I understand, you had no alibi when Andrew was getting stabbed.'

'Eh? What you talking about?' Toby said, looking appalled. 'I didn't kill Andy! Why would I? He—'

Toby bit off the rest of the sentence with an audible snap of his teeth, but he might as well not have bothered. Hillary merely smiled and finished it for him.

'He was your dealer, the supplier of the necessary white powder. And it's common sense that a drug addict wouldn't cut off the source of his supply by killing his dealer. Right?' she offered.

Again, Toby shot his head around to give the room a quick scan, but the clink of cutlery and the chatter of his noisy customers hadn't abated much. And nobody was paying the least attention to them, naturally. Why would they?

'I told you — I'm off all that now. It's all behind me. But yes, since you ask, no addict is going to off their dealer. It doesn't make sense, does it?' he challenged.

Hillary's lips twisted. 'Unless they got desperate — or greedy. After all, if you meet your dealer in the woods, you've got to suppose he's got a bit of a stash on him, right? And what if, on that day, you didn't have any money to pay him?'

'I told you, I always had the money,' Toby whispered, beginning to look truly afraid now. 'Look, I didn't kill Andy. I swear.'

'You weren't at school or college or whatever that day, though. DI Barker checked,' she pointed out. 'Your mother tried to feed us a line that you were ill in bed all day,' she added sceptically.

'So what? I skived a day off! It was summer and hot. Big deal.'

'So where were you?'

'Who the hell knows!' Toby hissed. 'I was probably a bit high, like, and just zoned out sunbathing in the meadow. I can't remember. I told that copper as much at the time. And he couldn't find any proof that I went anywhere near the woods that day,' he added triumphantly, 'otherwise he would have arrested me, right? Right?'

Hillary sighed. Because, depressingly, Toby Truman was right.

'Go back to work, Toby,' Hillary said flatly. 'And try and stay out of trouble, for your mother's sake if nothing else. She still loves you and cares about what happens to you, even if nobody else does.'

Toby shot her a look full of venom and pushed the chair noisily away from the table as he got up to go. He was just about to stomp off, but instead he paused.

'You know, I reckon whoever offed Andy did the world a favour. I hope you never catch him.'

And so saying he stalked back to the bar, the hero of his own little world.

For a moment, there was silence at the table.

Then, 'I need a drink,' Gareth said flatly.

Hillary grinned. 'But not here?'

'No, ma'am,' Gareth agreed soberly. 'Not here.'

* * *

As Hillary drove Puff into Kidlington, Gareth was surprised when she drove past the entrance to HQ and carried on into town.

'Where are we going, ma'am?'

'To get that drink,' she said succinctly.

Gareth stiffened a little in the passenger seat. 'I didn't really mean I needed a drink, ma'am,' he said quietly. 'I don't drink all that much, to be honest. Not with the medication I have to take.'

Hillary nodded. 'Relax, we can both have something soft. I just want to introduce you to the Black Bull, which is our local hangout. A lot of us coppers drink in there. And I just need to wash the bad taste out of my mouth before going back to HQ.'

Gareth nodded. Now *that* he could understand.

CHAPTER NINE

The Black Bull wasn't particularly full, since the lunchtime rush was long over. However, since a lot of police officers staggered their mealtimes anyway, and often preferred to eat when it wasn't so busy, Hillary wasn't surprised to see that there were still three vaguely familiar faces seated at a table at the back of the room.

Typical of the breed, they'd chosen a dim corner, where they could sit with their backs to the wall and have a more-or-less uninterrupted view of the comings and goings in the main salon.

Hillary noticed that her own presence was instantly noted, but that their curiosity quickly became focused on her companion. She knew one of the men — a forty-something with a shock of sandy hair and a face full of freckles — from a raid on a house many years ago, where there'd been a bit of gunplay. During which, she'd very narrowly managed to avoid getting shot in the bum, of all places. She still bore the scar at the top of her leg where the bullet *had* creased her though.

Of course, they'd all been younger then.

As she went to the bar and ordered orange juice for both herself and the new boy, she wracked her memory for the name of the sandy-haired officer, and by the time she'd paid for the round, she had it. Brian Foley — probably now a sergeant, she guessed, from his appearance and manner. He didn't have the look of someone who had risen — or had wanted to rise — to an inspectorship.

With him, the two younger men had the look of long-time DCs who were waiting to pass their own sergeants' exams.

They were talking about a case they were working on, and clearly didn't expect Hillary to join them. So all three fell silent as Hillary said something to Gareth, and then they both looked over towards their corner and started walking towards them.

Gareth felt their eyes assessing him as they got closer — noting the scar on his face, the walking stick and limp, and the way he held his left arm out of the way by his side. His eyes were flat and even and he allowed a brief smile to cross his lips as Hillary greeted them.

'Hello, what's this? A meeting of Reprobates Anonymous?' she opened cheerfully.

'Yeah, we thought we'd keep it up, since we heard you were a founding member, guv,' Brian shot back with a wide grin.

'What can I say?' She shrugged modestly. 'Nice to see there are no shortage of members. This is Gareth Proctor, formerly a soldier in the British Army, and now slumming it with the likes of me in the CRT as a civilian consultant.'

'How is it down in the Black Hole of Calcutta?' one of the others, whose name she didn't know, offered cheekily. Short, chubby, with a slightly bulbous nose and all-seeing blue eyes, he nudged his chair over as he spoke, allowing room for Hillary to pull out a chair of her own.

Gareth, after a slight pause, lifted a chair from the next table with his right hand and sat down. He carefully rested his heavy, round-headed walking stick within easy reach and lifted his drink — deliberately — with his scarred and slightly misshapen left hand. He was pleased that it didn't wobble.

'Well we're allowed to come up for air every now and then,' Hillary answered the question with a roll of her eyes. 'But my main job is to make sure the new recruits don't try and make a run for it when they see the light of day. Hence I have to keep an eye on them . . .' She nodded her head towards Gareth, who smiled around the rim of his glass. 'But don't let us interrupt you. I just thought I'd bring Gareth over so he could get a taste of how real coppers work, as opposed to us has-beens. And you all looked like such prime examples,' she said with a somewhat mischievous smile.

The third of the trio, a tall, slender man with thinning fair hair and slightly protruding eyes, gave a snort and sank about a quarter of his pint of low-alcohol lager in one gulp.

'Right. It's not as if he can learn anything with you, guv, sorting out *murders*,' Brian said drolly.

'So, what are you all working on at the moment then?' Hillary asked, settling back in her chair, ready to hear the latest. Although her days working bread-and-butter cases were long gone, it didn't mean that she couldn't still feel nostalgic for them now and then.

'Someone's been lifting heavy farming equipment out Cropredy way, guv,' Brian obliged. 'Combine harvesters worth hundreds of thousands of quid, being loaded and driven away at night. The poor farmers are going spare. The odd tractor here and there is bad enough, but this has got really out of hand.'

'Doesn't anybody notice?' Gareth asked, thinking of the giant machines he sometimes got caught behind whilst driving down narrow country lanes. Surely it wasn't easy to nick one of those?

'Farms are out in the middle of nowhere, by their very nature. Unless the farmer lives on site, who is there to see or notice a big off-loader? Or hear the noise of engines?' Brian pointed out.

'I don't suppose the farmer had security worth noting?' Hillary enquired.

'Poor sod did his best,' Brian sighed. 'But by the time the alarm was triggered, and we got out there, the buggers were gone. It's only ten minutes from the motorway out that way and . . .' Brian Foley shrugged. 'So right now, we're stretched as thin as the skin on a rice pudding, trying to stake out as many places as we can. You know, farms that have a lot of high-end machinery. Lovely — sitting out all night in a perishing cold van, watching the foxes and badgers on a thermal camera! Oh, we'll catch the buggers sooner or later, but . . .' He reached for his pint, and then glanced at Gareth with that studied nonchalance that instantly warned the former soldier of what was coming.

'So, you got banged up fighting in the army then?' Brian asked amiably.

'Uh-huh,' Gareth agreed just as amiably. 'An IED. I was lucky — I got to come home. Two of my mates didn't.'

He took a sip of orange juice and waited.

The men mulled that over in silence for a moment, then Brian sighed. 'So, how are you enjoying your new job? The guv here giving you jip, is she?'

Hillary grinned. 'He's only been on the job three days. So I'm still taking it easy on him.'

Everyone laughed at the likelihood of that happening, and good-naturedly joshed him about still being wet behind the ears. But by now, Gareth was fully relaxed, as Hillary had expected and hoped. Men used to working in a unit very quickly learned how to form bonds with their fellows. And after their rather distasteful interview of earlier, she thought the new boy could do with a boost.

She tuned out a little as Gareth asked about what other stuff they were working on, and let her mind wander. Who was still on the preliminary interview list? Well, Chloe Dalton and her father Sean, for sure. In many ways, Sean Dalton seemed to have the best motive for wanting Andrew Feeley dead and had certainly been one of Barker's prime suspects. Always providing it was one of the boy's nearest and dearest who'd done the deed, that is. She still couldn't rule out a desperate junkie or a rival gang of some sort.

When they got back to HQ she'd ask Claire to go with her to interview Chloe. She wanted to get her take on whether or not she thought Andrew Feeley had physically bullied his little sister or had been content with verbal abuse. From what the boy's own mother had said, Andrew had bitterly resented her. But had it gone as far as him causing her actual bodily harm?

She hadn't got the sense from Karen Feeley that she had ever found bruises or unexplained injuries on her young daughter. And her instinct told her that Karen wouldn't have allowed it to continue if she had. Since she'd had the courage and will to kick Malkie Comer out of her life, she must have had the backbone, when the chips were down, to do the same to her son.

But when it came to stuff like that, Claire Woolley really came into her own. So she'd like her opinion when—

Hillary's musings halted abruptly as, out of the corner of her eye, she noticed Gareth stiffen. Instantly, she tuned back into the conversation that had been going on around her.

'You know him then?' the chunky man said, looking at Gareth speculatively.

'There were a lot of us in the army you know,' Gareth countered with a twist of his lips.

'What's this?' Hillary interrupted sharply.

'The dead soldier in Reading, guv,' Brian said, sounding slightly surprised. It wasn't like Hillary Greene not to be on the ball. And then he remembered that Steven Crayle was not that long dead, and instantly felt guilty.

He hadn't known Superintendent Crayle personally, but any man who finally brought down that bastard Dale Medcalfe deserved respect. Especially when he'd given his life doing it.

'Oh, yes, I remember hearing about that,' Hillary said, glancing at Gareth curiously. 'He was attacked outside a pub, wasn't he?'

Gareth hesitated for a bare instant, wondering if he should admit to knowing all about it, then instinctively decided not to, and shrugged casually. 'I think so, ma'am. I haven't been following the case that closely.'

'He wasn't still serving, if I remember rightly?' she turned to Brian, who nodded.

'No, my mate who's working the case reckons he came out of the service about six months before, so factoring in the date of the attack, he'd have last served nine months ago.'

Nine months, Hillary thought. Around the same time that the new boy had been near-fatally wounded overseas and shipped home. Could there possibly be any connection? But then, as Gareth had pointed out, there were a lot of people in the army.

'If I remember rightly, wasn't the victim . . .' Hillary paused. 'What was his name again?' She raised an eyebrow at the group in general.

'Lucas Yates, guv. Aged thirty-four, divorced, no kids,' the fair-headed man supplied obligingly.

'Right,' Hillary nodded. 'This chap Yates was fairly drunk, wasn't he, when he left his last pub? He'd been on a bit of a pub crawl?'

Brian nodded. 'Yeah. My mate reckons he must have pissed off some gang of yobbos or other, because they found him in the back of the alley, all beaten up and kicked to hell. The working hypothesis is that he'd been too far gone to realise that he should have put discretion before valour. Probably mouthed off to the wrong yob, and they decided to put him in his place. Only things got out of hand.'

'He died of his injuries a few days later, right?' she asked, beginning to remember the details better now. As she spoke, she was aware that Gareth was still very tense.

Well, there was nothing surprising in that, she supposed. Even if he hadn't known the victim personally, the thought of a fellow soldier going through combat and active duty but then dying at the hands of some thugs after a night out back home in Blighty must have stuck in his craw.

'Yeah. Like I said, they reckon he was probably too sloshed to put up much of a fight. Although there were indications of bruising on his knuckles that showed he'd got in one or two hits of his own,' Brian said admiringly.

'Are they close to making an arrest?' Gareth heard himself say, and hoped he didn't sound as desperately interested in that answer as he actually was.

'Hard to say,' Brian shrugged. 'So far no witnesses have come forward. People don't like to get involved, not when it comes to grassing on gangs. Stands to reason, I suppose. They don't want to end up getting their own heads kicked in, do they?'

Hillary, still watching the new boy closely, said, 'No CCTV or traffic camera footage worth a damn?'

'Nah, guv. The alley wasn't covered. And there weren't any reports of incidents on the night of any vehicles driving erratically away from the scene.'

Hillary nodded. 'Is it still active?' she asked. It had, if she remembered rightly, been nearly three months since the former soldier's death. By that time, most DIs would have been forced to put it on the back burner.

Brian gave the what-can-you-do shrug that said it all. More often than they liked, police officers had to give up on a cold trail, whether they liked it or not. They simply weren't staffed, or funded, to be able to spend too much time on any one case. It was as frustrating as hell, and nobody sitting at the table — with the possible exception of Gareth — was at all surprised by the number of police officers leaving the force, being too angry or dispirited to carry on doing the job they had loved. If the government didn't start funding the police service as it needed to be funded, then Hillary for one wouldn't like to lay any bets on what might happen.

Gareth, aware that a trickle of sweat was running down his back, shifted slightly on his chair and reached for his nearly empty glass.

He was careful not to look at Hillary Greene. He'd already observed for himself how nothing escaped her notice and he didn't want to take any chances.

He was glad when the topic moved on to another case of supermarket robberies in Thame.

* * *

Outside, in the car park, Hillary got Puff going first try, and drove back to HQ in silence. But her mind was far from quiet.

She was sure that she hadn't imagined Gareth's reaction when they were discussing Lucas Yates's case. And there was something in his diffidence about it that rang distinct alarm bells in her head. Or was she overreacting, she felt compelled to ask herself. Just because another one of her former civil aides, Jake Barnes, had joined the CRT because he had an agenda of his own, it didn't mean to say that she should start suspecting everyone! After all, what was the likelihood of lightning striking twice in the same place?

No. She couldn't let herself get paranoid. As she indicated to turn into the HQ parking lot, she told herself to forget about it.

* * *

Back in the communal office, Hillary told Gareth to type up the interview notes with Toby Truman for the Murder Book.

'And when you've done that,' she added, 'see if you can track down the current whereabouts of Frankie Lamb. He was sleeping on a friend's couch at the time of the original investigation so he'll be long gone from there now. If he's even still alive, that is.' Hillary jerked her head to indicate the area where the IT and forensics technicians worked the majority of non-investigative cold cases. 'If you run into any problems trying to get into the databases, ask one of the boffins to help you out. They'll gripe and groan, but secretly they like to impress the newbies.'

Gareth nodded. 'Yes, ma'am.'

Hillary turned to Claire and explained why she wanted her to come and give her an overview of Chloe Dalton. As expected, Claire was glad to get out of the office.

* * *

Less than ten minutes later, Claire turned off the roundabout at the entrance to the historical town of Woodstock and looked around with a sigh. 'Prime real estate round here, guv,' she grinned. 'And I don't just mean *that* place.' That place being Blenheim Palace, the hangout of the dukes of Marlborough, which had just become visible off to their left, set in its massive and impressive grounds.

Hillary eyed the magnificent pale-stone palace and smiled. She wouldn't like to foot the electricity or heating bill for that pile.

'Chloe works for a solicitors' firm in town, right?' Hillary asked. 'It's going to be fun trying to find a parking space.'

'At least most of the tourists have buggered off by this time of year, guv,' Claire said hopefully.

Of course, in spite of Claire's optimism, they had to park a good ten minutes' walk from where Chloe Dalton was now working on her career path towards becoming a solicitor.

Choosing to work in the legal profession had been an interesting choice for her, Hillary mused. Had her teenage brush with the law triggered her interest in that side of things? Or did the daughter of working-class parents see the profession as a way of making a good living?

As they pushed through the main door of a small but modern office block and found their way towards the offices of Gillingham, Singh & Braine, Hillary found she was rather curious to see how the younger sister of their murder victim had turned out.

CHAPTER TEN

Both Hillary and Claire were struck at once by Chloe Dalton's exceptional beauty. Now in her early twenties, she stood at about Hillary's height, but moved with an unconscious elegance that came from having a naturally willowy and graceful figure. Her lovely café-au-lait complexion was perfect, and a careful but sparing use of blusher made the most of her seriously high cheekbones. Her nose was narrow, and perhaps her least attractive feature, but her heart-shaped face, luminous brown eyes and well-shaped mouth provided ample distraction.

She was one of the very few people that Hillary had ever met who could probably have become a model, and a successful one at that, if the camera loved her as much as the naked eye.

Chloe had already risen from behind a small desk in her small office overlooking a modern cul-de-sac of new-build houses when her secretary tapped on the door and showed them in.

Their witness was clearly only a junior member of the team here, but Hillary got the feeling from both the receptionist and the secretary that she was well regarded in the small firm. It boded well for her ability to pass the articles needed to become a fully qualified solicitor, and Hillary wondered if her ambitions stopped there, or if she intended to go on and try for the Bar at some point.

She was dressed in a charcoal-coloured, well-tailored suit, snowy white blouse and neat, square-toed shoes with a modest heel. She wore no jewellery.

'Thank you, Becky. Would you like some tea or coffee?' she asked, looking politely from Hillary to Claire.

Hillary shook her head and glanced at Claire, who took her cue from the boss and also declined. With a smile Chloe dismissed the secretary, who had to be ten years her senior, and indicated the chairs in front of her desk.

'Please, sit down. I'm trying to think which case I'm currently working on that might require a visit from the police? We do mostly civil law here at . . .'

'Ah, no, this isn't business. Well, ours, but not yours,' Hillary qualified, quickly showing her ID. 'I hope your receptionist didn't give you the wrong idea. I'm a former detective inspector at Thames Valley, now working as a civilian consult on cold cases. We've just reopened your brother's case.'

'Oh. Yes, Mum said you'd been to see her,' Chloe said, her eyes flickering slightly as she resumed her seat.

She sounded genuine enough, but as Hillary smiled, she also had to wonder. Had this very beautiful young woman *really* thought that they'd called on her because of some legal matter she was dealing with? Or had she guessed right away why they were here? And if so, why all the shenanigans?

'How can I help?' Chloe asked brightly. She was sitting very straight in her chair, and her hands were folded neatly together in front of her on top of her desk. Her gaze was level, and her eyes told Hillary absolutely nothing.

'I'm sorry if I have to ask questions that may become distressing, Miss Dalton,' Hillary began. 'And I'll try not to keep you any longer than we need.'

She paused, giving the other woman time to reassure them that she was happy to give them all the time they needed. But it didn't come. Instead, Chloe continued to watch her closely.

'I understand from your mother that Andrew had . . . well, issues. Mostly with your father, Sean?' It had only just begun, but Hillary was sure this interview was going to be a little bit tricky. And not only because Chloe was studying to become a solicitor, thus giving her a professional advantage over the general public when it came to police interviews, but because Hillary had the feeling that this woman was not going to give away anything at all unless she could help it.

Which didn't necessarily mean she had anything to hide, Hillary acknowledged. But it certainly made her life that little bit more difficult.

Chloe smiled slightly, and after about a second's thought, inclined her head. 'Yes, I think that's true to say. It's my opinion that Andy was very close to his own father when he was little. I'm not sure I ever met the man, though. On the rare occasions when he came to visit Andy, they always met well away from the house. Mum didn't want him in her home, you see? But yes, I learned from a very early age that Andy really had problems with Dad. *My* dad, I mean.'

Hillary nodded. 'He played up?'

'Yes.'

'To the point, sometimes, of getting physically violent?'

Chloe glanced down at her clasped hands, then back up to Hillary. Again she was in no rush to answer, and took her time to consider her response. After a pause, she sighed slightly. 'When he got bigger, perhaps when he was fifteen or sixteen, he tried it on with Dad a couple of times. But Dad wasn't having any of it, and gave back as good as Andy tried to dish out. So he soon stopped.'

'You mean he then confined his nastiness to verbal abuse?'

'Yes.'

'Racial abuse?' Hillary asked quietly.

Chloe's level gaze didn't falter. 'I'm afraid so.'

'How did your father react to that?'

Chloe shrugged and shifted slightly in her chair. 'Dad had had years of it by then. I imagine he became more or less inured to it. And when Andy was just a kid, a little kid, I mean, I suppose he tolerated it simply because he had to — for Karen's sake, as much as anything else. When Andy became an adult . . . well, let's just say everyone was relieved when his friend sold him the static caravan and he moved out of the house.'

Hillary nodded. 'I dare say *you* would have preferred it if he'd moved farther away than just to the end of the garden?'

Chloe smiled slightly. Again, there was that expected pause before she replied. 'I can't deny that,' the beautiful young woman conceded. 'But housing around here . . .' she shrugged helplessly and looked out of the window at the gleaming Cotswold stone houses across the narrow road. 'Take those for instance,' she nodded her head towards the window. 'Detached, three bedrooms. Nothing special. But they've probably all got a price tag of half a million or so. Woodstock is a very desirable town to live in. And Oxfordshire villages maybe even more so, having such good links with both London and Birmingham. There's no way ordinary working families can afford to live here anymore. Andy, being just a teenager, was lucky to be able to buy even the caravan.'

Hillary nodded. 'But then Andy wasn't entirely without means, was he?'

Chloe dragged her eyes back from the houses, and again regarded Hillary steadily. Finally she said, 'You're talking about his alleged illegal activities, I take it?'

Hillary couldn't help but smile. Now there was the voice of a solicitor-in-the-making.

'As far as I know, my brother was never convicted of any crimes,' Chloe concluded carefully, her tone neither defensive nor aggressive but simply matter-of-fact.

Hillary nodded, forced to play the game at her pace, but not really liking it. 'All right. But for clarity's sake, let us just stipulate that your brother was dealing drugs, and probably played a part in a number of local burglaries and the theft of some of his neighbours' cars.'

Chloe smiled, but said nothing.

Hillary, sensing she would get no nuggets of gold on this subject, shifted the focus slightly. 'I would imagine Andy's hatred of your father boiled over to extend towards yourself as well?'

Chloe mulled that over silently for a while, and then smiled slightly. 'Yes, I think that's fair to say. Although he didn't hit me like he did Dad.'

'He verbally abused you?'

'Yes.'

'From an early age?'

'Yes.'

'Can you give me an example?' Hillary pressed patiently.

The beautiful woman paused for a moment, perhaps mentally running through a list for a good choice, or perhaps merely playing for yet more time. Then she shrugged. 'Mostly his bullying was pretty generic. He seemed to resent pretty much everything about me — being the youngest, being a girl, being the centre of his mother's attention. He used to call me "the parasite" and constantly told me that I was good for nothing. But I think, looking back on it now as an adult, it was obvious that he didn't have a high opinion of women in general, so maybe I shouldn't have taken it so personally.'

Hillary nodded and glanced at Claire. 'Learned behaviour?' she murmured, and Claire nodded, attracting the glance of their witness for the first time. Seeing Chloe focus on her, Claire smiled slightly.

'We recently interviewed Andrew's father,' she explained, 'Malcolm Comer. You said you never met him, and for that you should be thankful. Let's just say that the apple didn't fall far from the tree in Andy's case.'

Chloe nodded. 'That doesn't surprise me,' she said, and at last showed some emotion as a brief look of something — anger, maybe pain, or a combination of both — flickered across her flawless features. 'From what Mum let drop once or twice by mistake, I got the impression that her first partner used to hit her.'

'Did *Andy* hit her, do you think?' Claire slipped in easily.

'No, I don't think so,' Chloe said, clearly taken aback by the question and answering it at once. It was, Hillary thought, the first spontaneous answer she'd given during the interview so far. 'I'm trying to be fair, and I think Andy loved our mum. Well, as much as you could say he loved anything or anyone,' she nevertheless had to qualify.

'But you maintain that he never hit you?' Hillary asked curiously. 'I find that hard to believe. Bullies usually pick on those they perceive to be the weakest.'

Briefly Chloe's face tightened. And this time, neither Claire nor Hillary had any trouble interpreting the cause of her response. Fear. It was one of the most recognisable emotions that police officers encountered when talking to both victims *and* perpetrators.

'I don't think he ever *hit* me, exactly,' Chloe qualified cautiously. 'Obviously I can't say that with any accuracy, since I don't have memories of my early childhood — say before the age of five. But from what I *can* recall, he never actually punched me.'

'But he did do other things?' Hillary pressed.

Chloe sighed. 'Well, a bit of pushing and pinching, and sly kicking. You know, the sort of things siblings sometimes get up to. Kids can be nasty, can't they?'

'But that sort of behaviour usually takes place between children of similar ages,' Claire put in gently. 'There's a difference between, say, a nine- and ten-year-old fighting because of jealousy or resentment, and a boy of fifteen picking on a child of seven or eight. That's not so much sibling rivalry as an assault.'

Chloe sighed. 'It never reached the magnitude of an assault. Like I said, it was more a case of casual cruelty. If I walked by and he was within arm's length he might reach out and pinch me hard. Or trip me up when I walked past his chair. Or bang into my shoulder, hard, when we passed each other in a narrow space. That sort of thing. It didn't take me long to learn to just not go near him.' Chloe shrugged.

She was giving the impression of a calm and collected individual, but Hillary couldn't believe that a child would have had this aplomb.

'And this happened all throughout your childhood?' Hillary asked.

'Pretty much.'

'And your mother didn't try to stop it?' Hillary tried not to sound judgemental, but she thought she saw a flash of irritation in the younger woman's eye.

'Mum never saw it happen,' Chloe confirmed a moment later, her voice as animated as Hillary had ever heard it. And, as if aware of that fact, Chloe visibly forced herself to relax, and added, in her normal, carefully even tone, 'Andy was too clever to let her catch him out.'

'You never told her about it?' Claire slipped in, a shade sceptically.

Chloe hesitated, and both women had the feeling that she was contemplating an outright lie, as opposed to the verbal fencing that she obviously preferred. But then she spread her hands in a helpless gesture. 'At first I did,' she reluctantly admitted. 'When I was very little. But, really, what could Mum do? She told him off, and she made an effort to make sure we weren't left alone together, if possible. But if you've ever raised a family, you know how impracticable that is. And if she really laid into him, it only made him more sullen and more vindictive, and more inclined to treat me worse than if she'd said nothing. And she could see that. So in the end, she had to back off.'

Hillary nodded. 'And so you learned that you had to stand up for yourself?'

Chloe regarded her hands for a moment, and then sighed wearily. 'Oh, I learned ways to keep myself safe. I often went to a friend's house down the street to play right after school, for instance, and only went home when I was sure that either Mum or Dad would be home. In the holidays, I never hung around the house or garden, but always stayed with my friend or went into town. And then there was Felix. He helped look out for me, when he was older.'

Chloe paused, a genuine smile hovering around her lips for the first time. 'I haven't thought of Felix in . . . gosh, years now. Funny how you lose touch with old school friends, isn't it, when you start your working life? He only lives in Banbury, but . . .' She shrugged.

'Felix was your boyfriend?' Hillary asked.

'What? No. Yes. I mean, he was a friend, and he was a boy, but we never dated or anything like that,' Chloe clarified. 'He lived in Tackley then too, so we went to the same village primary school together, and then on to the local comprehensive in Kidlington. We were in the same class, but as I've known him since I was five, I never thought of him romantically.'

And I'll bet that wasn't Felix's choice, Hillary thought wryly. Even as a gangly and awkward adolescent, this girl still would have been stunning.

'You said he helped look after you?' Hillary prompted. 'What did you mean by that exactly?'

'Oh, he'd stand up for me if Andy started . . . you know, kicking off.'

'When you say stand up for you — do you mean he and Andy would come to blows?'

'No! Well, not actual blows,' Chloe modified. Annoyingly, she took a long moment to regain her calm before continuing. 'Like I said, my brother was a snide, sneaky kind of creature. But he had a healthy regard for his own skin. And Felix was always big for his age, and played rugby and did boxing and stuff. So it never really came to a physical, knock-down, drag-out fight. It was just that sometimes Felix would see him try to trip me up, or kick me, or whatever, and he'd get in the way. You know — suddenly step between us so that the pinch couldn't reach me, or what have you. Not that I ever had Felix come to the house — these events would usually take place outside in the garden, or in the village.'

'And what did Andy think of that?' Hillary asked. 'When Felix prevented him from hurting you?'

Chloe flushed slightly. 'He used to call Felix names. You know . . . the usual racial slurs.'

'Felix is black?'

Chloe nodded.

'I'll bet Andy didn't like it, that you had someone looking out for you?'

Chloe shook her head. 'Not much, no.'

'But you maintain he never got really violent with you?' Hillary watched her reaction closely.

Chloe, however, merely shrugged. 'I think, deep down, Andy knew that if he went too far with me, Dad would kill him.' She smiled slightly, then the look froze on her face and turned to one of horror as she realised the import of what she'd just said. 'I don't mean that literally, of course,' she said hurriedly. 'I just used that as a figure of speech. A commonly used phrase, nothing more.'

Hillary nodded but said nothing. Now that she finally had this extraordinarily self-possessed woman on the run, she wasn't going to do anything to stop the momentum.

'I just meant that Dad would have given him a hiding, that's all,' Chloe insisted, then, realising that didn't sound too good either, added with growing anger, 'Oh, I'm not saying he'd have ever really *hurt* him. Just that he wouldn't have stood for it if he did me a bad injury. That's all I meant.'

Hillary nodded. 'But your father must have known that Andy was treating you badly? You say your mother couldn't do much to help but presumably you told your father about the abuse as well?'

Chloe blinked, then looked down at her hands. She saw that her fingers were gripping each other so hard that her knuckles had turned white, and with a visible effort forced them to loosen. 'I never told him anything about it,' she said flatly.

And, perhaps for the first time, Hillary was sure that the girl had just lied to her. And if Sean had known that his problematic stepson was bullying his own flesh-and-blood little girl, she couldn't see him standing for it.

But from the way Chloe's lips had now firmed into a tight line, she realised that she would never get the dutiful daughter to admit to anything that put him in a bad light.

Abruptly, she changed tack again. 'So what can you remember about the day that Andy died?' she asked. 'To begin with, did you notice him behaving any differently in the days or weeks prior to when he was stabbed?'

Chloe, obviously relieved to be off the subject of her father, thought for a moment, then shook her head. She had long dark hair that she kept piled up high on top of her head in an attractive chignon, and the movement made it sway slightly. 'Not that I can recall. He was just his usual nasty self. I remember — and it must have been only a week or so before it happened — that he made some snide remark about how he was sick of me acting like I was some sort of a princess, as if I thought I was entitled to the best of everything. I think Mum had just bought me a rather expensive pink dress to wear at some party or other, so that might have been what set *that* off . . .' Chloe shrugged one shoulder eloquently. 'Anyway, he said something about how I "wouldn't be around much longer" to be a pain in his arse.'

'*A death threat*?' Claire couldn't help but interject.

Chloe again shrugged, as if it had been nothing. 'Probably. He liked to say things to scare me, especially when I was a little kid. He was always looking at me and making out that he was plotting to do something evil to me. That used to freak me out completely, I can tell you. Which is why he did it, of course. To be honest, I had become almost immune to that sort of thing by the time he died.'

'On the day he was killed you were at school?' Hillary swept on.

'No. We should have been, but it was one of those teacher training days. Parents hated them, but we kids loved them — an extra day off, and in summertime too.' Chloe's lips lifted in a smile of remembrance. 'It was a really hot day, I remember that. Me and my friend, Donna went swimming in the river.'

Hillary knew that the friend had been interviewed and recorded in DI Barker's original report. She also remembered that Chloe's alibi for the time of her brother's death wasn't particularly airtight. The two girls had indeed been swimming during the afternoon, but neither girl had taken their watches or mobiles to the river. They hadn't wanted to leave them unattended whilst they swam. Which meant that the friend in question couldn't swear to the time that Chloe had left her to go home for something cold to drink.

So, theoretically, this girl, who had now grown into such a beautiful woman, could have cut through the woods. It was a hot day, and it would have provided the shadiest — if not the quickest — route back to her home. But would a teenage girl who'd just gone swimming bother with such considerations?

But just suppose she had, Hillary mused. And Chloe had had the bad luck to come across her bullying, hateful big brother in those woods. Perhaps Andy had just made a sale to some junkie, and realised his little sister had seen it?

He wouldn't have been best pleased by that if she had. Perhaps he might even have begun to worry that Chloe — who he knew had no reason to feel any loyalty towards him — would go to the police with her tale? And if they could convict him it would certainly put him away for a few years — which Chloe would have been only too delighted to see happen.

So say he threatened her. He might even have drawn his favourite knife and waved it about just to reinforce the threat. By Chloe's own testimony he liked to scare the life out of her.

But then what? Would a young teenage girl really be able to get the better of a man in his twenties in a knife fight?

Putting aside such speculations for later, Hillary sighed. 'You were at home when the police officers came to inform your mother of what had happened?'

'Yes.'

'Had you seen your brother that day?'

'Only at breakfast. He'd come over for a bacon sandwich.'

'You never saw him again after that?'

'No.'

'What did you think of Jade? Andy's girlfriend?' Hillary threw in abruptly.

As she'd hoped, the self-possessed young woman looked momentarily disconcerted by this sudden, seemingly random question. 'Jade?' Chloe frowned slightly. 'Well, I don't know. I mean, I didn't have much to do with her really.'

'She lived at the bottom of your garden,' Hillary pointed out mildly.

'Yes. But . . . well, she was Andy's girlfriend, wasn't she? She was older than me, and pregnant. I was, what, fourteen? We lived in different worlds. Besides, Andy wouldn't have liked it if we'd become friendly.'

'But she was nice enough?' Hillary asked. 'To you?'

'Oh yes, on the rare occasions our paths crossed.'

'Did you ever see Andy hit her?'

'No. But like I said, we moved in different worlds. I was a schoolgirl, and like all teenagers, I imagine I was too self-absorbed to notice or probably even care what she must have been going through. And around that time I was really infatuated with this boy I'd just met. He was nearly eighteen, so he was a bit older than me and he hung around with Andy for a while, and he was absolutely *gorgeous*. Well, you can imagine!' She gave a half-embarrassed laugh. 'I was so flattered that he paid any attention to me at all, because at that age you can feel invisible, can't you?'

Chloe sighed and then shrugged. 'So I was really caught up in my own little drama. It was getting pretty heavy at one point, because he was making it clear that he wanted to get serious. And I was half-terrified and half-elated. So my biggest concern then was should I lose my virginity or should I keep it for Mr Right? The talks me and my friends had over that issue . . .'

Again, she sighed and shrugged. 'So, as you can imagine, I didn't really pay much attention to Jade and her problems. Looking back on it now, though, I can't imagine that living with Andy and being pregnant was exactly a walk in the park . . .' Chloe paused. 'I wish now that I'd been less caught up in my own little soap opera and had been more friendly towards her.'

'Do you have any idea who might have killed your brother, Miss Dalton?' Hillary asked, wondering if Chloe's implied feelings of guilt towards Jade Hodson were real or not. With this woman, and her beautiful and often mask-like face, it was hard to tell.

They were back to the routine of long, thoughtful pauses between questions again, Hillary noted a shade impatiently, as Chloe waited a moment before answering. 'I always thought it was someone he did business with,' she said quietly.

'A junkie? Or a rival criminal?'

'Either, I suppose.'

Hillary glanced at Claire to see if her colleague had got any other questions, but a quick eye flick from Claire told her that she hadn't.

'Well, thank you very much for your time, Miss Dalton. If you think of anything else . . .' Hillary went automatically into her usual spiel, and a few minutes later, Claire and Hillary were once more outside on Woodstock's quaint streets, making their way back to the car.

'Well, what do you think?' Hillary said, once they were back in the privacy of Claire's car. 'Was she abused?'

'Well, she admitted as much, guv,' Claire said a shade pedantically, but added almost at once, 'but I know what you mean. Did the perp do more than inflict the odd kick or pinch?'

'Uh-huh?'

'In my opinion, probably not,' Claire said, after some thought. 'But I'm not infallible, guv,' she added with a laugh.

'None of us are,' Hillary conceded. 'But I agree with you. I think our murder victim made her young life miserable, but I think he was probably too scared of running foul of his stepfather to be really violent with her.'

'Yeah, she didn't like it when we started talking about good old Dad, did she?' Claire observed. 'Think she's scared he did it? Took the knife off her brother and lashed out when Andy pushed him just that inch too far?'

Hillary grunted. 'It's got to have crossed her mind, surely? Always supposing she didn't do it herself.'

Claire, who was far too experienced and wily to pooh-pooh the idea of a fourteen-year-old girl being capable of stabbing someone, sighed heavily. 'I take it you want me to find out all I can about her knight in shining armour, this Felix character?'

Hillary grinned. 'You can read my mind, Claire.'

Claire rolled her eyes and reached for her seatbelt. 'Do you mind if I stop off at Sainsbury's on the way back, guv? I want to get some duck breasts and a fancy dessert. My better half is bringing a pal home for dinner, and I promised I'd push the boat out.'

'Sure, fine.' Hillary nodded absently. And then wondered. When was the last time she'd eaten a proper meal?

Perhaps, instead of making do with a can of Big Soup and a bread roll for her supper, she'd treat herself to a meal at The Boat instead. After all, they let her leave Puff in their car park all year round. It was time she gave the pub a bit of proper patronage.

She carefully didn't let herself recall the last time she'd eaten a meal out, because it must have been with Steven.

'Want to come, guv?' Claire said. 'The more the merrier.'

Hillary blinked. 'Sorry? What was that? I was miles away.'

Claire sighed. 'Never mind, guv. Just a thought.'

CHAPTER ELEVEN

The next morning Gareth's leg felt stiff and painful — more so than usual. The weather had turned damp and was colder than it had been recently, which probably accounted for it, he supposed. He had the usual bowl of muesli for breakfast and winced his way down the single flight of stairs, the scent of last night's fish and chips from the shop below making him feel slightly nauseous. He supposed he'd get used to the smell eventually, even though he would probably never eat fish and chips again!

The small one-bedroom flat above the shop was ideal for now though, which was probably just as well. He still had child maintenance and alimony to pay, and would have for some years to come, so the chances of him being able to move out to anywhere bigger or better any time soon were pretty remote.

He walked to his car, then, seeing that he still had plenty of time before having to be at the office, he went right on past it. Walking to the end of the small line of shops, hoping he'd be able to walk off the stiffness and the pain a bit, he turned at right angles and did another circuit, before arriving back at the car, feeling a little less tentative in his walking.

At least he didn't have to brace himself for pain at every step.

With a relieved sigh, he slid behind the wheel and drove carefully into work. It was almost impossible to think that in just two more days he'd have completed his first week on the job. And since he'd joined the army right after leaving school, it literally constituted his first ever nine-to-five, Monday-to-Friday job. Almost an office job.

He smiled at the thought and, held up at a red traffic light, glanced casually out of his side window. It was a typical autumn day: grey, damp, chilly and miserable. A whole world away from the one thousand or so British troops who were still in Afghanistan right now, assisting the Afghan National Security Force. Of course, it was their remit to advise, now, and — since 27 October 2014 — not to take part in any active duties.

But he'd still rather be there than here, sitting in his cold car with his leg hurting, contemplating another day . . .

Abruptly, and before he could slide any further down the slippery slope to self-pity, he pulled his thoughts to a halt. It wasn't even as if he had any reason to complain.

Working at Thames Valley Police HQ was turning out to be a real eye-opener, even for a civilian consultant. Working with Claire was a doddle, even though he'd been worried a little bit that he might not find it easy working with non-army personnel, especially a middle-aged lady like Claire. What, after all, did they have in common? But he could see that they would become friends, and with that would no doubt come certain bonuses, which meant that he was already anticipating the time when she'd be having him over to her place for Sunday lunch, meeting the hubby and being force-fed roast beef and Yorkshire pud!

And even a complete novice like himself could see that working with Hillary Greene was a real privilege. It hadn't taken him long to see just how highly regarded she was, not just by the likes of Rollo Sale, but also by the rank-and-file. During the course of the week, a number of officers, of all ranks and from a number of divisions, had made it clear he'd fallen on his feet being given a job with her.

The lights changed to green and he pulled off the handbrake and battled his way slowly through the rush-hour traffic, thinking about his new boss and the case they were working on. He was so green at all this that he had absolutely no idea how well — or how badly — it might be going. As far as he could tell, they were just treading the same old ground already covered by the original investigation and getting nowhere fast. And unless he was being totally dim, they didn't seem to have come up with any new clues or leads at all.

Not that it wasn't fascinating to watch and learn as witnesses were questioned by such a consummate expert as former DI Hillary Greene, but exactly *what* was it accomplishing?

Having such a short commute to work left him with little time to contemplate things further, and when he arrived at the office and found Claire already at her desk, he gave a quick look at the clock. It reassured him that he was ten minutes early.

'Don't worry, you're not late,' Claire confirmed, grinning at him.

'The boss in?' Gareth asked. It was a testament to how well he was beginning to fit in that Claire knew immediately that he meant Hillary, not Rollo Sale.

'Course she is,' Claire said. Since losing her life partner, Hillary Greene was always first in and last out. 'I think you . . .' She broke off as she sensed someone approaching the open door, and a moment later Hillary glanced in.

'Ah, good. Gareth. I want us to get cracking and talk to Sean Dalton, get his take on things. He's beginning to look like the one with the biggest motive for wanting Andrew Feeley dead.'

'You think he's our prime suspect, ma'am?'

'Possibly,' Hillary said cautiously. 'Once we've questioned all the main witnesses, and I've had a chance to mull things over, we can start thinking about who else we might need to have a chat with. How would you feel about taking the lead in one or two sessions?'

Gareth tried not to look surprised — or worried. But he wouldn't have been human if he didn't feel a moment of unease. On the other hand, he reminded himself, this was why he'd chosen this job over the other, more mundane options, wasn't it? So that he could make a difference and contribute something again?

'Yes, ma'am,' he said briskly, even as these thoughts ran like quicksilver through his mind.

Hillary, though, wasn't fooled by the prompt, seemingly confident response. 'Don't worry, it won't be anything too major,' she reassured him. 'And I'll brief you thoroughly before we start, make sure you know what I want covered and what questions and techniques are likely to work best. And if I spot something you've missed, I can always take over where you've left off. It's time you started to get a "feel" for things. There's only so much you can learn by watching and listening.'

Hillary, seeing him stood almost to attention beside his desk, could only hope that as he gained more experience, he'd start to lose some of that stiffness and think more like an investigator than a soldier. And the only way *that* was going to happen was to chuck him in at the deep end and let him figure out how to swim.

'All right then. For this morning's interview though, it's the usual routine,' she reiterated. Sean Dalton was far too important a witness on which to let the new boy cut his teeth. 'Watch, listen, learn. Claire, how did the dinner go last night?' she added, in an abrupt change of topic.

'Great, guv, thanks.'

'Right then. Back to Tackley,' Hillary said to Gareth, who was already reaching for his coat.

* * *

She noticed Gareth wince as he settled into Puff's passenger seat, but said nothing when he had to reach down and physically pull his left leg inside with both hands. She noticed he was careful not to meet her eye. Was the poor sod really wondering if she was regretting him getting the job on her team? Was he scared that she thought he was going to be a liability? She had the nasty feeling that doubts like that were something he had to deal with on a regular basis.

But there was no point in saying anything. It would only embarrass him further. The only way to help him build up his confidence, she knew, was to just let him get on with things, and come to realise for himself just how much he was needed. She was sure it wouldn't take him long to realise how understaffed the police service really was, and how grateful the CRT was to have any help at all.

With that cheerful thought, she headed back to the farming community and village in the folds of the Oxfordshire countryside.

It was what her dad would have called 'damping' by the time they reached Tackley, the sort of weather that couldn't be said to be dry, but on the other hand, it wasn't actually raining either. The sort of weather that could make you wet through without you noticing it. Consequently, she was careful to zip up her green waterproof waxed jacket as they walked the short distance down the road to where Sean Dalton now lived. The place was almost at the other end of the village from his old family home with Karen, but she still found it slightly odd that the divorced man had chosen to stay so close by to his ex. Even given the fact that he still worked at one of the farms nearby.

The cottage was made of local stone, and had a grey slate roof and charming dormer windows and was set back a little off the road. Like Debbie Truman's abode, it would almost certainly have been built by one of the landowners for his farm workers back in the day, although, according to the background check, the current owner and resident of the house was a widower who was self-employed as an accountant.

No doubt he'd still been glad of a permanent lodger to help pay the household bills. Or had the two men been friends? Perhaps, being a widower, the homeowner had simply been glad of the company?

She stood under the meagre shelter of a narrow porch and rapped sharply on the knocker. The man who answered was probably somewhere in his early sixties, with close-cropped white hair and a goatee beard.

'Mr Fletcher?' she asked amiably.

'Yes.'

Hillary smiled. 'We're here to see Sean Dalton. I telephoned him last night to arrange an appointment, so he is expecting us.'

'Oh yes, of course. You're the people who are looking into his son's murder case again?' He looked at them with keen interest, but immediately stepped back against the wall of the narrow hall, indicating the set of stairs which immediately faced them. 'Sean's rooms are all upstairs so go on up. He is in. The spare bedroom has been converted into his sitting room — first on the left.'

'Thank you,' Hillary said, hearing a door above them open. As she climbed the stairs, she became aware of a large presence up ahead, looming over her. By the time she'd gained the landing, with Gareth behind her very firmly holding onto the rail as he climbed, Chloe's father was watching them thoughtfully.

The cottage wasn't large — it probably had three bedrooms, and the room Sean Dalton showed them to was tiny but decorated pleasantly enough. 'Please, sit down. Sorry there are only the two armchairs.'

'I'll stand,' Hillary said at once, before Gareth could make the offer. She saw the new boy hesitate a moment before walking to the smaller of the two armchairs and lowering himself gratefully down. He tried not to think about how nice it was to sit and get the weight off his legs.

Sean Dalton, having noted Gareth's injuries, watched him with a slight frown, then turned abruptly to Hillary. 'Karen said you'd been to see her. Chloe too. You're the one in charge?'

'Yes. We're talking to everyone involved, Mr Dalton,' Hillary confirmed.

'And now it's my turn?'

'Exactly. Please, won't you sit down? My colleague will take notes,' she added. Gareth, taking his cue, quickly withdrew his notebook and pen.

'Thanks, but I prefer to stand too,' Sean said. He was, Hillary noted, a big man, but not a fat man. Not quite six feet tall, he had powerful shoulders and upper arms, which made sense considering he'd worked a physically demanding job for all of his life. Even with the advent of labour-saving farm machinery, she was well aware that you still needed to be fit and have your fair share of stamina to work on a farm. She herself was a country girl, born and bred.

His once black hair was now turning grey. He was clean-shaven, and dressed in a thick pair of black trousers and a matching black woolly jumper. He walked to the window and glanced out, then turned and leaned against the wall next to the aperture.

Hillary had no intention of taking the spare seat, and instead moved to lean against the wall opposite him. The light — what there was of it on the overcast autumnal day — was now in her face, casting his details into negative light. It meant that she couldn't see his facial expressions at all, and she wondered if he'd done that deliberately, or if he'd just struck lucky.

And she didn't think this man had been born particularly lucky.

'Chloe painted a rather ugly picture for us yesterday, Mr Dalton,' she began, realising that there was very little point in shilly-shallying about with this man. 'Of her childhood, having Andrew Feeley for a brother.'

'Half-brother,' he corrected at once.

'Yes. Half-brother,' Hillary conceded. 'By the sounds of it, he wasn't in any way brotherly at all towards her, was he?'

Sean grunted. 'Little bastard,' he said quietly.

Hillary felt herself relax slightly. Well, at least he wasn't going to be hypocritical about it, which could only be of help. 'You never got on?'

Sean laughed suddenly. 'Now that's an understatement. The thing is, I never stood a chance with him. He was only six or so when I met Karen, and he hated me on sight. I think he would have hated anyone Karen took up with after his father went inside, but the fact that I was black really gave him something to rant about. My working on the land didn't help either. When he got older he regarded those who made a living through honest, physical work with contempt. According to him we were all chumps.'

'As opposed to someone like himself? A drug dealer, thief and pimp?' she said, pulling no punches.

Again, Sean Dalton gave a brief bark of not particularly amused laughter. 'An entrepreneur, if you please,' he said sarcastically. 'That was how the little bastard always referred to himself. As a businessman — a self-employed professional.' Sean shook his head in disgust.

'According to DI Barker's reports, you were working the land the day Andrew was killed?' Hillary prompted.

Sean nodded. 'What else would I be doing? It was a bloody hot day, the troughs needed to be filled.'

'You work for . . .' She paused, for a moment not able to recall the name of the farmer who employed him.

'Colin Woodbridge. Yeah, I've worked for him for nearly twenty years now. A good bloke.'

'He must rate you then,' Hillary said blandly.

'He does.'

'Trusts you to get on with things? To do your job well?'

Sean frowned, not seeing where she was going with all this. 'Sure. Why wouldn't he? I've been doing it for years, like I said.'

'So he wouldn't waste his time checking up on you, and overseeing what you were doing?'

'Ah,' Sean said, finally getting it. 'And yeah, you're right. That day, just like all the other days, he told me what he wanted done, and then got on with doing other jobs himself. And so, yeah, I didn't have anyone who could vouch for me around the time Andy was getting himself knifed in the woods.'

For a moment there was a heavy silence as the brutal words — and the imagery they conjured up — seemed to settle in the air. As if acknowledging the ugliness of it, Sean sighed heavily.

'Look, I didn't kill him. I know he made our lives a misery, but I wouldn't . . . And I'm not saying he deserved what he got, though at times . . .' Again the big man stumbled to a halt, shoulders drooping, as if being unable to express himself properly was wearing him down. 'Like I told that first detective, I was in the field opposite the water meadows, pollarding some willows along the river. I could see the woods from where I was, but not close enough to see who came and went. I heard Chloe and that friend of hers larking about a bit further downstream but I couldn't put a time to it when she left either. I *told* DI Barker all this,' he said impatiently.

Of course, he *hadn't* told DI Barker about seeing Debbie Truman out and about that afternoon, walking that dog of hers along the hedge line, before setting off across the water meadows towards the stand of trees where they'd found his stepson's body. Why should he have? He liked Debbie well enough, and she had enough troubles as it was with that dopehead son of hers, without him making more waves for her.

And he wasn't about to tell this latest detective about seeing her either. Well, not unless he absolutely had to, he thought uneasily. But if things turned dire, then maybe he might just have to? It was one thing to look out for your neighbours, but if your back was to the wall, it was those nearest and dearest to you who had to come first, right? Everybody knew that.

He broke off with a heavy sigh. 'Look, I really don't see the point of dragging all this up again,' he said. 'Can't you just leave it well alone? It was years ago, and we've all moved on with our lives. Raking it all up again is causing everyone a lot of pain and hurt.'

'You don't care that Andrew's killer was never caught?' Hillary asked, making sure her tone sounded sharp and surprised. Though she wasn't in the least surprised at all. In fact, given what they were beginning to learn about the sadistic nature of the dead man, she would be surprised only if she came across someone who *did* seem to care what had happened to him.

'I don't—' Sean said quickly, then just as quickly broke off. Again he shook his head, a shade helplessly. 'I just don't think going through it all over again will do any good, that's all. My Chloe doesn't need it, not when she's all set to do so well. And Jade and little Briana certainly don't need reminding of it all. Or Karen. The whole damn village is beginning to talk about him again, just when things had returned to normal. Now everyone's looking at us sideways again, or saying how sorry they are for our trouble. It's . . . depressing. Frustrating.'

'Even dead, he's still making problems for you it seems,' Hillary commiserated softly.

Sean Dalton shot her a quick, angry look. 'Is there anything else?' he challenged.

'Do you have any idea who killed your stepson, Mr Dalton?'

'I always assumed it was someone he crossed in his so-called business,' the big man said flatly.

'Ah yes — the stranger. Everyone keeps telling me the same thing,' Hillary remarked blandly. 'But I've worked many murder cases, Mr Dalton, and you'd be surprised how often this mythical "stranger" never existed at all. Nine times out of ten, people are killed by those closest to them. Like stepfathers.' Of course, Hillary knew the statistics were different when drug dealers were involved, but she wanted to rattle him a bit, see what she could unearth.

Sean shrugged. 'You think I don't know I'm a suspect?' he asked wearily. 'How could I not be? Everyone knows

Andrew hated me, and made my family's life a misery. Of course people wonder. But I didn't kill him,' he insisted.

'Not even to keep your daughter safe?' Hillary asked gently.

Sean Dalton stiffened angrily. 'I kept Chloe safe, don't you worry about that!'

'He used to bully her, she tells us, especially verbally. Calling her racist names. Even making vague death threats against her.'

Gareth moved a little forward on his chair, his eyes on Sean Dalton's big, callused hands, which were now clenching and unclenching into fists. He glanced at his walking stick, making sure it was within easy reach.

Hillary too was watching her witness closely. Whilst it often paid to make hostile witnesses angry, in the hope that wrath would lead them into saying things they'd prefer to keep secret, there was always the risk that you could provoke them into actually attacking you.

But for all the big man's tenseness her instincts told her that neither she nor the new boy were in any real danger.

'I know what the little bastard was like,' Sean gritted. 'I don't need you to tell me.'

'Did you know he didn't confine the abuse to just words?' Hillary pressed. 'She told us that he used to pinch her, and try and trip her up. Barge into her, trying to knock her over.'

Sean took a long, shaky breath. 'Nothing got past me, I can assure you. And when the little bastard tried it on, I quickly made sure that for every bruise he gave my daughter, he sported ten more himself. Believe me, he quickly got the message. For all his nasty, big-man talk and bragging, that boy was a coward. He might have been happy dishing it out, but he didn't like it when it came to taking the knocks himself.'

'So you admit to beating your stepson?' Hillary asked quietly.

Sean looked at her for a long, silent moment. 'I ain't admitting nothing. Besides, how would you prove it now, after all this time, if I *had* given him as good as he tried to give out to our Chloe?' he challenged.

Hillary smiled grimly. How indeed? 'You can understand that it matters, Mr Dalton,' she began reasonably. 'If you were in the habit of, shall we say, physically disciplining your stepson every now and then, what's to say that it didn't get out of hand that last time? That Andrew, maybe not wanting to take any more knocks, drew his knife on you?' She paused, making a show of thinking things out. 'You know you would have a legitimate case of self-defence if that's what happened?'

Sean smiled wearily. 'Good try. But I never saw the little bastard at all that day. I was never in the woods that day, and I never stabbed him. And that's all I'm saying.' His chin thrust out as he stared at her levelly, daring her to call him liar.

Hillary let the moment hang, then smiled slightly. 'All right, Mr Dalton, that will be all for now. But we'll be out and about in the village for some time yet, and we may need to speak to you again.'

She didn't miss the way the man's broad shoulders slumped slightly as the tension went out of him. 'Of course. I'll be either here or working on the farm,' Sean told them quietly. 'Or in the pub, sometimes.'

Hillary nodded and turned. Gareth snapped shut his notebook and struggled a little to get to his feet. The chair had been lower than it looked.

Sean Dalton stayed by the window and watched them leave the room, then, a few moments later, looked down on their slightly foreshortened figures as they left the cottage and walked down the garden path.

He wondered idly if the blond man had been in a car smash or something. A quiet sort of bloke, he looked competent. Funny, Sean couldn't recall him saying a word. You had to watch out for the quiet ones, wasn't that what people said?

But it was the woman who worried him the most. She had the look of someone who was clever and painstaking, the sort who never missed a trick and wouldn't stop poking and prying about until she had found out something.

And the thought of her poking and prying about — and what she might just find — brought him out in a cold sweat. There was no doubt about it now, there was something he needed to get done — and quickly. He'd been content to let things lie all these years, thinking they were all safe and sound, especially when DI Barker and the original team had pulled out of the village with nothing to show for all their pains. And once they'd gone, it had seemed sensible to just let sleeping dogs lie. If you started messing with things, you never knew just who might see . . . But now . . . yes, now, he thought with a frown, he had better get on and retrieve the evidence, just in case.

And destroy it good and proper, once and for all this time.

CHAPTER TWELVE

Hillary and Gareth arrived back at the office at just gone noon to find a note from Claire left on her desk.

Up in the canteen putting on the feed bag. You might want to join me. Had a bit of time on my hands so decided to dig a bit deeper into Frankie Lamb. Here's a hint — never was a man so misnamed.

They headed upstairs and spotted Claire at once, sitting over in one corner, reading a magazine whilst working her way steadily through what looked like a shepherd's pie.

She amiably made room on the table for them as they approached, Hillary with just a cup of coffee, and Gareth with a cheese bap and a glass of orange juice.

'Anything interesting from the stepfather, guv?' Claire asked the moment they sat down, and Hillary nodded to Gareth, letting him do the talking. As she suspected, he gave a clear but concise report, missing out nothing salient but perhaps lacking a little on the nuances.

It was probably the military way, but both women knew that a lot of good stuff could be missed by ignoring nuances. But Hillary was fairly sure the former soldier would quickly learn as much.

When he had finished his account, Hillary turned to Claire and said, 'Frankie Lamb?'

Claire rolled her eyes. 'Another right prince. I can see why him and Andrew Feeley were such good mates.'

'He's got form?' Hillary asked.

'Natch, and lots of it,' Claire sighed. 'Small-time drug dealing, and four counts of breaking and entering. Petty thieving. Most of that stemming from his late teens to early twenties. He's now, allegedly, been going "legit," and hasn't been inside for nearly five years.'

Hillary grunted, but said nothing. She knew as well as Claire that the likelihood was that the ex-con had simply become savvy with age and thus hadn't been caught recently, rather than that he'd genuinely learned his lesson and was now on the straight and narrow.

'Did you manage to track down his current address, Gareth?' Hillary asked, turning to him.

'Yes, he's in Bicester, guv.'

Now was her bloody memory at fault again, or wasn't Toby Truman currently living in the ever-expanding market town as well? She'd have to check later, to be sure. 'It's a popular place,' she said thoughtfully. 'A lot of our persons of interest seem to have landed up there,' she felt safe in adding.

'Probably coincidence, guv,' Claire said, nodding. 'It is our fastest growing town, or so the local news keeps telling me. Every time I go in to do some shopping they've flung up another housing estate somewhere. They'll be building bungalows in the cemeteries next!'

Hillary wouldn't have been surprised, but was distracted from her usual worries about all the building on the green belt. 'Any evidence our Mr Lamb and Toby Truman know each other?'

'Nothing obvious. They live in different parts of the town, and never served time together in the same nick.'

'OK. He's in employment?'

'Not at the moment, guv.' Claire forked a spoonful of minced lamb and mashed potato into her mouth, chewed thoughtfully and quickly swallowed. 'On benefits. He did have a job up to three weeks ago, but he was on a zero-hours contract, and the company's feeling the squeeze. So it was cut the vulnerable staff, last in first out, the same old story.'

Hillary nodded, sipped her coffee and then turned to the new boy. 'So, Gareth, I was going to wait until next week to give you your first shot as lead interrogator, but I suppose there's no time like the present.'

Gareth blinked. 'Ma'am?'

'You up for doing your first interview? With our friend Mr Lamb? You and the witness are more or less of the same age group, so he's likely to feel more comfortable talking to you. We need to get information out of him, but men like Frankie tend to get funny ideas when challenged by a female authority figure. They either start to play silly buggers or turn nasty.' And she wasn't feeling in the mood to put up with either scenario right then. Besides, it was time the new boy got his feet wet. 'It'll be interesting to see just what Frankie has to say about the bad old days and his dear old dead pal. What's more, if you take the lead, it'll give me more scope to watch and listen and see if I can pick up on any tells. So you lead off, and if necessary, I'll step in and finish.'

Gareth took a quick sip of orange juice and nodded, his expression deadpan. 'What line do you want me to take with him, ma'am?' he asked, hoping he sounded as if he wanted clarification, rather than being desperate for a clue.

Hillary smiled, not fooled for a moment by all the stoicism. But there was not much truly helpful advice she could give him. Every investigator had to find their own technique, and learn by trial and error what worked best for them. But there were some general truisms, she supposed.

'A lot of it you'll have to play by ear. Try and take your cue from the witness. If he seems loquacious, just let him have his head and babble away, but try and keep him on topic. If he's surly, ask specific questions and keep asking them until he gives you a satisfactory answer. We already know from the original team's reports that Frankie wasn't in Tackley on the actual day of the crime, having been seen out and about drinking in Oxford, so he's not in the frame for it. Mind you, his drinking buddies weren't the most reliable and might have been telling porkies on his behalf. But as far as DI Barker could ascertain, he had no motive for wanting to kill Andrew, so he was never much of a person of interest.'

'Right, ma'am,' Gareth said. It sounded simple enough. But then, in his experience, what sounded simple enough very rarely was when you actually had to go and do it.

'Didn't Barker think our Frankie was probably on Andrew's payroll?' Claire put in, scraping the crust from around the sides of her dish. She'd always liked the burnt bits best!

'More than likely,' Hillary agreed, pleased that she had no trouble recalling the original SIO's notes on Andrew's business operations. 'He had a lot of "friends" hanging around him who were probably errand boys. He almost certainly paid them to do the dirty work and take any falls if necessary. It'll be one of the main reasons why he never did time himself. He probably kept any users sweet with free fixes as well.'

'In which case, Frankie wouldn't have killed the goose that laid the golden eggs?' Gareth said, just to show them that he'd caught on. 'Was he a user himself?' He directed the last question at Claire, who thought for a moment, and then shook her head.

'Nothing suggests he was. Or if he was, he was never an obvious addict.'

'OK, when you've finished, we'll go,' Hillary said, nodding to Gareth's half-eaten bun.

Claire grinned at him as he took a hasty bite and chewed frantically. 'Didn't think you were going to get such a thing as an actual lunch break, did you?' she teased.

'And whilst we're out and about, Claire, you can make sure that we've got contact details for Chloe Dalton's protective school friend,' Hillary said with a wry twist of her lips. 'I have a feeling he might have some interesting things to tell us. You found out his last name yet?'

'Not yet, guv,' Claire admitted.

Gareth wagged a finger at her playfully.
Claire wagged one back.
Hillary watched the children play and smiled patiently over her coffee cup.

* * *

Frankie Lamb lived in a new-build block of four-storey flats overlooking the Bicester Village train station. This railway stop was a relatively new addition to the town, which had previously only been served by Bicester North. But when the high-flying, very lucrative Bicester Village shopping mecca had been built, it was quickly decided that a new stop was needed to help cope with the vast influx of mainly overseas customers.

Naturally, the development of the station had led to tiny-roomed blocks of flats springing up on every scrap of land available nearby, and it was to one such depressingly nondescript block that Hillary and Gareth made their way.

The lifts in the tiny lobby were clean and working, but Hillary couldn't help but wonder how long that would last.

The former 'bestie' of their murder victim lived on the third floor, in a corner unit, and was actually in when they knocked on his door. Hillary had half-expected to have to roust him out of a local pub or pool room somewhere.

Frankie Lamb looked more like a fox than any relative of a sheep, with reddish-brown hair, a sharp pointed face and alert light brown eyes. He wasn't big, standing a few inches shorter than Hillary, but he had a wiry, naturally fit-looking build that would probably stand him in good stead should he ever manage to reach old age. 'Yeah?'

He looked from Hillary to Gareth, his eyes noting the scar on the face of the male half of the duo, and then dropping to his walking stick. Hillary knew he hadn't missed seeing the slightly misshapen left hand either. And the fact that this man had automatically checked Gareth out to see what kind of a physical threat he might pose, should it come to violence, told her a lot. He was the kind who didn't miss much at all — the sort who was always watchful for something that he might turn to his advantage, constantly alert for a weakness that could be exploited. She wouldn't have been at all surprised to learn that blackmail was his favourite pastime. Which would explain how he could afford to live in even the smallest of flats all by himself; for even before being invited in, she would have bet money that this man had no need of a flatmate in order to try and help him make the rent.

Even as she was thinking all this, Hillary reached for her ID and displayed it, prompting Gareth to do the same. This they did without a word, and also without a word, Frankie Lamb studied them closely.

'Says here you're civilian. Not proper plod?' he finally said, but he didn't sound belligerent so much as simply wary.

'Yes, that's right,' Hillary agreed amiably.

'So I don't have to talk to you?'

'No you don't,' she confirmed, still amiably.

'Right then.' He nodded, withdrew his head and shoulders and began to shut the door.

Before he could complete the action, Hillary said mildly, 'But you might be interested in why we're here.'

'I doubt it,' Frankie Lamb's voice came casually from behind the closing wooden barrier.

'It's about a blast from the past,' Hillary added rapidly, knowing she had only moments before the door was shut in their faces. 'We're reopening an old murder case. A friend of yours, as it happens.'

As she'd hoped, the almost closed door ceased its final inward movement, and then, after a significant pause, moved back in the opposite direction as Frankie's face reappeared again, head cocked a little to one side, pale eyes gleaming brightly. 'Yeah? Murder, you say?'

Good old curiosity, Hillary thought gratefully. There was nothing quite like it.

'Who's that then?' Frankie added, when she remained silent.

'Just how many murdered friends do you have, Mr Lamb?' Hillary enquired with a smirk and a raised eyebrow. She knew his sort only too well. Try anything heavy or authoritarian and they'd just spit in your face — either literally or figuratively. But show a bit of playfulness, intrigue them, tease them along a bit, and you could usually appeal to something in their nature to get them interested.

Frankie looked at her for a moment, and then grinned. 'Now that you mention it, I don't. This is about poor old Andy then, yeah?'

'Yes. Can we come in and chat about the old days?'

Frankie's eyes narrowed. 'Sure. So long as this is all about Andy?'

'It is,' Hillary promised.

Frankie Lamb pulled the door aside to reveal that the builders hadn't bothered to include even a token nod to a hallway. Instead, the door opened directly into the main living space. They stepped inside, and Hillary glanced around. An open archway in one corner revealed glimpses of a tiny kitchenette. Another door no doubt led off to an even tinier bathroom. A quick glance around confirmed that the sofa converted into a bed. The space had that neutral light beige colour of new builds and everything still looked unnaturally clean and pared-back. She wondered how long Frankie had been living here.

'Well, take a seat then,' Frankie said. He himself moved to the two-seater sofa. Hillary pulled out a hard-backed chair, one of two that flanked a small table that was obviously being used for dining, leaving the room's only armchair to Gareth.

She pulled out a notebook and pen and waited.

Gareth, knowing that was his cue, took a slow deep breath, and said. 'You and Andrew Feeley were tight, is that right?'

'Sure,' Frankie said, turning his attention to the younger of his visitors. 'I first met him at comprehensive school. He was a bit wild, even then. You know, had a bad rep, which is always irresistible, right? I suppose he was something of a Robin Hood figure. Naturally, a lot of us were drawn to him.'

'Except that Robin Hood supposedly robbed the rich to help the poor,' Gareth pointed out, trying to echo the easy-going tone he'd observed Hillary using in her past interviews. 'From what the original investigator into his murder thought, it seems Andrew preferred to keep his ill-gotten gains for himself.'

Frankie laughed suddenly, a rather distracting, high-pitched giggle that sat oddly with his laid-back, self-confident demeanour. 'Well, you can't blame him for that! Everyone has to make a living, don't they?' he asked reasonably.

Gareth's lips firmed into a tight line at this, and Hillary tensed a little, worried that he'd let his indignation get the better of him. But she need not have worried as the former soldier forced himself to merely nod. 'I believe you used to work for him?'

'Work for him?' Frankie echoed, almost teasingly. 'No, I wouldn't say that exactly. We were mates, see. We hung around. Drank a bit. Played cards for money sometimes. You know, stuff.'

'Sometimes in Tackley, the village where he lived?' Gareth clarified.

'Yeah, that's right. A right hole in the middle of nowhere.'

'You were staying in Kidlington at the time?'

'Yeah. Hardly a metropolis,' Frankie said scornfully, 'but at least it had a bit of life in it.'

'I'm surprised you used to hang out in a dead hole like Tackley then,' Gareth said.

Frankie shrugged his narrow shoulders. 'What can I say? Andy liked it. He said it was quiet and private like.'

'Ah. So his . . . customers . . . felt safe, going there to buy from him?'

Frankie shrugged again. 'Wouldn't know nothing about that, mate. Like I said, we hung out in that caravan of his mostly.'

'And Andrew never paid you for doing little odd jobs for him?'

Frankie Lamb grinned. 'That's right. He didn't.'

Hillary could tell that the little scrote wasn't going to be drawn on that line, and was relieved when Gareth made it plain that he had also sensed the same thing, by changing his line of questioning.

'If you hung out at his place, you must have known Jade Hodson, his girlfriend?'

'Yeah, met her a couple of times.' Frankie shrugged. 'Can't say I really took to her much.'

'Oh? Why not?'

'She didn't like me,' Frankie admitted bluntly with another grin.

Hillary, taking notes, thought that showed exceptionally good judgement on Jade's part, but kept her amusement strictly to herself. So far the new boy was doing quite well, and she didn't want to throw him off his stride.

'What was Andrew like?' Gareth asked next. To his ears it sounded a bit lame, but right at that moment he couldn't think of anything else to ask.

'Andy? Well . . . like I said before, he was a bit of a wild card to be honest. You never quite knew what he was going to do next, know what I mean?'

'I'm not sure that I do,' Gareth said, deadpan.

'Huh. I mean, don't get me wrong, he was always a good laugh and all that. But I reckon he had a kink somewhere.'

'A kink?'

'Yeah. You know, up here,' Frankie said, tapping his temple. 'Me, see, you give me enough dosh for some good nosh, plenty of booze, and spending money to keep the ladies satisfied, and I'm happy. I take life as it comes, and make the most of it. I don't much care about anything else. I reckon most of us are like that, if we're honest with ourselves. But Andy . . . he seemed to take a lot of things personally. Feel a lot. You know, really take things to heart. When he got pissed, he got really angry, like pacing-and-punching-the-walls angry. Or when something funny happened, sometimes he'd laugh until he went red in the face and could hardly breathe. You know?'

'He was emotional?'

'Yeah, sort of,' Frankie said dubiously. 'But hard with it. No, you know, I reckon you've got that wrong. More often than not he was the exact opposite — totally unemotional, I mean. Like a robot. Ah hell, he was sort of all over the place, I suppose,' he added, sounding annoyed with himself for not being able to make it clear what he meant. 'He kinda reminded me of a character from a Quentin Tarantino film, you know? All cold and sod the consequences sometimes, as if nothing could touch him one moment. And then prepared to slit your throat if you said something that touched him on the raw. I'm not explaining this very well, am I?'

Gareth resolutely refused to look at Hillary Greene for help, though he was beginning to feel as if he had no idea where to go next.

'We know he had issues with his family set-up,' Gareth clutched the first straw he could think of. 'Especially with his stepfather. Tell us about that.'

'Oh yeah,' Frankie agreed at once. 'Andy really hated him. Mind you, I think he kept most of his real venom for that little sister of his. Poor kid. He had a real down on her. You ask me, he had mummy issues.' Frankie nodded wisely. 'That's what all the shrinks say, isn't it? He resented his little sister having all of Mummy's attention.' He grinned across at Hillary.

Hillary didn't rise to the bait.

Gareth cleared his throat. 'So he resented the attention his mother spent on Chloe, you say?' he kept on doggedly.

'Oh yeah. He used to sneer about "the little princess." He was always complaining about her. Mind you, not long before he carked it, he'd begun to hint that he had got something on the brew about her . . .'

'Oh? Any idea what?' Gareth asked quickly, as Hillary too pricked up her ears.

'Nah, no idea,' Frankie shrugged, disappointing them both. 'But he was sort of . . . gleeful about it. You know, like a kid hugging a great secret to himself. Whatever it was, the poor cow would have gone through it, I can tell you that. But then he got stuck with his own knife, so I reckon she had a lucky escape. To be honest, I wasn't that interested when he got all squirrelly. You just sort of had to accept that Andy had a kink, like I said, especially about women, and let him get on with it. I used to just zone him out whenever he began spouting off. Like I said, I like women.'

He again glanced at Hillary, as if expecting approval. Hillary continued to scribble down her notes.

'We know that some of Andrew's customers were women. Is it true that he used to let some of them pay for their gear by pimping them out?' Gareth asked.

Hillary made a great show of shifting in her seat. Gareth shot her a quick look, realised he'd done something wrong, thought about it for a moment, and then came up with what he thought was the probable cause.

You never gave out information, only asked for it. He could remember Superintendent Sale telling him that shortly after he'd been given the job. It was rule number one. Damn!

Frankie, unaware of his unease, gave that slightly unnerving, high-pitched giggle again.

'Oh yeah. That was Andy all over. You ask me, he got a kick out of seeing people humiliated. I remember, there was this one girl living in the village who must have pissed him off somehow, 'cause he told me that he was gonna make it his mission to get something on her just so that he could . . . well . . .' Frankie, suddenly realising that he might be leading himself into that particular brand of hot water that barristers called 'accessory before the fact,' hastily bit off the rest of it. 'But that was Andy all over,' he finished, somewhat lamely.

'You knew him well. Do you have any ideas who might have killed him?' Gareth asked brusquely, not wanting to give the witness time to ruminate on the fact that inviting the cops in for a chat might not have been such a good idea after all.

'Nah. But I can tell you this, I was surprised when I heard about it,' Frankie said.

'Oh? Why?'

'Well, Andy was nobody's fool, was he? He was always careful. For a start, he carried that knife with him everywhere, didn't he? He knew how to look after number one, all right. And he wasn't too proud to leg it, if he thought that was what was needed. So I just can't see how he could have let himself be lured into the woods and then stabbed.' Frankie sounded genuinely bewildered now. 'He was a total bastard, see? I would have thought, in a fight, it'd be the other poor sod who'd come off worse.'

Gareth nodded, then was finally forced to glance across at Hillary to see if he'd forgotten anything, and hand off to her. Hillary, not wanting to knock his confidence, made a show of closing the notebook. There were one or two questions she would have asked, but if she needed to, she could always come back and take another run at Frankie Lamb herself.

'Thank you for your time, Mr Lamb,' Hillary said mildly, getting to her feet.

Frankie grinned amiably at her, and led her to the door. 'I didn't mind. It was kinda nice, talking about the good old times.'

Hillary blinked. Years spent hanging around with a twisted character like Andrew Feeley were the good times?

Once outside, she took a long, slow breath, and then headed down the short corridor to the lifts. Once the doors had opened and they were inside, Gareth hit the ground-floor button and said, rather sheepishly, 'Sorry about . . . you know, mentioning the pimping. We never let on information about the case. I do know that.'

'Don't do it again,' Hillary said mildly.

'No, ma'am.'

'All in all, you did well.'

'Thank you, ma'am.'

'So how was it? Your first interview?'

Gareth sighed. 'It felt . . . odd.'

Hillary nodded. She tried to remember her very first interview and was a little disconcerted to find that she couldn't.

CHAPTER THIRTEEN

When they got back to HQ, Claire had come up trumps with a name and recent address for Chloe's friend Felix Wainbridge, now living in Banbury, the market town to the north of the county.

'Well done,' Hillary said, standing in the doorway. 'Gareth, if I give you my notes, think you can type up the interview with Frankie Lamb for the Murder Book?'

'Yes, ma'am,' Gareth said, knowing he'd have no problem, since he was still feeling a little flushed with success right now and that almost every word was imprinted in his mind.

The last time he'd felt such job satisfaction was when he'd finished stage 1 of his basic training, and then gone on to please the corporal overseeing his combat training.

After that, he'd found himself pitched into combat zones mostly in hot remote places, and had been too busy concentrating on staying alive rather than earning brownie points with his superior officers. Nevertheless, the sergeant of his troop had obviously seen something in him, for he'd recommended him to the staff sergeant for Intelligence training.

He could still remember that feeling of satisfaction he'd felt when he heard he'd been accepted to work in Intelligence. Funny that he should get the same sort of feeling now when all he'd done was ask some low-level criminal a few questions. Or maybe it wasn't that surprising? Even though Andrew Feeley had been no great loss to society, he suddenly realised that he really wanted to find out who had killed him. And why. It somehow mattered.

Hillary, unaware that the new boy was taking a brief trip down memory lane, handed over her notebook, snapping him out of it. As he sorted himself out behind his computer, she gave Claire a brief oral report, then added, 'I want you to go back to Tackley and ask around. See if you can find out which girl Frankie Lamb was talking about.'

'The one who must have pissed him off?' Claire clarified.

'That's the one,' Hillary confirmed.

'Bit of a long shot, isn't it, guv?' Claire asked sceptically.

Gareth broke off from his typing to watch and listen thoughtfully. In the army it was practically unheard of for privates to question superior officers, and he couldn't help but think of himself and Claire in that light, with Hillary being, say, a second lieutenant with Rollo Sale as captain. But obviously things had to be much more relaxed in a civilian office environment, where bouncing ideas off each other was a vital part of the job. Certainly Hillary Greene hadn't taken the least offence by Claire openly second-guessing her.

He knew from the grapevine that Hillary Greene had a long-standing, close but professional relationship with Commander Donleavy, who, in his own mind, had to be a general, at least. Perhaps that gave her a certain amount of invulnerability not available to lesser mortals? Although from what he'd observed so far, Hillary didn't need to hide behind anyone's skirts.

'Sure it is, but it's a lead that DI Barker's team didn't have, so we have to follow it up,' Hillary responded. 'And in a village like Tackley, it shouldn't be that hard to narrow down the possible candidates. Gossip and news travels fast in a village, remember. Even though she's probably moved away by now, I'll be surprised if you can't find someone who knows who she is.'

Claire nodded, but still didn't look impressed. 'I still can't see this being a woman's crime somehow, guv. Our vic didn't carry that knife around with him for fun — he must have been proficient with it. Whereas your run-of-the-mill village girl . . .'

'Would have had a father, probably. Or even an older brother or two? Not to mention an irate boyfriend. None of them would have liked the thought of the village bad boy paying so much attention to their girl,' Hillary slipped in, and Claire grinned and slapped her forehead with her hand.

'Right. Sorry, being a bit slow on the uptake today, guv,' Claire said. 'You want me to get on it now?'

Hillary glanced at the clock. There was still an hour and a half until knocking-off time. 'You might as well. Mind you, you might not find many people at home at this time of the day. Most of them will still be at work.'

'Ah, but what I need is a little old lady,' Claire said, and winked at Gareth as she grabbed her bag from the desk and her coat from the back of her chair. 'Can't beat a nosy old biddy for knowing which girls were the naughty ones. And being only too happy to spread the dirt to an inquiring copper.'

'Good luck,' Hillary said with a smile, and went back to her stationery cupboard to prepare her progress report for Rollo Sale.

* * *

It was nearly dark when she left the building at just gone five. She wanted to go into town to do some shopping before going back to the *Mollern*, so for once she left at a reasonable hour. It was just as she was approaching Puff, parked under a horse-chestnut tree that was busy dispensing with its leaves, that she heard a gaggle of voices, one of which she recognised.

She paused, turning to look across the dark wet tarmac and rows of cars to where a group of uniformed men and women stood under one of the streetlights, laughing and talking. Only three of them were in civilian clothes, and one of them was definitely Gareth. Although they were near enough for Hillary to hear some words, they were just far enough away to make the conversation more of a general burble than anything comprehensible.

She was glad to see the new boy wasn't having any trouble making friends and networking. He'd need all the contacts he could get if he was going to make a career in law enforcement.

She delved into her handbag for her keys, and was half-turning away to slip the key into the door handle (no fancy key-free nonsense for the ancient Volkswagen!) when one word caught her attention.

Reading.

For a moment she paused, hesitating in front of her car. She couldn't be sure, but she thought it was Gareth who'd been doing the speaking. Instantly, her mind went back to the lunch at the Black Bull, and the talk about the murdered soldier in the nearby Berkshire town. Hadn't she thought then that the new boy seemed more than ordinarily interested in hearing about the case?

She was feeling vaguely tired, and part of her simply wanted to get out of the damp evening air and into her car, go and do her chores and go home and collapse in front of the telly.

Another part of her made her stand still and listen intently. With a sigh, she put the key back in her bag, and careful to stick to the shadows in the car park, made her way cautiously towards the chattering group.

When she was confident that she could hear better, and that none of the more eagle-eyed and experienced members of the group had spotted her approach, she leaned against a large black van and waited.

The main topic of conversation seemed to have turned now to a dawn raid that had gone off that morning, and which had netted three of the officers present a large haul of stolen goods from one of the city's industrial estates. Someone was being ribbed for falling over a stack of high-tech televisions, resulting in the inevitable breakage of several sets and the scattering of their prey like mice spotting a cat.

'Course, who got stuck with the bloody paperwork needed to sort out all that?' one male voice said plaintively as everybody laughed.

'Oh come on, Bazzer, I've said I'll take your next callout for when United play on Saturday! Not that Oxford is known for its hooligans,' the culprit shot back good-naturedly.

'Yeah, yeah,' a laconic voice wafted across the dark, damp night air.

'So, has anybody heard if they're any closer to arresting someone for that soldier's murder over in Reading?'

The voice definitely belonged to the new boy. And, as a change of topic, it wasn't that subtle. Hillary frowned. Whatever it was that was bugging him about the death of a former comrade, he was clearly anxious for more news. Obviously his first attempt to talk about it, the one that she'd overheard when she'd been about to get into her car, hadn't succeeded in getting him any information, hence his need to now ask the question outright.

'Jess might know,' a voice spoke up after a moment's thought. 'Jess, ain't your better half working on that case?'

'He's not my better half anymore — we broke up last month. Bloody hell, keep up with the latest gossip, Keith, you moron,' a plaintive female voice piped up.

There was more general laughter, then the same woman spoke again. 'Last I heard, they might have had a witness who saw the vic talking to someone on the street after leaving the last of the pubs on his pub crawl. Why?'

'Oh, no reason. We ex-squaddies like to keep up with stuff when it concerns one of our own, that's all,' Gareth said nonchalantly. Like all people who worked in Intelligence, they never admitted to intelligence-gathering. 'So, you think they stand a chance of getting somewhere then?' he pressed.

'Maybe,' Jess said, but was clearly not interested.

Gareth, taking the hint, said casually, 'Speaking of Reading, do you think they stand any chance in the play-offs?'

The talk turned eagerly to football and Hillary moved away, making her way back to Puff as surreptitiously as she'd left him. This time she slipped behind the wheel and sat there thinking for a moment or two.

The new boy had been wise to back off and change the subject when he did. Trying to pump coppers for information was not a good idea. It never took them long to twig what you were doing.

She frowned slightly in the darkness, not liking what she'd heard, but still disinclined to give it too much credence. So what if the new boy was interested in hearing about the murder of a former soldier? Like he'd just said, it wasn't so surprising that he'd be interested.

Yeah, right, a little voice snorted at the back of Hillary's head.

With a sigh, she gave in to the inevitable, and ran through her mental list of the cops that she knew in Reading and who owed her a favour. It didn't take her long to come up with one or two possibilities.

Wearily, she put the key in the ignition and switched on the headlights. When she got back to the boat, she'd have to put in a few calls and see if she could find someone to do her a favour and just have a little nose around the murdered soldier case on her behalf. Just to see if there was anything in the wind that pinged on her radar.

It was probably nothing.

But it was always best to make sure.

And with that thought, she lifted the handbrake, slipped into gear and swore at Puff roundly as he shuddered, coughed and went silent.

A few muttered remarks about the charms of a second-hand Astra that she'd seen for sale in a car show room's front window that morning did the trick though, and a minute or so later she headed out onto the main road, and joined the growing stream of rush-hour traffic.

* * *

Friday morning brought an unexpected phone call from Malkie Comer.

It took Hillary a moment or two to recognise his voice, but when she did, she leaned back a little in her chair and reached for a notebook.

'Mr Comer, how can I help you?' she asked mildly.

'You told me to call you if I should remember something. About Andy, I mean.'

Hillary's heart picked up a little, but only a little. She'd had too many phone calls in her career that had sounded hopeful at first, only to end up disappointingly fizzling out into nothing.

'And have you remembered something?' she chivvied him along.

'Yeah. Well, it's not much. I mean, that's why I didn't mention it before. He was only a schoolkid, kicking off, talking big, the way they do.'

Hillary took a long, slow breath, reminded herself that patience was a virtue and all that jazz, and tapped the pad with her pen. 'Schoolkid?' she prompted.

'Yeah. That mouthy little black git that used to hang around with the princess,' Malkie's unlovely voice rattled across the line, followed by a smoker's hacking cough. Hillary imagined that Malkie had only just got up and was probably standing in the kitchen in his boxers, puffing on his first fag of the day. The unappealing thought of Malkie Comer in his boxers almost made her gag, but she stifled the reflex.

It took her only a moment to decipher the message. 'The princess being Chloe Dalton, I take it?'

Over in Swindon, Malkie grunted.

'And the mouthy schoolkid . . . ?' She had a fair idea of who he was talking about, but she wanted to see what he would say.

'How the hell should I know?' Malkie bellowed belligerently. 'I couldn't care less who Karen let her precious little darling hang around with, let alone remember their names! And I don't say that I took it seriously at the time, when

Andy told me all about it, because I didn't! And neither did Andy, come to think of it. He just laughed it off.'

Hillary sighed, trying to sort out the less-than-clear statement into some sort of order. 'All right. So, what was it that this unnamed schoolkid did or said that you've only just remembered?' She kept her tone of voice sceptical and disinterested, mainly because she knew it would rub Malkie the wrong way, thus making him even more eager than ever to come up with something, just to have the satisfaction of feeling he'd put one over on her. But in reality, her heart had slowly begun to do that anticipatory little pitter-patter again.

'Oh not much!' Malkie's voice drawled sarcastically in her ear. 'He only threatened to kill my lad, didn't he?'

And with that, he must have slammed down the receiver with a great deal of smug satisfaction because the only thing Hillary could hear now was the dialling tone once more.

She hung up thoughtfully. No doubt, over in Swindon, Malkie was standing by the phone, confidently expecting her to ring back, all excited, begging for more details.

More fool him.

Hillary was in no mood to indulge him, but talking to Felix Wainbridge had now just been raised to the top of her to-do list.

* * *

Hillary let Gareth drive in his car to Banbury. Although she could tell the car had been adapted to help him overcome the problems caused by the weakened left side of his body, he seemed to have no difficulty in driving longer distances. Which was good to know. Sometimes their cold cases required them to travel further afield than the area covered by Thames Valley.

'Did Claire find out where Felix works, ma'am?' Gareth asked as they idled at the traffic lights just outside Adderbury.

'Yes — at a mobile phone shop not far from the Cross.' Banbury Cross, of the nursery rhyme fame, often disappointed tourists, who found it stuck on a roundabout in a busy market town that, at first glance, didn't look particularly medieval.

The famous monument was surrounded more or less on all sides by roads lined with shops, and they were lucky to find a parking space in a small car park a little up the road from it. The car park was situated on a sharp slope though, and Gareth was careful to walk steadily until he gained more level ground. He tried to pretend it didn't annoy him that he had to do so, but underneath he still felt bitter resentment at every compromise he and his new body had to make.

His face, however, showed nothing.

'This is probably the place,' Hillary said somewhat dubiously a few minutes later, after they'd turned down the main shopping street that would eventually lead to the market place. But mobile phone shops weren't exactly thin on the ground, unlike some of the big-chain shops that had all gone to the wall recently.

Barber's shops, on the other hand, she noticed, seemed to be doing all right.

Inside, a girl in her late teens who was obviously obsessed with facial jewellery was talking to a customer at the counter, going over all the features of the model that the customer had selected.

According to the metal-bedecked girl, the phone could do anything with the possible exception of launching a NASA satellite — and maybe it could even do that if the customer had the proper tech skills.

At one of the shelves closer to the door, a tall, lean black man was busy stacking neat boxes of the shop's wares into a glass-fronted cabinet.

She walked closer to him and, when he turned to acknowledge her presence, said quietly, 'Mr Wainbridge? Felix Wainbridge?'

For a moment he looked disconcerted, having expected them to ask him a question about the merchandise. Then his look moved from Hillary to Gareth, then back to Hillary again, and he nodded to himself.

Hillary wondered who it was that had warned him that he could expect a visit from the police sometime soon. And the obvious answer, of course, was his old school friend Chloe.

'Yes?' he said mildly.

Hillary discreetly displayed her ID, and Gareth promptly followed suit. When Felix barely glanced at them, but immediately looked around to see who might be watching them, Hillary was sure she was right. This man had been warned well in advance that he would need to prepare himself to answer questions about the murder of Andrew Feeley.

'I'll take a break. We can sit and talk on one of the benches by the church,' he nodded back up the road. 'It's not raining, is it?'

'No,' Hillary agreed. For once, intermittent sunshine was doing its best to dry some of the dampness of the previous days, but she doubted it had had much luck. Still, if the witness preferred to sit on a damp wooden bench, she wasn't going to argue.

'Chantal, I'm taking a coffee break, OK?' he called to the other side of the shop.

'Sure,' the girl said, barely breaking off her spiel to her young male customer, who seemed to be more fascinated by her line of nose studs than the handset she was demonstrating.

Felix disappeared briefly behind a discreet door in the back wall of the shop, returning less than a minute later, shrugging his arms into the sleeves of a blue-and-white anorak.

They said little as Felix led them up the busy pavement towards the church, and then through a set of large wooden gates. Being right in the middle of the town, the place of worship didn't have a particularly large graveyard, but sure enough there was a wooden bench set back by an ivy-clad wall, situated under a slightly dripping yew tree.

Hillary hoped one of the drops wouldn't magically find its way down the back of her neck, as they usually seemed to.

'Thames Valley are taking a second look at the murder of Andrew Feeley, Mr Wainbridge,' Hillary began, once they were all seated. Gareth, to minimise the contact of his trousers with the damp and potentially dirty bench, was sitting right on the edge of the seat. He suspected that it wouldn't be long before this somewhat awkward position started to make his legs ache.

'I see,' Felix said blandly.

'You knew Andrew's half-sister Chloe very well, I understand?' she used as her opening gambit.

Felix smiled and nodded. 'Yeah. Little Chloe Dalton,' he mused softly. 'How's she doing these days?'

'Don't you know?' Hillary asked mildly. 'I was sure you must have talked to her only recently.'

'Nope,' Felix said, with what sounded to Hillary to be surprising sincerity.

She turned a little on the bench to observe him more closely. Steady brown eyes looked back at her.

'I had the impression our visit wasn't much of a surprise, Mr Wainbridge,' she challenged him pointedly.

Again Felix smiled. 'It wasn't,' he admitted readily. 'Karen phoned me, oh, a couple of days ago now. She said the police were reopening Andy's case.'

'The case was never closed,' Hillary corrected automatically. It was a common mistake the public made, thinking unsolved cases were officially 'closed' after a certain time period. But her mind was much more focused on wondering why Karen Feeley had felt the need to warn Felix, of all people.

'Ah,' Felix said. He looked at the church tower, his eyes moving over the clock.

'Did she have any specific reason to call you, Mr Wainbridge?' Hillary prompted.

'Karen?' Felix turned to her again and shrugged. 'Not really. She was worried about the effect it would have on Chloe, I think.'

'And why would she call *you* about that? Did she think you could help her? Are you and Chloe an item?' To think that he'd asked *her*, Hillary, how Chloe was doing these days . . .

Felix laughed. 'You're barking up the wrong tree there, Mrs . . . er . . . Greene, was it?'

Hillary nodded.

'Nah, I haven't seen Chloe since we left school. I've been living with my partner, Suzie, for . . . uhh . . . must be getting on for six years now. And before you ask, we weren't an item at school either. Me and Chloe, I mean.'

'And how did you feel about that?'

Felix gave a short guffaw, as if looking back at his younger self was genuinely amusing. 'It made me want to chew the wallpaper,' he admitted wryly.

'You seem to have got over it well,' Hillary pointed out with a dry smile of her own.

Felix shrugged. 'Sure, I hung around her, hoping . . . well, you know what all teenage boys hope for,' Felix said with another laugh. This time at his own expense. 'But Chloe just never saw me like that. And if I didn't take those hints to heart, catching her doing some heavy petting with that loser Ian Kendall sure as hell opened my eyes good and proper. Still, I can't say that it didn't break my heart, at the time.'

Felix gave another amused laugh.

At the mention of this new name — Hillary was sure it didn't appear in DI Barker's original case file notes anywhere — she pricked up her ears. 'Oh? Another school friend of yours?'

'Nah. He was older — he'd left school and was probably going to college by then or something.'

'So he'd be what — eighteen, nineteen?' Hillary pressed.

'Yeah, I reckon.'

'That's some age gap when the girl is underage. She wasn't yet fifteen, was she?'

'Hell no. But you don't need me to tell you that girls grow up way faster than boys,' Felix pointed out.

'So you're saying Chloe was sexually active when her brother was killed?'

'Nah, I don't think so,' Felix corrected her. 'I think she was just, you know, experimenting. Beginning to explore her own sexuality maybe. My sister Janice was friends with her, and if she'd been having sex she'd have told Janice for sure, and Janice never could keep a secret, bless her.'

'But you asked her — Janice, I mean — about this boy, Ian Kendall, right?' Hillary challenged him with a knowing smile. 'You wouldn't have been able to resist pumping your sister for news about what Chloe was up to.'

Felix grinned. 'Sure I did,' he admitted. 'That's how I know it hadn't progressed beyond the heavy petting stage.'

'And did she and this boy become an item?'

'Nah, don't think so. I think it fizzled out when Andy died.'

Hillary slowly nodded. 'And you didn't manage to snare her on the rebound?'

Felix laughed. 'I wish!'

'So you remained just her friend?'

'Yup. That's me. Good ol' Felix, the best friend.'

'Who used to protect her from her big brother sometimes?'

For a moment all three sat in the quiet churchyard in silence. They were so quiet that they could hear, just off to the right, a female blackbird rootling through some fallen leaves in search of grubs and worms.

Then Felix sighed. 'Sure, I used to have to come to her rescue sometimes. That brother of hers was bad news with a capital B and N. But then, if you're investigating him, you probably already know that.'

Hillary nodded. 'We heard he used to bully Chloe. Pinched her, tripped her up, that sort of thing.'

'Yeah. But it was mainly verbal abuse. He knew if he really hurt her, her father would be down on him like a ton of bricks.'

Hillary nodded. It was nice to have Sean Dalton's take on the Feeley family affairs confirmed by an outside source.

'But fathers aren't always on hand to see what their kids get up to,' Hillary pointed out. 'The life of a teenage schoolgirl and the life of a parent are very different. It takes another school pal to have an insider's knowledge about what really went down.'

Felix sighed. 'Yeah, I'd say that was a fair statement.'

'So how often did you have to play the knight in shining armour, Felix?' Hillary asked bluntly.

'Often enough. Mostly, like I said, Andrew just spewed his vitriol and left it at that. But Chloe was a tough kid, and she was used to it by then. It never used to affect her much — especially since Andrew was foul to everyone, not just her. And she was a beautiful and popular girl, so that helped.'

'So she was self-confident you would say?'

'Yeah, I'd say so. She was good at schoolwork too, you know, so the teachers rated her. All of that helped. She was never isolated, like some kids who suffer from bullying.'

'And you helped her most of all?'

'Sure, when I could.'

'Ever hear Andrew threaten to kill her?' The question, asked in a quaint English churchyard, in a quaint English town, in the middle of a colourful and bright autumn day, should have sounded shocking. But somehow it didn't. Even the female blackbird continued to toss up leaves and search for her lunch as if nothing untoward had happened.

Felix slowly nodded. 'Yeah. Sort of. I mean, not actually "I'm going to kill you" threats. Just sort of taunts and vague hints. You know — "you won't be around for long" or "enjoy it while you can". You know, that sort of thing.'

'One of our witnesses said that, not long before he died, Andrew seemed to have been plotting something nasty, something that was probably aimed at Chloe. He seemed sort of gleeful, as if hugging a secret to himself. Did you ever notice anything of the kind?'

'Nah, can't say I did,' Felix said, after a short, surprised moment of thought. 'But then, I never made it a priority to be around Andrew — quite the opposite in fact. I did my best to avoid him at all costs. But it wouldn't surprise me. That kid had a real twist in his make-up somewhere. He had a way of winding people up. You know?'

Hillary nodded.

'The school had a teacher training day the day that Andrew died, is that right?'

'Yeah, I remember we had the day off. It was summer, and we were all happy as Larry to get a day off.'

'Did you see Andrew that day?'

'Nah! The only one I saw from the village that day was Toby Truman. He was just going back into this garden. He looked a bit goofy and glassy-eyed to me. Me and a mate . . . Dwayne Chalmers, hung out, playing games at his place. Then we went into Oxford that afternoon.'

Hillary nodded. 'Do you know where Dwayne is now?' she asked. She didn't think DI Barker's original investigation had paid too much attention to Felix or his alibi, and she wanted to rectify that. Especially after meeting this self-possessed, slightly laid-back man, who seemed to be going out of his way to be helpful, in a curiously non-committal sort of way.

Felix once more looked at the church tower. 'Dwayne died last year. Cancer,' he said flatly.

'I'm sorry to hear that,' Hillary said. She had not mistaken the slight pause her witness had given just before he'd mentioned Dwayne's name. And, of course, a dead friend couldn't prove — or disprove — an alibi.

Felix looked at her knowingly. 'Yeah. I can see how you would be.'

'You were what . . . fourteen, fifteen when Andrew was killed?' she pressed on, her voice as bland as his own.

'Fifteen.'

'I imagine you were big for your age?'

'I grew up fast, yeah.'

'Did much sport at school?'

'Yeah. Rugby and tennis mostly.'

'So you were fit and strong?'

Felix smiled, still looking at the church clock. 'Uh-huh.'

'Did you come across Andrew Feeley in the woods that day?'

'Nope.'

'Do you have any idea who killed him?'

For a moment, Felix visibly hesitated. Then, realising that he did, slowly smiled again. 'We all had *ideas,* Mrs Greene. Most of the village seemed to think one of his junkie customers did for him, so they could get their fix and not have to pay for it.'

'Do you *know* who killed him?' Hillary patiently rephrased the question. This time, Felix didn't hesitate.

'No, I don't know who killed him. And do you know what?'

Hillary raised an eyebrow.

'I don't care,' Felix said. And gave her another amiable grin.

CHAPTER FOURTEEN

Toby Truman was not best pleased to see them back again and this time, after abandoning the bar and his less than pleased colleagues, he led them a shade sullenly outside to one of the garden tables.

Needless to say, on a cool autumn day, nobody was outside eating, and they had an uninterrupted view of the roundabout, with its constant traffic and the scent of petrol fumes. Nice.

'What now, for Pete's sake? Do you *want* to get me fired?' Toby grumbled, sitting down on a white plastic chair, wincing a little as he realised that he should have made sure it was dry before parking his backside.

'No, but that's what sometimes happens when you tell us porkies,' Hillary said sharply.

Beside her, Claire reached for one of the laminated menus, running her eyes wistfully down the list of choices. It was the usual fare — burgers, chips, grilled meats and salads. The hunter's chicken looked good, she mused but knew that Hillary wouldn't be happy with her if she indulged her grumbling tummy by ordering something.

'What do you mean?' Toby said, looking from Hillary to Claire warily.

'I mean,' Hillary sighed, 'you weren't exactly honest with us about your activities on the day that Andrew was killed, were you? And unluckily for you, you were seen,' she added, her voice flat and hard, and left it at that.

As she'd known he would, Toby began to sweat and look panic-stricken. He swallowed hard, several times, his Adam's apple bobbing up and down in his neck like a demented yo-yo. No doubt he was frantically going over the fatal day in his mind, trying to remember who it was that might have seen him.

Would he have been worried, or relieved, to know that it had been the schoolkid Felix Wainbridge?

Hillary herself wasn't that impressed, as she had the feeling that Felix's very casual mention of seeing Toby had been meant to deflect her attention away from himself and Chloe. Of course, that didn't mean he'd been lying. And from the way her witness was reacting now, she was fairly confident that he hadn't been.

'I dunno what you mean,' Toby said feebly at last.

Hillary sighed and looked across at Claire. 'I hate it when they lie to my face,' she said plaintively.

Claire grinned. 'I know what you mean, guv. It feels so disrespectful, dunnit? Like they think you were born yesterday. It's aggravating.'

Her eyes went to the drinks menu, wondering if they did those lovely thick milkshakes here. They were a bit of a nemesis for her, those ice-cream-laden drinks. She could never resist the damn things.

'You were seen, Toby,' Hillary reiterated, her voice going hard. 'That afternoon, going back to your house, all glassy-eyed and happy-hippy.'

'Happy-hippy?' Claire repeated, slightly startled. She shot Hillary a look and saw that her guv'nor's lips were twitching. On cue, she began to laugh herself.

It totally disconcerted the young man to watch the two women openly laughing at him, for at first he flushed red, then went rather pale.

'Come on, Toby,' Hillary sighed wearily. 'We're not interested in a drugs buy you made eight years ago. But we know you must have seen Andrew sometime shortly before he died and bought from him, and that *is* something we want to know about. So spill what happened, what or who you saw, and anything else that you can remember about Andrew and the woods that day. Then we'll get out of your hair.'

For a moment Hillary thought he might actually do just that, but then common sense took over and he began to look stubborn. 'I dunno what you're talking about. And your witness must have had rocks in their head. I never went anywhere near the woods that day. I didn't even see Andy.'

'Did you kill him?' Hillary asked flatly, as if he hadn't bothered to deny it.

'No!' Toby squeaked. He straightened up in his chair, looking properly frightened now, and shot glances from one of them to the other. 'You can't pin that on me!'

Claire, more to keep her eyes off the menu than for any other reason, kept her eyes fixed firmly on him, staring at him unsympathetically.

'Honest,' he added, a shade pathetically. 'Andrew scared me, see? He was a scary bloke. I only ever went near him when I wanted some . . . I never saw him that day.'

'So the witness who saw you returning to your house that day was lying to me?' Hillary raised her voice at the end, turning it into a question. 'And just why would he or she do that?'

Toby's shoulders slouched again, and his mouth went into a straight, hard line. 'I never said they were lying. Just that they were mistaken, that's all,' he muttered.

The two women looked at each other. 'Do you want me to arrest him, guv?' Claire asked mildly. It was a total bluff, of course. She didn't have any power of arrest, any more than Hillary did, since neither of them were actively serving police officers anymore. When it came time to make arrests, Hillary had to ask Rollo to either send a sergeant or come and do the honours himself. 'We can get him for impeding the course of an investigation, if nothing else,' Claire threw out off the top of her head. 'Maybe attempting to pervert the course of justice?' she added hopefully.

Hillary never even blinked, but turned to look at Toby thoughtfully. 'It'll be an awful lot of paperwork,' she objected.

'Look, I never killed anyone, all right,' Toby objected, sensing they were only playing with him, but not quite sure. And the last thing he wanted to do was get himself back on the Old Bill's radar. 'OK, so I probably *was* out sometime that day,' he temporised reluctantly. He nodded. 'Yeah, I think, now I look back on it, I probably was. Yeah, I might have been out in the garden, because I saw Mum come back with the dog.' He was happy with his effort. It sounded vague enough, and reasonable enough, to keep him out of trouble.

Hillary leaned back in her chair and crossed her arms over her chest. 'Go on. Fairy tales have always interested me.'

'No, honest. I was in the front garden and she came back with the dog,' Toby said, anxious to please and embellish. 'Muttley, its name was — you know from that old cartoon series *Wacky Races*? Dick Dastardly and all that stuff. Mum loved that as a kid, so when she got a dog of her own she called it Muttley. He's gone now, but she was really fond of him. Scruffy, Heinz-variety thing, you know?'

Hillary wasn't finding Toby's sudden verbal diarrhoea particularly entertaining. Even if she had rather enjoyed the cartoon series herself as a kid!

'Everyone tells us that it was very hot that day,' Hillary pointed out flatly. 'And conscientious dog owners don't usually go walking their dogs in the heat of the day. Try again.'

'No, I know, that's why Mum always took him down the shady route through the trees—' Suddenly Toby Truman broke off and went back to swallowing hard again.

Claire glanced at Hillary.

Hillary sighed. Would there be much point in going back to Debbie Truman and asking her if she'd been in the woods that day, walking her dog in the shade? Call her unduly sceptical, but she didn't think there was.

On the other hand, she was inclined to believe Toby — oh, not about his assertion that he hadn't bought any drugs from Andrew that day. But about seeing his mother with the dog.

She rubbed the side of her nose tiredly. As DI Barker had learned years before her, there were no shortage of suspects without alibis in the Andrew Feeley case. There was just not one scrap of evidence worth a damn! So perhaps it was a good thing that she thought she might just have a handle on this case at last.

Maybe.

Wordlessly she got up and walked away. Claire, with one last wistful look at the menu, sighed and followed her. Neither one of them looked back to see what their witness had made of their abrupt departure.

'So where to now, guv?' Claire asked as they climbed into her car.

'Back to the station. It's Friday. You and Gareth get off for the weekend early. I need to do some thinking.'

Claire didn't need telling twice. Whilst she liked her job, she liked skiving off early along with everyone else.

So it was that, at three o'clock that afternoon, Hillary Greene sat alone in her tiny stationery cupboard of an office, thinking hard. And the more she let her mind weigh up the pros and cons, the more she thought it possible — just possible — that with a bit of luck, they might be able to close the Feeley case.

Of course, with no forensics, it would all come down to them being able to get a confession. And that, Hillary thought, leaning back in her chair as the afternoon darkened around her, might just prove to be a mite tricky.

She opened a new folder and began to make careful notes, making her case on paper, looking for flaws, trying to see where the best potential lay for gaining additional evidence. She was meticulous. She was, after all, in no hurry to participate in the general exodus of the building going on all around her.

For her, the weekends weren't so much a reward as something that she just had to get through.

This weekend, for instance, she would probably take the *Mollern* up to Banbury and moor up somewhere near the shopping precinct on Saturday night. Maybe do a little Sunday shopping, then travel back down again. It wasn't that there was anything she particularly needed, but since canal narrowboats were supposed to do only 4mph, travelling passed the time nicely.

* * *

As Hillary Greene sat at her desk, patiently putting together the pieces of the Feeley case, Gareth drove back to his flat, contemplating the weekend with more enthusiasm.

He would be seeing his daughter tomorrow, for one thing, which was always a bonus that cheered him up and reminded him that he was lucky to be alive. And then there was the fishing trip with Jason. Which probably wouldn't be such a joyful occasion. He could only hope that he'd find his old friend in a better frame of mind than he had in recent months.

And this time, he wouldn't ask him anything about what might have happened in Reading. Because he was not sure what he would do about it if he learned more than he bargained for.

Besides, he was almost sure that he was making a mountain out of a molehill.

Probably.

* * *

Jade Hodson was also thinking about the weekend at that moment, as she set about making her daughter's tea. She'd promised Briana that they could go to the new Westgate shopping centre in Oxford, so that they could have a grown-up lunch in one of the roof terrace cafés that had been built there. There was an American-style diner that Briana really liked.

As she checked her purse to make sure that she had enough cash to pay for the treat, her eyes strayed once more to the old apple tree.

And she shuddered.

All that blood . . .

She shook her head, and the memory, firmly away. The police would soon stop nosing around, asking their worrying questions. They had before. They would again. Wouldn't they?

* * *

Sean Dalton spent a short time on Saturday morning doing that little job he'd been putting off, and could put off no longer. He felt a lot better when he'd done so.

* * *

Chloe and her mother spent Saturday afternoon baking in Chloe's modest flat in Woodstock. Neither of them mentioned Andrew's name. And if either of them felt as though they were living in a sort of breathless limbo, just waiting for something devastating to happen, neither of them mentioned that, either.

* * *

Monday morning dawned with a bright blue sky and cheerful sunshine, as if the previous few days of grey drizzle and chill winds had never happened.

The weather, however, wasn't doing much to cheer up Gareth. As he settled himself behind his desk, automatically responding to Claire's cheerful greeting with a forced one of his own, he turned on his computer screen with blank, unseeing eyes.

The weekend had not gone as he'd hoped. Oh, being with Fiona had been great, and he was more than happy to still be Number One in his little girl's eyes. Even seeing Trisha again had been OK. Their break-up hadn't been particularly acrimonious, and he was glad, sort of, to see her happy and getting on with her life.

He suspected that she had some new fella hovering in the background somewhere, and had been relieved, if slightly surprised, to find that he hadn't felt unduly hurt or jealous about it. Which only went to show, he supposed ruefully, that Trisha had been right when she'd said that they hadn't been in love with each other, as a couple, for some time. So no wonder their marriage had ended.

He sighed, scrolling through his emails without enthusiasm. So far, he hadn't found another woman to share his life with, but then to be fair, he hadn't been actively looking for one, so that was no big surprise. He supposed he'd get around to it eventually. But that wouldn't be easy, since hovering at the back of his mind like an annoying, whining little gnat was the vague worry that no woman would find him attractive now; not with the scar on his face and his mangled left hand. However, plenty of people had told him that the scar wasn't disfiguring, and that he was still good-looking and a desirable 'catch.'

Gareth couldn't help but smile internally at the phrase. Why did people say that? And did he really want to be 'caught'?

But it wasn't the state of his love life that was worrying him so much as the ongoing and worsening situation with his friend Jason.

For a start, his old army buddy had been late when Gareth had arrived to pick him up, and he was sure he could smell booze on his friend's breath. It had probably been a consequence from Saturday night's drinking — at least he hoped it was — but it hadn't been a great start. Early-morning rising shouldn't be a problem for a former soldier, and the fact that his old pal was having trouble getting out of bed in the morning spoke volumes about his mental attitude.

Plus, Jason had had the same lecture about booze being a depressant as he had, when he'd been undergoing his own rehabilitation. But whereas he'd taken it to heart, and kept his drinking very carefully controlled, he suspected Jason didn't give a toss, and still drank to excess on a regular basis.

Worse, once they'd got to the river and set up their fishing rods, he found his friend to be morose and moody, not to say almost belligerent. It hadn't boded well for a day's peaceful fishing, and sure enough, before long, Jason had begun to talk about what army officials tended to call 'the incident.' The 'incident' that had led to his own physical injuries, and Jason's mental ones. He simply wouldn't leave it alone.

Of course, Gareth had tried to talk him down, to be positive, to point out all the good stuff. They were alive, weren't they? Back home? They were still young, with so much to look forward to, and plenty to enjoy.

But that only seemed to make his friend angrier. Didn't he care, Jason had almost screamed at him at one point, that it needn't have happened? Didn't he care that he was going to walk with a stick for the rest of his life because of some stupid bastard's incompetence — and worse, downright cowardice?

Gareth moodily stared at his emails with unseeing eyes, feeling his own sense of injustice and frustration rise. Because of course he *cared*. Of course he was *angry*. Of course he often thought about their former colleague, Captain Francis Clyde-Brough, who'd been forced out of the army under a distinct cloud, without a pension or an honourable discharge. Because of his bad decisions and mismanagement, men had died. But Francis had simply walked away without a scratch and gone back to living the good life in Reading — mostly living off family money, or so the grapevine told it.

And of course Gareth resented him. Bitterly. He'd never liked him, even before the incident. He'd been the kind of fourth-generation soldier who thought he owned the bloody regiment, a Sandhurst graduate who acted as though he was Lord Kitchener reincarnated. An arrogant prat who was nowhere near as good an officer as he thought.

But it had never crossed Gareth's mind to seek him out and *kill* him.

The trouble was . . .

He sighed heavily. He knew that Jason had not only thought about it, but in the first dark months after their discharge, had talked endlessly about actually *doing* it.

At first, Gareth had let him talk and make his plans, thinking it would help his mate to vent his spleen. Didn't everybody say it did more harm than good to keep rage bottled up? It had never once, in those early days, ever occurred to him that Jason might actually have meant what he said.

But as time went on, Jason just seemed to sink further and further into gloom and the booze, and his anger never seemed to go away. Sometimes he actually seemed to vibrate with stress and rage.

And still Gareth had persisted in believing it would all turn out OK, stubbornly insisting to both himself and all their friends who still gave a damn that Jason just needed time. That he would come through it all, and that the frightening behaviour would eventually stop.

But then Clyde-Brough had turned up dead. Beaten to death outside a pub after going on a pub crawl.

When he'd first heard the news, he could remember how he'd gone cold, thinking that Jason had finally broken down and done what he'd been fantasising about for so long. And then he'd heard on the news how a gang of youths had become the prime suspects, after witnesses had seen them hanging about in the vicinity, bent on causing trouble.

And he'd allowed himself to relax at last, sure now that he had nothing to worry about. That he'd been an idiot, in fact, to even think his mate could have been involved. And as if to reinforce that feeling of relief, the very next time he'd seen Jason, Jason had laughed about how Clyde-Brough had got what he deserved at last. And how he wished that he'd been there to see for himself the arrogant prick pick a fight with a bunch of kids who didn't give a toss about his rank or high-status bloody family.

Which might not have been a particularly nice sentiment, but had surely been a human one?

His friend's honest reaction had even made Gareth feel a little guilty that he had ever even entertained the thought that Jason might have done something really stupid.

And yet in spite of all that, ever since Clyde-Brough's death, every time they met, Gareth had found himself watching his friend, looking to see the expression in his eye, wondering if it was all an act, and then kicking himself later for being so damned lame and disloyal.

And that particular fault, as far as Gareth, Jason or any other soldier was concerned, was the ultimate betrayal. Being disloyal to your mates was simply unthinkable.

And so they had continued to hang out, fishing, playing table football on an old machine of Jason's, playing cards, drinking a little, watching football and swearing at the players, who were always useless and never deserved their absurd pay cheques.

And Gareth would try not to wonder about what had happened to Francis Clyde-Brough that night in Reading.

Except this time, yesterday, Jason had barely talked to him. Gareth had tried everything he could to coax something out of him, even if it was only hostility, but he just hadn't been responsive. He'd simply sat, fishing listlessly, drinking a few bottles of beer and ignoring Gareth as if he wasn't even there.

So now here he was, worrying himself sick, trying to work out what this latest development meant. Because what if the unthinkable *had* happened, and Jason *had* gone to Reading all those weeks ago and let loose all his rage on the man who was responsible for the incident that had ruined both their lives? What if Jason *had* killed him after all?

Sitting in his new office at Thames Valley Police HQ, with his new colleague working alongside him, Gareth suddenly felt utterly alone.

Because there was yet another thought, hammering away gently but persistently at the back of his brain and demanding to be heard. A thought he was desperately trying to ignore because he didn't want to face up to it.

If Jason confessed to his best mate that he'd killed Clyde-Brough . . . what would he, Gareth, actually do about it?

It was ironic that he was now working for the police because he knew that the one thing that he would never do, *could* never do, was betray him to his brand-new employers.

It just wasn't in him.

It went against the code.

He'd never be able to meet his reflection in the mirror again.

So what would he do?

'Is the boss in yet, do you know?' Claire's cheerful voice finally cut through his self-enforced nightmare, and he dragged his eyes from the screen.

'Sorry,' he said, trying to sound rueful. 'I was miles away there for a moment.'

'No kidding,' Claire grinned. But she hadn't missed how pale he looked, or how tired either. For a while there, it had looked as if he had the weight of an elephant sitting on his head. 'Everything all right?' she asked gently.

'Yeah. No, it's fine,' Gareth said, and laughed, shaking his head. Because, when you got right down to it, it probably *was* all fine, wasn't it? After all, he didn't *know* that Jason had done anything at all, did he? The problem might well exist only in his own head.

But as he shook off his gloom and tried to convince himself that he was worrying about nothing, it was probably a good job that he wasn't a fly on the wall in Hillary Greene's office right at that moment. Because knowing that she was on to him wouldn't have done his already taut nerves any good at all.

* * *

Hillary reached for her ringing phone automatically, her eyes on her computer screen. Unlike Gareth, however, she'd actually been reading her emails and absorbing the information they contained. So it took her a moment to recognise the voice on the other end of the line.

'Hello, Hill. How are things in the rarefied atmosphere of lofty Oxford today then?'

Hillary grunted. 'The sun is shining and the spires are duly dreaming.'

Laughter came down the phone line and the familiar bellow allowed Hillary to place him. 'Geoff, thanks for getting back in touch. That was quick!'

'As if I could ignore a plea from the woman who taught me all I know. Well, about nabbing crooks anyway. Can't say your advice on my sex life was ever worth a damn.'

Hillary laughed. 'Since when did tomcats with the moral compass of a sewer rat ever need advice about amour?'

'OW! That hurt. I'm not that bad . . . well . . . not since Tracey got her hand on the family jewels anyway.'

'I hope she keeps a tight hold on 'em,' Hillary said vindictively. And then, small talk over, she got briskly down to business. 'I take it you've been asking around for me about the Clyde-Brough case?'

She'd done a little research of her own on the case in Reading before asking her old crony, Geoff Wadley, to sniff around more fully for her. Geoff had worked under her for a few years, back when she'd been a sergeant and he a lowly newly promoted detective constable. Even then she'd appreciated the man's ability to blend into any background and gain information, seemingly without even asking questions. He just seemed to absorb information like a sponge, as though by osmosis. It had been a rare trait that she'd spotted, appreciated and helped him to cultivate, and which had ultimately helped him to his quick promotion up and away to better things.

Now he sat in a lofty superintendent's office in Reading, and as such, had overall charge on the death of the former soldier, which had made him a good candidate to be her eyes and ears when she'd been considering who to ask for the favour.

'Yeah, I've put out a few feelers over the weekend,' Geoff admitted. 'Like I said when you first phoned, the DI working on it seems confident that it was gang-related. Captain Clyde-Brough was just in the wrong place at the wrong time, and probably said or did the wrong thing. But I did do a bit of sniffing around of my own — and I have to say, I enjoyed myself thoroughly doing it. You forget what it's like to actually get your hands dirty when you ride a desk . . .'

'Yeah, yeah, you can skip the nostalgia,' Hillary interrupted with a laugh. 'Some of us poor sods never did get to ride a desk, you know.'

Over in Berkshire, in his nice, spacious, light and airy office, her old friend laughed heartily. 'Yeah, right, like that was ever a big ambition of *yours*! OK, down to brass tacks. No, I couldn't find any mention anywhere in any of the reports that Clyde-Brough had been seen in the company of former soldiers. Nor had anyone working the case reported coming across anyone who seemed to be fishing for information about it, or nosing around asking questions. I don't suppose you know something about the case that I don't?' he asked hopefully but doubtfully.

Hillary grunted. 'If I did, you'd be the first to know about it,' she pointed out.

'Goes without saying,' Geoff agreed. 'So why the fishing expedition?'

Hillary grunted. 'Let's just say I have a nasty suspicious mind, and I'm glad to find, in this case, that it wasn't justified.'

'*What*? Could it be that the great Hillary Greene got it wrong?' He sounded scandalised.

'Are you trying to say that I'm not infallible after all?' Hillary shot back, sounding even more shocked to her core.

'As if I'd dare!'

'I should bloody well think not. That's the trouble with cocky detective constables. They grow up into blasé superintendents and forget their place.' And before he could get in the last word — which was something she remembered he loved to do — she hung up on him, grinning widely.

Then she sighed with satisfaction. Well, at least that was one bogey she could forget about. Whatever interest her new recruit had in his ex-colleague's death, at least he wasn't actively pursuing it. Which was good to know. The last thing she needed was to have a problem with Gareth Proctor.

* * *

Rollo Sale glanced up as Hillary tapped on his door and entered. 'You wanted to see me, sir?' she asked briskly.

'Hmm? Oh yes,' Rollo said, initialling the bottom of a report and throwing down his pen. 'I thought you might like to know that the search warrant you requested has finally come through.'

For a moment Hillary remained silent.

'You know — the one you asked for, allowing you to dig up the Feeley garden in the vicinity of an apple tree? I've asked for a couple of uniforms to do the digging,' Rollo explained.

'Yes, sir, I remember,' Hillary said slowly. When she'd asked for the warrant she'd been playing a hunch, as well as making sure she'd left no stone unturned. Almost literally, in the case of a warrant to dig up a garden! Now though, if she was right about who had killed Andrew Feeley and why, the search warrant almost certainly wouldn't turn up anything useful.

But she didn't think it would be politic to say so to her boss, who had had to go through the hassle of getting it for her in the first place. So she smiled and nodded appreciatively, and said, 'Thank you, sir, I'll get on it right away. I'll take Gareth with me. It'll be a good experience for the new boy to see a ground search done well.'

'OK. Let me know if anything comes of it,' Rollo said, turning his attention back to yet another report.

'Yes, sir,' Hillary said, and she took the warrant from his desk and left the office thoughtfully. As she walked back to her own office, she shook her head wearily.

'What a damned waste of time,' she muttered under her breath. Which, as it turned out, just went to show how truly fallible she was.

CHAPTER FIFTEEN

Hillary and Gareth arrived at the Feeleys' garden about half an hour later, following a patrol car containing two somewhat gloomy constables. Not that she could blame either of them for being less than impressed to get the assignment. Digging was hard work and she was very glad she didn't have to do it anymore.

The garden, after its recent soaking, was looking a little sodden, but it was still a pretty enough sight in the bright, clear autumn sunshine.

She paused to knock on Karen's door since, technically, she was the owner of the land they were going to search, even if the garden area outside Jade Hodson's static caravan was probably regarded by both women as being Jade's.

There was no response inside the house to her knocking, however. Hillary then moved around to the back of the property, following the uneven garden path towards the rear of the large garden, where she noticed that a new black water butt stood by the shed, catching the occasional drips from the guttering. The sight of it made Hillary pause and look at it thoughtfully.

Apart from an inch or so at the bottom, it was empty of water.

Hillary frowned. 'Now that's just sloppy,' she muttered disapprovingly under her breath.

'Ma'am?' Gareth said, not quite catching it.

She shook her head and nodded towards the caravan. 'Nothing. Come on, let's hope that Jade is in, otherwise we'll have to hang around to serve the warrant.'

But when they walked onto the veranda and tapped on the door, it was Karen who answered the summons, not the younger woman.

'Ah, Ms Feeley. I'm glad we found you,' Hillary said, handing over the search warrant. Briefly she explained what it was for, and what they would be doing.

'Digging under the apple tree?' Karen repeated blankly, staring past her at the two young men in uniform, who, given the nod from Hillary, had already set off for the tree in question. 'But what on earth for?' she asked, clearly perplexed. 'Hey, Jade, the police are here,' she called back over her shoulder. 'They're digging up the garden of all things!'

There was a rapid movement inside, and then Jade appeared looking over Karen's shoulder, her big blue eyes going round with fright and her face going deathly pale.

'What? Where?' she said. And then she saw the constables underneath her apple tree, and she began to sink to the floor in the doorway as her knees gave out underneath her.

Karen gave a concerned cry and quickly bent over her. 'Jade, love, what is it? Do you feel all right?'

Jade began to sob quietly and hopelessly.

Hillary took one astonished look at her, and thought, *Damn, this is going to complicate things.*

* * *

'Guv, we've found something.' One of the constables, a tall youth who'd had his nose broken not so long ago, shouted from beneath the tree. It was about ten minutes after they'd started digging, and Karen, Hillary, Gareth and Jade were all sat around the kitchen table in the static caravan, with the window open to admit some fresh air. Not that the colour seemed to be in any hurry to return to the younger girl's cheeks.

After the girl had stopped crying, Karen had told Jade to be quiet and not say a thing, and then had insisted on making them all tea, heaping sugar into the young girl's cup, obviously a believer that hot sweet tea was good for shock.

Hillary was inclined to let Karen have her head, and had made no demur, even when she'd told Jade to keep quiet.

Gareth, feeling out of his depth, had said very little, but he was surprised that Hillary Greene wasn't being assertive. He couldn't quite figure out what was going on. Obviously, Hillary had had good reason to ask for a search warrant for the garden, and from Jade Hodson's reaction, it was also a fair bet that his new boss had scored a direct hit of some kind.

So why had Hillary looked so surprised, and then almost annoyed by the young girl's spectacular collapse? And why had she allowed Karen Feeley to monopolise the situation? Why was Hillary not pressing the advantage and demanding an explanation for Jade's behaviour?

Instead, she seemed content to just sit and wait. True, Gareth could tell from the way she would occasionally frown or give an almost infinitesimal shake of her head that Hillary Greene was thinking furiously. But just what it was that she was thinking, he had no idea.

Now, with the shout of triumph coming from outside, Hillary rose quickly. Gareth, not sure whether he was supposed to go with her or stay and guard the suspect, half-rose too.

Hillary waved him back. 'Stay here,' she said curtly. 'Don't let the witnesses confer.'

'Yes, ma'am,' Gareth said, relieved to have clear orders.

He sat down and watched the women with what he hoped was a friendly but neutral expression. Karen, clearly nervous, kept shooting looks from him to Jade, as if she expected him to produce handcuffs and haul her off to jail at any moment.

Jade herself looked simply dazed. She drank her tea mechanically, but Gareth couldn't tell if she was really aware of what was going on outside.

Whatever the hell it *was* that was going on outside.

Hillary walked towards the apple tree, where the two constables, looking quietly pleased with themselves, moved to one side to allow her to see into the hole they'd excavated between two major roots of the apple tree.

At first glance, it hardly looked a prepossessing sight. There was no buried treasure gleaming golden or jewel-bright amongst the dank, rich soil; no sinister bones or human skull grinning up at them. Only a twisted, dirty tangle of material, partially rotted, and showing, here and there, a few tentative shades of different colours.

From that, Hillary could tell very little about what it was, but she could make a damned good guess. Unless she was very much mistaken, and she didn't think she was, what she was looking at was the remains of a brightly patterned summer dress. And when the forensics people were allowed to do their thing, she suspected that they might well be able to find bloodstains on it. And if they were very lucky, match it to Andrew Feeley's DNA.

Hillary sighed heavily. 'Damn it,' she said, with feeling.

Her reaction was clearly not what either of the uniformed men expected it to be, for they looked at each other warily.

Catching it, Hillary forced herself to smile and nod. It was not, after all, their fault that this new discovery threatened to derail her investigation. 'Well done, lads. I'm calling in SOCO, so once they've arrived you can get off.'

'Guv,' they said, giving her a curious look as she moved off. Once she was out of earshot, she didn't doubt that their speculations would run riot.

Hillary reached for her mobile, hesitated for a moment as she ran through her options, and then made a brief plan of action, and hit Rollo Sale's number.

'Sir, it's Hillary,' she said crisply, the moment he answered. 'We've found fresh forensic evidence at the Feeley site. I need a SOC team. We'll also be bringing in Jade Hodson for questioning on suspicion of murder.'

After a startled pause, her superior officer said briskly, 'Right. I'll arrange for an interview room.' He sounded pleased.

But Hillary doubted that he'd sound pleased for very long.

'Sir,' Hillary said flatly and hung up.

She knew that Rollo, as a serving police officer, would have to be present at the upcoming interview, but she was also pretty sure that he'd let her take the lead. And that was going to be vital.

Jade Hodson would have to be handled very carefully, or she might just muck things up well and truly.

Hillary walked back to the caravan slowly, thinking furiously, going carefully over her conclusions as to who she believed had killed Andrew Feeley, and why. Trying to pull them apart, trying to tease out any inconsistencies or mistakes she might have made.

But she didn't think she was wrong.

Finding Jade's almost certainly bloodstained clothing was definitely a blow that had come out of the blue, and just when she needed it the least, but she couldn't let it derail things. If only she hadn't asked for that damned search warrant . . .

Unless . . .

Her already slow steps became even slower. Perhaps, if she played it right, and she had a bit of luck on her side, the clothes turning up now might actually play right into her hands? It would all depend on what Jade Hodson had to say for herself in the interview room. That was going to be key.

Straightening her shoulders, Hillary walked back to the caravan. Inside, all three of them looked up at her as she entered. Gareth was openly curious but wary. Karen looked unbearably anxious. Jade still looked blank.

'What was it? What did you find?' Not surprisingly it was Karen Feeley who shot out the questions. 'What's going on?'

'Jade,' Hillary said quietly. 'I need you to come to the police station with me to answer some questions. Do you think you can do that?'

Jade blinked a bit, then nodded docilely, even as Karen said explosively, 'No! She can't. Briana will be home from school soon. Who's going to look after her?'

'I'm sure you'd be happy to do that for her, Ms Feeley,' Hillary said.

'No, I'm going with Jade. I'm not letting her go alone,' she said stubbornly. As she spoke, she reached out and closed her hand over the younger girl's. Jade responded by clutching her fingers and smiling gratefully at her.

Hillary nodded. It wasn't surprising that a young woman, raised without a family of her own, had come to look on Karen Feeley as her own mother. She was, after all, the grandmother of her child, so they were sort of related, in a way.

Gareth never expected Hillary to agree to Karen's demands, so he was visibly surprised when Hillary nodded and said, 'All right, Karen. You can ride with us, but you'll need to call someone to pick Briana up from school.'

'I'll call Sean,' Karen said at once. 'He's ploughing up by the main road, he can be here in a few minutes.' She was already scrolling down her phone as she spoke.

Briefly, her voice shaking with stress, she told her ex-husband the situation. From their half of the conversation it was clear that Sean was happy to look after the child, and from the way Karen muttered 'yes' and 'all right' a few times, it was also obvious that he was giving her some forceful advice on how to handle the situation.

Again, Gareth glanced curiously at Hillary. He may not know a lot about detective work yet, but he'd done some courses after being hired for the job, and he knew that this was all very unorthodox. Usually, police officers went to great pains to keep witnesses separate and not give them the chance to communicate or confer with each other.

Karen hung up and slipped her phone into the pocket of the jeans she was wearing. She smiled bravely down at Jade.

'Come on then, love, let's get this over with. I'm sure it's all a fuss about nothing, and you've got nothing to worry about. It's not as if,' and here she shot Hillary a look, 'you've done anything wrong, is it?'

Jade gulped and went, if it were possible, a shade more pale.

* * *

Claire was waiting in the office when they got back, having been given a brief update by the superintendent. She was, naturally enough, agog with curiosity, and pumped Gareth for a blow-by-blow account of what had happened as she led him to the viewing room.

Behind the one-way glass, Gareth could see a simple table and set of chairs, and a recording device. Inside, Rollo Sale was already seated and waiting. Hillary Greene was probably still upstairs, 'processing' Jade.

To Gareth and Claire it seemed to take ages for both women to enter the room, but in fact, it had probably taken no more than ten minutes.

Gareth supposed that Karen Feeley had been left kicking her heels in the waiting room, and doubted she would have liked that much. On the way back to HQ, she'd told Jade that she should wait for a solicitor and say nothing until one arrived, promising to find one for her in the next hour or so.

Jade had nodded, and looked as if she was listening, but Gareth wasn't so sure. He could tell by her body language that she was feeling defeated, tired, and had probably lost any will to fight. As a soldier, he'd seen that reaction in many shocked, war-weary people.

As the two women entered and Jade was seated, Rollo Sale ran through the correct procedure for the recorder, gave Jade Hodson the usual recital as to her rights, and then said quietly, 'Miss Hodson, Mrs Greene is going to interview you. It would be in your best interests to co-operate with us. Do you understand all that I've just said to you? Please speak clearly for the recorder.'

'Yes,' Jade said. Her voice was calm but seemed to have very little substance to it, and Claire wasn't surprised to see Rollo fiddle with the volume control.

'Do you need a glass of water, Jade?' Hillary spoke for the first time, and Claire felt herself tense. This was the point where suspects either demanded a solicitor, clammed up altogether or else elected to speak.

Jade shook her head.

'The suspect has just shaken her head,' Rollo Sale said.

'Oh, sorry. No, I don't want any water,' Jade said, turning her head a little towards the recording device.

'All right, Jade. Now, as you know, we've just come from your caravan and the garden surrounding it,' Hillary began. 'We had a search warrant to dig around under the apple tree, near to your home.'

Hillary paused, and Jade, after a moment of uncertainty, said, 'Yes. That's right.'

Hillary smiled and nodded. 'Good. You're doing very well, Jade. I can tell you now that we found something buried in the earth under the tree. Do you know what that was?'

Jade sighed. 'I suppose it was the clothes I was wearing that day.'

Beside Gareth, Claire let out a relieved sigh, and murmured 'yes' under her breath. This was clearly going to be plain sailing.

'By that day, you mean the day your partner, Andrew Feeley, was stabbed to death in the woods near the village where you were living?' Hillary clarified carefully for the tape.

'Yes,' Jade confirmed listlessly.

'Can you tell us how the clothes came to be buried beneath the apple tree please,' Hillary said gently.

'Yes. I buried them there myself.'

'Why did you bury them?'

Jade closed her eyes and shuddered. 'Because of the blood. There was so much blood.'

Hillary nodded calmly. Beside her Rollo Sale listened attentively, but said nothing.

'Andrew's blood?' Hillary asked, still in that soothing, gentle tone that Gareth found oddly unsettling. Perhaps it was because he was so used to orders being barked at him that he found the subtlety of the situation going on in the room beyond him completely alien.

'Yes. Andy's blood,' Jade said, and gulped.

'How did you come to have Andrew Feeley's blood on your clothes, Jade?' Hillary asked, hoping her own tension didn't show. Because now everything hinged on what this traumatised young girl would say.

Oh, Hillary knew what she *should* say. She knew what she was *expecting* her to say. And, unless she was totally wrong about what had happened that hot summer's day eight years ago, she knew what Jade *must* say. But if she didn't actually say it then she was going to have an almighty fight on her hands.

The trouble was, she knew just how easy it was for shocked and vulnerable women to say whatever it was they thought you wanted to hear. Especially women who had been haunted by an event for years, and had probably suffered all sorts of violent emotions from guilt, to fear, to relief and everything in between. They were perfectly capable of saying almost *anything*. And sometimes it could bear very little resemblance to the actual truth.

'Because I held him in my arms,' Jade said, looking across at Hillary, her big blue eyes filling slowly with tears. She reached up and pushed a reddish-gold strand of hair from her cheek. 'He looked so alone, you see. Lying there in the woods. And so quiet. I'd never known him so quiet. For the first time, he didn't look angry or . . . He just looked . . . so alone.' Jade shrugged her shoulders helplessly. 'I don't expect you to understand. I don't know that I understood it myself. He wasn't always . . . kind to me, you know? And if I'd had somewhere else to go, I think I'd have left him in a heartbeat. But in *that* moment . . . seeing him like that . . . I just had to hold him. Do you see?'

Hillary felt the tension slowly drain out of her. Yes. It was going to be all right. She nodded gently. 'Yes, I think I do. Now, why don't you start at the beginning for us? How did you come to be in the woods, Jade? Did you go there with him?'

'Oh no.'

'Had you arranged to meet him there?'

'No, it wasn't like that. I knew he was going to the woods to meet . . . well, one of his customers, because I'd heard him on the phone, making the arrangement. And I wanted to talk to him away from the house. Karen's always been like a proper mum to me, and has always watched out for me. But sometimes . . . well, she could be a little too protective, you know? I wanted to talk to Andy about our baby's future, and I knew what I had to say would make him angry and I didn't want him to start shouting and for Karen to hear and come running.'

Hillary nodded. 'All right, we understand that. You needed to be sure you had some privacy. So you, what, left the caravan and went to the woods when you were confident that Andrew's business with his customers would be over?'

'Yes. I knew he often stayed on in the woods, drinking beer as a sort of celebration after he'd made a good sale. So I went and, and . . .'

But she faltered a little now, putting a hand up to her mouth.

'All right. Let's take it slow and steady,' Hillary said soothingly. 'You went into the woods. Did you see anyone else there?'

'No. Well, I think there was a woman walking her dog, further away across the meadow. It was hard to tell — she was keeping to the shady areas.'

Hillary nodded. It was very likely Debbie Truman that she'd seen, but she said nothing. 'All right. Was there anyone in the woods themselves?'

'No, I don't think so,' Jade said. 'At least, I didn't hear or see anyone.'

'So what happened next?'

'Well, I called out Andrew's name, but he never answered. So I began to walk down the path. I don't know if you've been in there, but there are several, well, tracks I suppose you'd call them, that go through the trees. Dog walkers, and the farmer, and deer and sheep and what have you, they all sort of make a right of way through the undergrowth. So I just followed them for a while, calling out to him, and after about . . . I don't know . . . maybe ten minutes, I . . . f-found him.'

She stopped speaking abruptly.

'Found him how?' Hillary asked after a moment's silence.

'Lying in the grass. He was all covered in blood. I didn't see the knife sticking in him at first. I just . . . well, I think I must have cried out, I was so surprised. I ran to him and knelt down beside him and shook him . . . his shoulder, I think . . . and called his name. I tried to wake him up, even though I think I knew, all the time, that he wouldn't wake up. That he *couldn't* wake up . . .'

Jade paused, her voice shaking badly, and took a long, gulping breath. 'That's when I sat down and sort of hugged him. I had his head in my lap . . . I stroked his hair . . . It felt like hours and hours, but I don't think it could have been. I don't know. After a while I just . . . well, got up and went home.'

Jade frowned. 'That sounds silly, doesn't it? *I got up and went home*. But at the time, I just couldn't think of anything else to do. Does that make sense?' She appealed first to Hillary and then to the straight-faced older man sitting beside her.

'Yes, it makes sense,' Hillary assured her gently. 'So you went home. Did anyone see you?'

'I don't think so. It was so hot that day that in the village most people stayed indoors.'

'And what did you do then? When you got home?'

'Well, it was when I was walking down the garden path to the caravan that I realised I felt all sticky.'

Jade shuddered and put a hand to her mouth. 'Oh, I feel sick remembering it.'

Hillary reached across and laid a hand on her hunched shoulder. 'It's all right. Just take deep breaths. Would you like a toilet break?' she offered.

But Jade shook her head adamantly. 'No. Now I've started I just want to get this over with.'

She leaned back in her seat, looking so pale that Hillary poured her a glass of water and put it in front of her. Jade smiled her thanks vaguely, but ignored it.

'I remember looking down at my hands, and seeing they were all red and sticky with blood. And then I saw my dress was the same. I . . . well, I freaked out a bit. I tore it off, right then and there, in the garden. I just left it on the grass and then ran to the caravan. I just wanted to shower. To wash it all off . . .'

Jade's voice faded for a moment and she was silent. Then she took a long, shuddering breath. 'I must have stood under the cold water for a long time. I kept shampooing my hair and soaping myself all over and then rinsing off and doing the same thing over and over again . . . Eventually, I left the shower and got dressed. I suppose I began to think . . .'

Jade shook her head. 'I knew I should have just phoned the police, all right?' she said, looking from Hillary to the older man whose name she had forgotten. 'I mean, I *knew* that was what I should do. But then I got scared. I began to worry. What if you thought *I'd* done it? Everybody knew that Andrew . . . well, wasn't kind to me. And I'd found him — and everybody says the first one to find the body is always a suspect, right? And I had blood on my clothes . . . I just panicked. I didn't want my baby to be b-born in p-prison . . .'

Jade gulped and put a hand over her eyes for a long, long moment, and then slowly lowered it and slumped back in the chair. She looked utterly spent. 'So I went outside and dug a hole under the apple tree and buried the clothes. And when the police came to tell me that Andy had been found, I said I'd stayed in the caravan all day. And from that day to this, I've never spoken about it to anyone. I've tried not to think about it. I've tried to pretend it never happened. And after a while, after the years began to pass, it almost began to feel like it *hadn't* happened.'

Jade smiled forlornly. 'Well, until you came back,' she added simply, looking at Hillary Greene.

Hillary nodded. 'Thank you, Jade,' she said simply. She turned to Rollo and nodded at the recorder. Rollo, after a slow moment, reached reluctantly forward and, for the benefit of the tape, said that the interview was being suspended and stated the time.

In the viewing room, Claire let out a long, slow breath. 'Phew!'

Gareth looked slightly puzzled. 'So that's it? Is it over?'

'Bar the shouting,' Claire told him confidently.

'So did she do it?' he asked uncertainly.

Claire nodded. 'Course she did.'

'You didn't believe her, about finding him already dead?' he pressed.

'That's what they all say,' Claire said flatly. 'Don't worry — you'll learn. She's a pretty kid, and you want to believe her. She sounds plausible. And the vic was such a tosser. All of that makes you *want* her to be innocent. But that doesn't make it so.'

She opened the door and walked towards Hillary and Rollo, Gareth on her heels. 'So I'll get back to my office and start on the paperwork,' Rollo was saying.

'The paperwork for what exactly, sir?' Hillary asked him quietly.

'For the arrest of Jade Hodson for the murder of Andrew Feeley of course,' Rollo said, looking at Hillary with a sudden sharpening of his gaze. 'What else?'

Hillary met his gaze head on, her eyes unwavering. 'Before you do that, sir, I think it would be a good idea if we talked to someone else first.'

And it was then that Detective Superintendent Roland 'Rollo' Sale felt the hairs on the back of his neck begin to stiffen.

Because he'd heard Hillary Greene use that certain, carefully neutral tone of voice before.

CHAPTER SIXTEEN

For a moment, he hesitated. He knew he had enough to charge the young woman sitting patiently in the interview room behind him. He also knew that his lead investigator, who had a success rate second to none when it came to finding killers, wasn't happy for him to do so.

And was silently asking him to trust her.

Which, of course, he did.

Slowly he nodded. 'Very well,' he said, his eyes never leaving hers. 'You want me to send a uniform to bring this other person in?'

Hillary, some of the tension leaving her shoulders as she saw that her superior wasn't going to be difficult, sighed gently. 'That won't be necessary, sir,' Hillary said. 'She's already here.'

'She?' Rollo repeated.

'Yes, sir,' Hillary said. 'The boy's mother.'

Beside Gareth, Claire said softly, 'Oh, man . . .'

* * *

Karen Feeley looked around the interview room like a cat that had just been taken from its own territory and set down in a totally unknown place. She looked around the meagre room with wide eyes and then, when Hillary indicated a chair, sat down reluctantly.

'Where's Jade? Is she all right?' Karen demanded. She was wearing black slacks and a white and orange striped jumper, her greying fair hair pulled back from her face by an orange scrunchie. Her hands trembled visibly as Rollo Sale sat down, turned on the tape, went through the same procedure as he had with Jade Hodson, and then leaned back in his chair. His attitude clearly said that this was Hillary's show, and she'd better not be wrong or muck it up.

'What's all this about?' Karen asked nervously, her brown eyes going straight to Hillary. 'I thought you'd brought me here to see Jade?'

'Jade is fine, Ms Feeley, she's given her statement. Right now, we want to talk to *you* about the death of your son, Andrew Feeley,' Hillary said clearly for the tape. Even though the superintendent had just apprised the woman of her rights the last thing she wanted was for some legal eagle to try and make out a case for entrapment or anything else.

'You don't have to talk to us, Karen, but I think it would be better for everyone if you did. Yourself included,' Hillary added gently.

Karen's eyes sharpened. 'Better for Jade you mean?' she demanded.

Hillary hesitated for a moment, tempted to use her concern for Jade as leverage, but then rejecting it. Any hint of perceived coercion on her part would almost certainly later be jumped upon in court.

'Better for all concerned,' Hillary temporised.

'What was it you found in the garden?' Karen asked warily.

Hillary spent a split second considering the pros and cons of answering her truthfully or dodging the issue. On the one hand, you never divulged information, nor did you let a witness dictate the direction of an interview by letting them ask questions and receive answers. On the other hand, anything that put pressure on the witness to confess was generally considered a good thing.

Instinctively, she felt that the second option had the edge in this instance, and sighed gently. 'I'm afraid we've found something that tends to incriminate Jade Hodson in the murder of your son, Andrew Feeley.'

'What? No, you can't have!' Karen said, shocked, reeling back a little in the chair, her eyes darting to Rollo, as if for confirmation, and then going straight back to Hillary. 'I just don't believe it,' she said adamantly.

'You sound very sure about that, Ms Feeley.'

'I am!'

'Why?'

Karen blinked. 'Why? Well . . . I mean, because that poor girl wouldn't hurt anyone. You can see that just by looking at her! Anyway, she's such a small thing,' Karen pounced eagerly. 'How could she have hurt Andy? He swatted her around like a fly.'

Hillary nodded. 'Yes. He was a bully where women were concerned, wasn't he, Karen? So you admit he used to hit her?'

Karen winced, then slowly nodded. 'Yes. All right, I admit it. He was . . . like his father in that way. I tried to get him out of it, but . . .' She gave a helpless little shrug.

'Did he ever beat on you, Karen?' Hillary asked mildly.

'No, never. He never raised a hand to me. I was his mum.' She sounded, to Hillary's acute and experienced ear, as if she was being truthful.

Hillary nodded. 'Now that *is* interesting. Which means that when you confronted him in the woods that day, he never threatened you with his knife?'

Karen opened her mouth to reply, then froze. 'What? *What did you just say*?' She again looked to Rollo, as if checking to see if he had heard it too. But Rollo Sale was staring mutely at her, his face a perfect blank.

'How can you say such a thing to me?' Karen turned back to Hillary, but her voice was weak, and didn't carry nearly as much outrage as she would have liked. 'Who kills their own son? What kind of a mother do you think I am?' she demanded, more firmly this time, clearly working up a head of steam. After all, it was far easier to cope with feeling angry than feeling frightened.

But Hillary wasn't about to let her rally her defences.

'The kind who had no other choice, Karen,' Hillary answered flatly. 'The kind who had finally been pushed to the limit, and beyond. The kind who had another, younger, much more vulnerable child to think about.'

At these words, Karen stiffened instantly, the colour bleaching out of her face. 'You leave my Chloe out of this,' she all but shouted.

But Hillary was already shaking her head. 'I'm sorry, but I can't. You must know that, Karen. Because this was all about Chloe, wasn't it? About protecting her?'

Karen sank back in her chair, her eyes widening. She reminded Hillary of a rabbit, watching the approach of a snake — fascinated, appalled, terrified, but somehow accepting.

It made her feel about two inches tall.

But she wasn't in this room to feel good about herself, a small, hard voice in the back of her head reminded her.

Leaning forward across the table, Hillary lowered her voice gently. 'It's all right, Karen. *I get it*. I really do. I understand. During the last week, I've been listening to so many witnesses, and they've all been telling me the same story. Putting the picture together for me. Laying it all out. How Andrew hated and resented his stepfather, and hated and resented his half-sister even more. How he used to torment her, physically and verbally. How he enjoyed making her life miserable.'

Karen took a deep breath, but said nothing, continuing to stare at Hillary fatalistically.

'And I can imagine what must have happened that day as well, to finally bring things to a head. I've pieced it all together you see,' Hillary carried on calmly, keeping her voice level and holding Karen's troubled eyes. 'You found out that Andrew had stepped up a gear in his campaign to destroy Chloe, didn't you? Because that's what he wanted to do, wasn't it? Destroy her? Nothing more, nothing less.'

Karen slowly shook her head, but Hillary didn't think she was trying to refute her claims. It was more a gesture of disbelief. As if she couldn't quite process the realisation that all her family skeletons were being laid bare.

'Now that she'd reached puberty, he wasn't content with just sly pinches and kicks anymore, was he? Or terrifying her with threats that she wouldn't be around for much longer.'

Hillary, seeing that Karen still wasn't ready to take that final step and admit her guilt, leaned back slowly, casually, and allowed herself to sigh softly. 'Do you want to know how we pieced it all together? How I know that it was you who must have killed Andrew, and why?'

Karen blinked.

Hillary took that for a yes. 'It's like I said before — simply through listening to what people told us. And by that, I mean really *listening,* and *understanding* what they were saying. You might have thought your lives were private, and nobody knew what went on in your family, but nobody lives in a vacuum, Karen. People heard, people saw, people wondered. And I've been spending my time listening to what it was they saw and heard and wondered, and from that I discovered the answer.'

Karen let out a slight, tremulous sigh, but still remained stubbornly silent.

'So, let's start at the beginning, shall we?' Hillary said encouragingly. 'I'll just go through it — don't worry, you don't have to say a thing, but you might want to correct me if I go wrong?'

Karen's big brown eyes wavered, her expression flickering a little, but still she remained silent.

Beside her, Hillary could feel the tension emanating from Rollo in waves, but she didn't dare look at him now.

'I think that on the day Andrew died, you knew that he was going to the woods to sell his poison. You're an intelligent and observant woman, Karen, and I think you knew your son and his routines pretty well. But you turned a blind eye to his activities on that day, just as you always had done before. So when he came to you that morning for his bacon sandwich, it was nothing unusual. But something happened, didn't it, Karen? Something happened that day that changed everything.'

Karen swallowed.

Hillary nodded. 'Now here, of course, I have to make a guess. An educated guess, I suppose you'd call it, but I think I've guessed fairly accurately. You overheard him saying something to someone, probably on his mobile phone, that made your blood run cold.'

'But how could you—' The words burst from her before she could stop them, and almost comically, Karen Feeley raised a hand to cover her mouth, as if to physically prevent herself from speaking.

'How could I know that?' Hillary finished the sentence for her with a wry smile. 'Well, I didn't know, not for sure, until you just confirmed it for me. And you don't have to tell me what he said, either, you see, because I already *know* what it must have been.'

At this Karen gasped and leaned back a bit, and again Hillary smiled wryly at her. 'Oh, not his exact words,' she reassured her. 'I wasn't there, obviously, but I knew, you see, what he had planned for your daughter. And I think you found that out too. On that day — the day he died. And it broke your heart, didn't it, Karen?'

Hillary paused as she saw the horrified expression creeping slowly over Karen's face as the mother of the dead man finally accepted the fact that Hillary wasn't bluffing.

It made her own blood run cold to see that expression in Karen Feeley's eyes. Never, in the whole of her career, had she wanted to discontinue an interview more than she did at that moment. To just get up and leave, and have someone else do the dirty work for her.

But she couldn't do that, of course, and so remained stubbornly seated. However, not for the life of her could she meet Karen Feeley's eyes as she swept on, electing instead to look down at her own hands, which were clenched together tightly on top of the table. The tension in the room was now palpable.

'It was Felix, Chloe's friend from school, who told us about a boy called Ian Kendall,' Hillary began, and heard Karen give another sharp intake of breath. Without pausing, and without looking at her, Hillary said casually, 'I can see you knew his name then? No doubt he was an addict and one of your son's customers. We were told how he was always hanging around with Andrew, which, as we know, can only mean one thing. After all, nobody was friends with your son because they liked his company, were they?' she added sadly.

Karen gave one soft, near-silent sob.

'It was Felix, again, who told us how, one day, he'd walked into a heavy petting session between Chloe and this boy Ian. Felix didn't think it had gone too far, figuring that Chloe was only experimenting a bit, you know, exploring her new feelings as she became a young woman. But he was worried, since Ian was eighteen or so, and Chloe would only have been, what, fourteen?'

Hillary paused, hoping for Karen to finally speak. But she encountered only silence.

'But sadly it wasn't anything that innocent, was it?' Hillary continued. 'And Ian himself certainly wasn't innocent either, was he? He had nothing but bad intentions towards your daughter. He fully intended to have sex with Chloe, and keep on having sex with her. And eventually, he was going to introduce her to drugs, wasn't he, Karen? Because that's what Andrew wanted.'

'Please stop,' Karen finally spoke.

'I wish I could,' Hillary said, perfectly truthfully. 'But I can't, not yet. You see, people who knew your son kept telling me that just before Andrew died, he'd been making plans for Chloe, plans that made him seem "gleeful." That was the word they used. As if he was nursing some wonderful secret. We know he hated Chloe, that he resented your marriage to

Sean, and took Chloe's birth as some sort of personal insult. So what better way could he punish both her and you than by turning her into one of his victims? We know he often forced his female customers to have sex for money in order to pay for his wares. And if he could add Chloe to his list of—'

'All right, all right, stop it!' Karen shouted. 'Yes, you're right, OK? I heard him on the telephone that morning, talking to that boy, Ian. Andrew was demanding to know if he'd . . . slept with Chloe yet. And he was urging him to get her to take some ecstasy — he said it was the perfect drug to start her off on. And I knew. I just *knew*! I knew what he wanted to do to her.'

Karen began to cry bitterly.

Hillary, exhausted, slumped back in the chair a little and let her cry. In fact, for two pins, she felt as if she could join in. She pushed a box of tissues closer to her and took a slow breath.

After a few minutes, Karen began to pull herself together.

'It's nearly over, Karen,' Hillary promised her gently. 'Shall I tell you what happened next?'

Karen shrugged her shoulders listlessly.

'All right. You either followed Andrew into the woods, and watched and waited whilst he conducted his selling business, or you waited at home until—'

'I followed him,' Karen interrupted flatly.

'All right. You saw him make his sales?' Hillary carried on quietly, talking her through it.

'Yes, to three men and two women. After the fifth one left, Andrew began drinking beer. He kept his . . . stuff . . . in an ice box, along with some food and drink. I guessed, once he'd started drinking beer, that there wouldn't be anyone else coming. So I walked out from the trees where I was hiding and went over to him.'

Karen paused, and for the first time in a while, Hillary felt able to lift her head and look fully at her.

'He was so surprised to see me. I'd never gone to the woods before, see,' Karen said.

Hillary nodded. 'Did you go there intending to kill him, Karen?'

'No! Of course not! I just wanted to confront him — to tell him that I knew now what he was up to with Chloe, and that I wouldn't stand for it,' Karen flared, then shook her head, looking baffled. 'I thought he'd be angry, or argue with me, or deny it or something. But do you know what he actually did?' Karen looked at her with wide eyes of incredulity.

'Tell me what he did, Karen.'

'He laughed at me. He *laughed*! As if it was nothing. As if getting one of his nasty junkies to seduce his own sister and get her hooked on drugs was *nothing*!'

Hillary nodded. 'That must have been devastating. To see how far he was gone.'

'It was. I just flew at him,' Karen said. 'I could hardly see, I was so angry! I remember screaming at him, and running at him, with my hand raised into fists . . . like this.'

She held out her hands in front of her, fists clenched.

Rollo stiffened slightly, his muscles tensing, but almost at once Karen let her fists fall to the table, as if the effort of holding up her arms was too much for her.

'And was that when he pulled out his knife?' Hillary asked.

Again, Karen's eyes widened. 'Yes, it was. How do you *know* that?' she demanded.

'It was just a good guess, Karen,' Hillary reassured her and shrugged. 'So what did you do when he pulled out the knife?'

Karen shook her head. 'I stopped dead for a moment or two. Instinct, I suppose. I'd seen the knife before of course, he was always showing it off. His bloody father gave it to him when he was only a kid. I ask you! A *knife* of all things! But he was so dead proud of it when he got it, always swishing it about as if it made him feel like a man, that I didn't have the heart to take it off him. But I'd always hated the sight of it, and seeing it again just made me so angry all over again.'

Wearily, she pushed a strand of hair out of her eyes. 'Without thinking, I just said something like, "Oh, give that stupid bloody thing to me," and snatched it out of his hand. He was so surprised, he just let me.'

'Then what happened?'

'I told him he had to leave Chloe alone, or else.'

'And what did he say to that?'

'He just sneered at me, and said, "Or else what, Mum? What are you going to do?" And then he laughed at me again. You know — taunting me. And I knew he was right. I couldn't stop him. I'd never been able to stop him doing anything before, no matter how hard I tried, or what tactics I used. I couldn't get him to stop selling drugs or robbing houses or stealing cars. And I wouldn't be able to stop him ruining Chloe's life either. I could see by the look in his eyes — so gloating, so . . . what was that word you used before?'

'Gleeful?'

'Yes. Gleeful. He just wouldn't stop. I could see it all playing out — Chloe having underage sex and falling under the influence of that awful boy. Becoming a rebellious teenager, getting into trouble at school, getting hooked on harder and harder drugs — drugs that Andrew would be sure to give her. I could *see* it in my head, playing out. And so I stabbed him,' Karen said simply, dully, her voice eerily matter-of-fact.

'He looked so surprised,' Karen said a moment later, when Hillary remained silent. 'But then, I think I must have done too. For this weird, really bizarre moment, we just gaped at each other in astonishment. You see, I hadn't *known* I was going to do it. I mean,' Karen shook her head, as if groping to explain it, 'I didn't actually think, *All right, I'm going to stab you.* The thought, the words, never even crossed my mind. I suppose it must have been my subconscious acting, because one moment he was stood there, jeering at me, and the next he had a knife in his chest.'

And that sheer unexpected nature of it had probably saved her life, Hillary thought, feeling a chill trickle down her spine. The fact that she'd given no indication of what she was going to do would have given her son no chance or time to react, to fight her off, to get possession of the knife back and probably attack her with it instead.

'For a second he just stood there, looking down at himself, at the knife handle sticking out of him . . . And then he looked at me . . . And I looked at him too, and then down at the knife handle. It was . . .' Karen shook her head helplessly. 'I just can't describe it. He didn't believe I'd do it, you see. *I* didn't believe I'd do it. But I had, and then . . . then he fell down and I turned and ran away. I didn't know what else to do. I just ran away from him . . . and what I'd done . . . I couldn't *believe* what I'd done. I still can't, all these years later . . .'

Karen leaned slowly forward and rested her forehead on her arms, which were stretched out in front of her on the table.

'I feel so tired,' she said faintly.

So do I, Hillary Greene thought woefully, but all she said was, 'It's all right, Karen, we're nearly finished now. What did you do when you got home?'

'I called— I took my clothes off. They were stained with blood — not much, but some. And I hid them.'

'They were buried under the water butt in your garden, weren't they?' Hillary pressed.

Karen raised her head, her eyes wide now in total wonderment. Hillary shook her head. 'No, I'm not a witch or anything. I just noticed, when we went out to search the garden, that the old water butt had been replaced. Sean did that for you, didn't he?'

'What? No!' Karen shot back in her chair, looking panicky now.

'You called him that day you killed Andrew, didn't you?'

'No!'

'And he came and helped you. Told you to shower. He buried your clothes under the water butt, didn't he? And when you had calmed down, he coached you on how to talk and act when Andrew's body was found. And sometime within the last few days, he came and removed the evidence and installed a new water butt, didn't he?'

'No! He had nothing to do with it. Any of it,' Karen whispered.

'Is that why your marriage broke up? Because, even though he knew you'd acted to save your daughter, he could never quite get his head around the fact that you'd killed your son?'

'No! Sean doesn't know anything about it. Any of it,' Karen insisted. But Hillary knew she was lying. And Karen knew that she knew. But Hillary was well aware that nothing would make this woman implicate the man she'd once loved. And who had once loved her.

Hillary sighed. They would have to bring in Sean and see if they could get *him* to crack. But, like Karen, she was feeling too exhausted to think about that right now. Perhaps she'd let Rollo Sale take care of that interview.

'Karen, Superintendent Sale is going to arrest you for the murder of your son, Andrew Feeley. Do you understand that?'

Karen nodded. 'Yes. In a way, I'm almost relieved. But I don't suppose you believe that.'

But Hillary, in fact, had no trouble in believing it. No trouble at all.

* * *

It was late before the team were ready to leave. Claire, Gareth and Hillary were sitting in the communal office. Rollo Sale was interviewing Sean Dalton, but Hillary doubted that Sean would admit to anything.

'Bloody hell, guv, that was really something,' Claire said, reaching for her coat and shrugging her arms into it. 'I thought when we found Jade's bloodstained dress it was all over. Bit of a coincidence that, wasn't it, both of them burying their clothes like that.'

'Coincidences do happen, as you well know,' Hillary reminded her crisply. 'And in this case, it nearly threw everything for a loop.'

'If only she'd been in time to see Karen coming back from the woods,' Gareth said. 'It would have saved them all from years of uncertainty. Albeit, I guess that would've thrown up its own set of problems.'

'Indeed it would,' Hillary observed dryly.

'You think a good brief will get her off with manslaughter, guv?' Claire asked. 'Due to diminished responsibility or extenuating circumstances or something?'

'I hope so,' Hillary said. 'There's certainly no case for premeditated murder anyway. That's why I made sure to get it on the tape, her saying that she didn't go to the woods intending to kill her son.'

'You gotta feel sorry for her though, haven't you?' Claire said, grabbing her bag. 'I mean, what a choice for any mother to have to make.' She shuddered, no doubt thinking of her own brood.

Hillary didn't want to think about it. 'Usually, when we close a case, we go to the pub for a celebratory drink,' she said to Gareth. 'But I don't think any of us are in the mood for that are we?'

'Not me,' Claire said glumly.

'Nor me, ma'am,' Gareth said. And then, after a pause, and thinking back on the gruelling and heartbreaking interview that he'd just witnessed, he said tentatively, 'Is it always like this?'

'No. Normally catching the bad guys feels great,' Claire assured him. 'Well, I'd better be off. Hubby will think I intend to let him starve.'

'Night, Claire,' Hillary said wearily, and Gareth echoed her.

'Night, guv. Gareth.'

'So,' Hillary said to the new boy, 'how do you like the job so far?' Her voice was heavy with irony.

Gareth looked at her thoughtfully for a few moments. Because of the Murder Book, he'd seen or heard or knew about everything that Hillary Greene had, but he had never made the connections. In the observation room, he'd listened and marvelled at the way she'd put it all together, and known that he'd never be able to do the same thing, no matter how long he was in this job.

And what a job it was. He'd thought that finding killers would be different to this. True, Karen Feeley's case wasn't the usual run-of-the-mill affair, even Claire had said as much. But even so . . . it took it out of him. He felt as if he'd just been put through an emotional wringer, so he could only imagine how his boss felt.

'Why do you do it, ma'am?' he finally asked her curiously.

Hillary Greene grunted a laugh. Now *there* was a question, and one she'd not bothered to ask herself for quite some time.

But after a moment's thought, the answer came back to her, just the same as it always did.

'Because some poor sod has to, don't they?' Hillary Greene said simply.

THE END

DI HILLARY GREENE SERIES

Book 1: MURDER ON THE OXFORD CANAL
Book 2: MURDER AT THE UNIVERSITY
Book 3: MURDER OF THE BRIDE
Book 4: MURDER IN THE VILLAGE
Book 5: MURDER IN THE FAMILY
Book 6: MURDER AT HOME
Book 7: MURDER IN THE MEADOW
Book 8: MURDER IN THE MANSION
Book 9: MURDER IN THE GARDEN
Book 10: MURDER BY FIRE
Book 11: MURDER AT WORK
Book 12: MURDER NEVER RETIRES
Book 13: MURDER OF A LOVER
Book 14: MURDER NEVER MISSES
Book 15: MURDER AT MIDNIGHT
Book 16: MURDER IN MIND
Book 17: HILLARY'S FINAL CASE
Book 18: HILLARY'S BACK!

MONICA NOBLE MYSTERIES

Book 1: THE VICARAGE MURDER
Book 2: THE FLOWER SHOW MURDER
Book 3: THE MANOR HOUSE MURDER

JENNY STARLING MYSTERIES

Book 1: THE BIRTHDAY MYSTERY
Book 2: THE WINTER MYSTERY
Book 3: THE RIVERBOAT MYSTERY
Book 4: THE CASTLE MYSTERY
Book 5: THE OXFORD MYSTERY
Book 6: THE TEATIME MYSTERY
Book 7: THE COUNTRY INN MYSTERY

FREE KINDLE BOOKS AND OFFERS

Please join our mailing list for free Kindle crime thriller, detective, mystery, and romance books and new releases, as well as news on Faith's next book!
www.joffebooks.com/contact/

Thank you for reading this book. If you enjoyed it please leave feedback on Amazon, and if there is anything we missed or you have a question about then please get in touch. The author and publishing team appreciate your feedback and time reading this book.

Our email is office@joffebooks.com

We hate typos too but sometimes they slip through.
Please send any errors you find to
corrections@joffebooks.com
We'll get them fixed ASAP. We're very grateful to eagle-eyed readers who take the time to contact us.

Made in the USA
Middletown, DE
12 November 2022